NAMED OF THE DRAGON

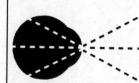

NAMED OF THE DRAGON

SUSANNA KEARSLEY

THORNDIKE PRESS
A part of Gale, Cengage Learning

GALE
CENGAGE Learning·

Farmington Hills, Mich • San Francisco • New York • Waterville, Maine
Meriden, Conn • Mason, Ohio • Chicago

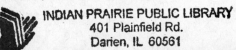

GALE
CENGAGE Learning®

Copyright © 1998, 2015 by Susanna Kearsley.
Thorndike Press, a part of Gale, Cengage Learning.

Thorndike Press® Large Print Romance.
The text of this Large Print edition is unabridged.
Other aspects of the book may vary from the original edition.
Set in 16 pt. Plantin.

LIBRARY OF CONGRESS CATALOGING-IN-PUBLICATION DATA

Kearsley, Susanna, 1966–
  Named of the dragon / by Susanna Kearsley. — Large print edition.
    pages cm. — (Thorndike Press large print romance)
    ISBN 978-1-4104-8426-0 (hardcover) — ISBN 1-4104-8426-2 (hardcover)
  1. Dream interpretation—Fiction. 2. Mythology, Celtic—Fiction. 3. Large type books. 4. Paranormal fiction. I. Title.
PR9199.3.K4112N36 2015b
813'.54—dc23
                                                          2015032556

Published in 2015 by arrangement with Sourcebooks, Inc.

Printed in Mexico
1 2 3 4 5 6 7 19 18 17 16 15

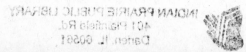

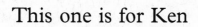

This one is for Ken

CHAPTER 1

Shine, little lamp, nor let thy light grow dim.
Into what vast, dread dreams, what lonely
  lands,
Into what griefs hath death delivered him
Far from my hands?

> — Marjorie Pickthall,
> "The Lamp of Poor Souls"

The dream came, as it always did, just before dawn.

I was standing alone at the edge of a river that wound through a valley so lush and so green that the air seemed alive. The warble of songbirds rang over the treetops from branches bent low with the weight of ripe fruit, and everywhere the flowers grew, more vivid and fragrant than any flowers I had ever seen before. Their fragrance filled me with an incredible thirst, and kneeling on the riverbank I cupped my hands into the chill running water and lifted them dripping, preparing to drink.

A shadow swept over me, blocking the sun.

Beside me the grass gave a rustle and parted, and out came a serpent, quite withered and small. It slipped down the riverbank into the water and opened its mouth, and as I knelt watching the serpent swallowed the river, and the flowers shriveled and died and the trees turned to flame, and the songbirds to ravens, and everywhere the green of the valley vanished and the world became a wasteland underneath a frozen sky, and the riverbed a hard road winding through it.

And the serpent, grown heavy and large, slithered off as the ravens rose thick in a chattering cloud that turned day into night, and I found myself walking beneath a pale moon through the wasteland.

I was looking for something — I didn't know what, but I'd lost it just recently . . .

And then, far off, I heard a baby crying in the night, and I remembered.

"Justin!"

The crying grew stronger. I started to run, with my hair streaming out like a madwoman, running, but always the cry came from somewhere ahead and I couldn't catch up with it. "Justin!" I called again, panicked. "Oh God, love, I'm coming. Hold on,

Mummy's coming."

But already I was losing him, I wasn't running fast enough, and then the road fell away and I fell with it, spiraling helplessly down through the dark into nothingness, hearing the cries growing fainter above me, and fading . . .

I woke with a jolt.

For a long moment I lay perfectly still, blinking up at the ceiling and forcing my eyes to focus through the stinging mist of tears. Outside on the pavement I heard footsteps pass with the brisk, certain ring of a businessman heading for Kensington station. The sound, small and normal, was something to cling to. I drew a deep breath . . . and another . . . reached my hand toward the lamp.

Light always helped, somehow.

Clear of the shadows, my room felt less cold and less empty. I rose, shrugged myself into my robe, and crossed to the window. The sulfurous glow of a late November night had given way to hard gray light that flattened on the line of roofs and chimney pots that faced me. In the street below, the stream of morning traffic had already started, sluggishly, as everywhere the houses yawned to life. It was morning, just the same as any other morning.

I pulled the curtain back an inch, and looked toward the fading morning star. It looked so small, so vulnerable. Another hour, and it would be forgotten. There wasn't anybody in the flat who could have heard me, but I spoke the words quite softly, all the same: "Happy Birthday, Justin," I said, to the tiny point of light.

It winked back, faintly, and I let the curtain fall.

CHAPTER 2

Go hence to Wales,
There live a while . . .
  — William Rowley, *The Birth of Merlin*

"Oh, Lyn, you can't be serious." Bridget Cooper flicked her auburn hair back in a careless gesture that distracted every man within a two-table radius, and glanced at me reprovingly. "You look like death warmed up, you know. The last thing you should do is take another transatlantic flight."

With anybody else, I might have argued that I'd slept straight through the New York flight two days ago, and that my next business flight wouldn't be until the twenty-first of January . . . but with Bridget, I knew, I'd be wasting my breath. Besides, I'd known her long enough to realize this was simply preamble.

Bridget never worried about anybody's

health except her own. And she never rang me at nine on a Monday, suggesting we meet and have lunch, unless she had a motive.

Bridget was a one-off, an exceptionally talented writer with a wild imagination that made her books for children instant classics, and a wild nature that drove the poor directors of my literary agency to drink. In the four years since I'd signed her as a client, Bridget's books had earned a fortune for the Simon Holland Agency, but her unpredictability had caused much tearing of hair and rending of garments among my colleagues. My favorite of her escapades — the day she'd kicked the BBC presenter — was now a Simon Holland legend. And I, who had survived four years and one week's holiday in France with Bridget, had risen to the status of a martyr.

Not that Bridget was so very terrible. In fact, if one didn't mind the occasional embarrassment, she could be tremendous fun, and time had taught me how to keep pace with her ever-shifting moods. Still, she did leave me wondering, sometimes, exactly who was managing whom.

Our lunch today had been a case in point. It had begun, reasonably enough, with a discussion of the plans for an animated television series based on the bestselling Llandrah books that had first launched Bridget's career. But by the time the waiter cleared away our starters, she had somehow shifted topics to the coming holidays.

"And anyway," she said, "who goes to Canada for Christmas?"

"Quite a lot of people, I'd imagine. All that snow . . ."

"There won't be snow," she told me, very certain, "in Vancouver. Their weather's much too mild." Taking another slice of bread from the basket between us, she tore it neatly into pieces. "No, you ought to come with me, instead, to Angle."

"Angle?"

"Pembrokeshire," she said. "South Wales. You know, where they had that big oil spill a couple of years ago." Bridget's sense of geography was, I'd learned, invariably linked to the six o'clock news and the Sunday tabloids. Name any town or village and she'd pinpoint its location in relation to a murder or a scandal or a natural disaster. Odd, perhaps, but undeniably effective. As it happened, I did remember the oil spill in question, and my memory flashed an image of a rugged stretch of coastline as she took a bite of bread and went on speaking. "James is minding a lovely old house down there — well, it's sort of three houses, really, but two of them have been knocked together to make one — right by the sea, with an old ruined tower in the garden. You'd adore it. Anyway, he's asked me for the holidays, and he said I could bring you along, if you wanted to come."

I didn't bother asking her who "James" was — I'd long since given up trying to keep track of Bridget's men. I simply shook my head, shifting aside so the waiter could set down my plate of risotto with fragrant spiced pumpkin. "I couldn't, I'm afraid. My brother would never forgive me."

She glanced up, clearly finding my excuse inadequate. "And how is dear Patrick the Protester? What's he on about this week? Saving the dormice? Blocking the bypass?"

"Battling the logging industry, actually. Chaining himself to trees. But only at the weekend," I explained. "He doesn't have so much free time, now he's married."

"Ah." Losing interest, Bridget took an experimental taste of her own dish of brightly colored pasta, chasing it down with a sip of red wine. "Mm, that's glorious. I ought to *marry* an Italian, they do brilliant things with food." The Italian waiter, hovering nearby, looked briefly hopeful, and I hid my smile with an effort, marveling again at the effect that Bridget had on men.

She was not, on close inspection, a beautiful woman. She had an ordinary figure, an ordinary nose dusted with freckles, an ordinary smile, and tilting eyes too impish to be called exotic. My brother, having met her, thought her "cute" rather than "pretty," though even he admitted Bridget had a certain something that was . . . well, it simply *was*. I blamed it on the auburn hair, myself. To believe a person's hair color could shape their personality might seem, at first glance, less than scientific, but I'd never met a redhead yet who didn't have the same allure — a sort of blend of vibrant energy and freshness that made those of us with brown hair feel ridiculously dull.

I smiled. "I thought you'd sworn off marriage."

"So I have," she said, remembering. "I'm thirty-four now, far too sensible to fall into the trap. And two ex-husbands ought to be enough for anyone. D'you know, that's one thing that I've always envied you."

"What's that?"

"Well, I'd rather be widowed, I think, than divorced. It's much tidier. Nobody skulking round, trying to make your life a misery. You're rather lucky, that way."

Only Bridget, I decided, would have

thought to tell a widow she was lucky that her husband hadn't lived. But her candid words, as usual, were not far off the mark. My marriage to the novelist Martin Blake had not been the greatest of successes.

"I sometimes wish," said Bridget, "that my number one would drive *his* car into a handy tree. He's being a right pain, lately. I'll be that relieved to get away for the holidays. And Dylan Thomas notwithstanding, I'm frankly seduced by the thought of a Christmas in Wales — especially the *singing* . . . d'you remember that Welsh choir we heard at the Albert Hall? Magnificent," she pronounced them. "I mean, how can one not admire a people who can sing like that?"

I smiled into my wineglass, thinking how my own assistant Lewis, who was Welsh, would have cringed to hear her say that. He frequently despaired of the stereotypes attached to his countrymen. "Singing, coal mining, rugby, and sheep," he'd told me once, in great disgust, "are the only things the bloody English think we know. Pure ignorance."

Bridget took another piece of bread and sighed. "I do wish you'd come. Fond as I am of James, he can be such a bore, sometimes. You'd be a good distraction for him."

"Oh, yes?"

"What I mean is, you'd be someone new that he could tell his stories to. They're fascinating stories, first time round. And I thought, since you waxed so rhapsodic about his last novel . . ."

My fork paused in midair. "I did?"

"Of course you did, don't you remember? When it didn't win the Booker, you called the judges a pathetic bunch of —"

"Bridget," I interrupted her carefully, setting down my fork, "this 'James' of yours . . . he wouldn't be, by any chance . . ."

"James Swift," she said, with a confirming nod.

I felt a sudden need for water. Reaching for my glass, I calmed the tiny racing thrill along my nerves that always signaled my professional excitement. "James Swift," I repeated the name, to be absolutely certain we were speaking of the same man — the man whose latest novel *should* have won the Booker prize; the man who, I felt firmly, was the closest thing to literary genius that our nation now had living. "I didn't realize you two knew each other."

Bridget's mouth curved, full of mischief. "One doesn't tell one's agent *everything,*" she said. "You're far too young. And anyway, I know how much you fancy his writing — I didn't want you pestering the poor man to defect to Simon Holland."

"Give over," I told her, "I'm hardly the pestering type. And I'm not so short on ethics that I'd try to lure an author from the agent he's already got."

"I see," said Bridget. "So you wouldn't want to know, then, that he's not exactly happy with his agent." She twirled up a forkful of pasta, the picture of innocence. "Or that he's thinking he might look round for a new one . . ."

"You are joking."

She smiled, sensing victory. "Are you *sure* you'd rather go to Canada for Christmas?"

"You really don't have any scruples, do you?"

"God, no. Horrible things, scruples," she said, with a shudder. "They get in the way of my fun." Reaching to refill her wineglass, she tested the weight of the bottle. "Nearly empty. We'd best have another."

"Oh, Bridget, no, I can't . . ."

But she'd already raised her hand to hail the waiter, who all but leaped across his other tables to reach ours, arriving slightly out of breath and wearing his most charming smile. Bridget, being Bridget, took no notice, though she did spare him an admiring look as he scurried off again to fetch her order. "The service here is really something, isn't it?" she asked; then, seeing my expression, raised an eyebrow. "What?"

"Nothing." I let it pass. "Only I can't drink any more wine, I've reached my limit. Some of us," I reminded her, "have to go back to the office."

"Yes, I know." Upending the first bottle over my wineglass, she poured out the dregs. "And it wouldn't help my reputation any, if I let you go back sober."

She needn't have worried. Her reputation was already unassailable. So much so that, two hours later, as I leaned against the cool mirrored wall of our office lift, my coworker Graham had no trouble guessing the cause of my unsteadiness. "Been to lunch with Bridget Cooper?"

"Mm." I kept my eyes closed while I nodded. "That obvious, is it?"

"Well, at least you managed to find your way back to the building," he congratulated me. "The last time I had lunch with her I ended up in Soho, doing most peculiar things with women's clothing."

"Did you really? I'd like to have seen that."

"I'm sure it's all on video, somewhere." The lift stopped with a shudder and Graham took my elbow as the doors slid open.

"Not my floor," I slurred.

"Yes, I know, but I can't let you go upstairs

in that condition. You'll have to hide out in my office, till you get your second wind."

Graham's spacious office, one floor below mine, was the war room of our film and television rights department. My book-shelves only had to bear the weight of books by my own clients, but Graham's shelves were stacked to overflowing with a dizzying collection of typescripts and bound proofs and published books, his wall-mounted schedules and half-buried desk completing the picture of organized chaos.

Ignoring the clutter, I sank into the cush-ions of the love seat in the corner, pushing aside a stack of catalogs so I could prop my feet up on the coffee table.

"Tea or coffee?" Graham offered.

"Tea sounds heavenly."

"Right," he said, and left me, returning several minutes later with two cracked and battered mugs. I'd just begun to drift, eyes closing, and the heat of the mug being thrust into my hands came as a bit of a jolt, but the fragrant steam revived me.

I took a sip and thanked him. "You're an angel."

"That's hardly the image I'm after," he said, with a smile, as he settled himself in his own padded chair. "I'd rather be seen as the devil incarnate — I get more accomplished, that way."

"Yes, I heard you'd been terrorizing my poor assistant lately."

"Vicious rumors," he denied. "Speaking of which, I don't suppose Bridget happened to confirm or deny her affair with that Formula One chap? No? Damn. I've got ten quid riding on that one." Swiveling his chair round, he faced me expectantly. "So, what's her opinion of the Llandrah series?"

"I think she likes it. She seemed quite happy they were wanting Julia to oversee the animation." That had been one of my concerns, as well as Bridget's. Julia Beckett's original illustrations for the Llandrah books had been so very beautiful that they'd become a living part of Bridget's text, and neither of us could envisage the stories being told without those same distinctive images.

"Yes, well, Julia is rather irreplaceable," said Graham, with a sigh. "Horrible shame that she went and got married — I'll never understand the female mind."

"She's very happy."

"No doubt." With a shrug that dismissed the irrational nature of women, he returned to the topic at hand. "So you think Bridget's pleased with the deal?"

"I think so, yes."

"But you're not sure."

"Well, we sort of got sidetracked," I explained, raising one hand to massage the veins pounding time at my temples. "You know Bridget. One minute we're discussing the contract, and the next I'm hearing all about her Christmas plans."

"Oh, yes? And where's she off to this year? Rome? Vienna?"

"Pembrokeshire."

"I'm sorry?"

"Some little place called Angle, in south Pembrokeshire."

"Of course," he said. "That would have been my next guess."

"Yes, well, you might laugh, but she's been asked to spend the holidays with James Swift, of all people. And she wants me to go with her."

Graham turned his head at that. "I hope you told her yes."

"I told her maybe." To his scandalized expression I explained: "It's my brother's first Christmas in Canada, Graham — my family's expecting me there."

He felt sure they'd survive. Turning away, he adopted a carefully casual tone. "You do know who represents Swift, don't you?"

"All the more reason not to go," I said.

"And miss the chance to lure away his

blue-eyed boy? You disappoint me." He glanced at me and smiled, taking pity on my situation. "I've been in this position myself, you know. I once had two invitations arrive by the same post — one to my eldest sister's anniversary supper, and another to this gala West End opening — both for the same night. In the end, I found that there was only one fair way to settle it." Fishing in his pocket, he produced a single penny and held it up for me to see.

"What, you tossed a coin?"

"It's the tried and trusted method." He defended his decision. "Saves a lot of mental aggravation. Here, you give it a go."

I caught the coin in a reflex motion, shaking my head. "Don't be daft."

"No, really. Heads, you do the boring family thing and go to Canada, and tails . . . Oh, hell," he said, as the ringing of his telephone cut in. "I'll have to take this, Lyn. Won't be a minute."

As he swung round in his chair to take the call, his back to me, I frowned, considering. He might be right, I thought — a toss of the coin did seem the only fair way to decide where I ought to spend Christmas.

And it only took four tries to make the penny come up tails.

CHAPTER 3

And so to the land's
Last limit I came —
> — Alfred, Lord Tennyson,
> "Merlin and the Gleam"

My mother didn't seem at all put out by my announcement. Sitting cross-legged on my sitting room floor the next evening, she measured out ribbon with one hand and bent forward, only half listening. "Of course I don't mind. Heavens, dear, you're twenty-eight now . . ."

"Twenty-nine."

"Old enough to do your own thing, that's my point. Could you just put your finger right here, on this ribbon? That's it." She finished tying the elaborate bow, and sat back to judge the effect. To my mother, wrapping Christmas gifts was a job that demanded absolute perfection. She'd been a window dresser once, and she still liked to make things beautiful. "That will have to do, I suppose." Setting the professional-looking parcel to one side she picked up a rugby shirt and shook out the creases. "Now then, who is this for?"

"Patrick. He desperately wanted an England home jersey." I glanced at her sideways. "You're *sure* you don't mind?"

"Darling, I've already told you . . ."

"I know, but you're wearing that look."

She raised her head and smiled. "You shouldn't be so sensitive to how I look, you know. I didn't live my life to please my mother."

"Yes, well," I said drily, "I doubt that you could have pleased Granny. *She'll* have something to say about my not coming to Canada."

"Your grandmother," my mother assured me, "will be far too busy putting Patrick's in-laws in their place to worry about you."

I'd met Patrick's in-laws the previous summer. They were very political, full of opinions and ready to argue. They'd lock horns with Granny the minute they met. "Oh Lord, I hadn't thought of that."

"So you see, it's just as well you won't be there," she said. "It isn't going to be a restful Christmas. I, for one, intend to buy a vat of sherry at the duty-free and keep it to hand." Reaching for another roll of ribbon, she glanced up, met my watching eyes, and sighed. "If I'm wearing any look at all, it's only because I'm a mother, and no mother likes leaving her child alone during the holidays."

I could understand that. She'd never had to worry about it before, because I'd never missed a Christmas with my family. Even during those brief, disastrous years of my marriage to Martin — ancient history now — when the simple act of sitting down to Christmas lunch became a kind of torture and my mother took to serving the turkey already sliced, for fear my father might do murder with the carving knife — even then, I'd always kept the ritual, shuttling back and forth between our tiny flat in Shepherd's Bush and my parents' home in Maidstone.

This would be the first year that I'd broken with tradition.

"And I suppose," my mother went on, rather carefully, "I'm just a bit concerned about you being on your own, you know, at this time of the year."

"I'm fine," I said. "And after all, it's been five years. I'm past the fragile stage." I'd been sitting too long. I rose rather stiffly, and stretched. "Shall I make us some tea?"

It was a tactic that I often used when I didn't want to talk about something, and I knew she wasn't fooled, but being my mother she didn't let on. And she didn't follow me into the kitchen, either — she let me have my privacy. Alone, I filled the kettle, forcing back the pricking tears. I'd never liked to cry in front of anyone, not even my mother, but my emotions weren't so easy to control so close to Justin's birthday.

That's how I preferred to think of it — his birthday. Not the day that he had died.

It seemed like yesterday, sometimes, as if the five years hadn't happened. I remembered every moment of my labor, being glad that my mother was there, being glad that Martin wasn't — he'd been dead three months by that time, and although I had gone through the motions of grieving I'd secretly felt like an enormous weight had lifted from my shoulders. Martin hadn't wanted the baby in the first place. Careless, he'd called me at first, and then selfish, and finally he'd gone along grumpily, showing no joy at the prospect of being a father. His death had somehow made the baby more my own.

I'd picked the baby's name myself, the day I'd learned I was carrying a boy. I'd spelled it out in brightly painted letters on the nursery door: Justin. I'd stocked the nursery shelves with clothes and books and cuddly toys, and planned the outings I would take him on, the places I would show him. I'd walked on air for weeks.

He'd been a big baby, nine pounds and three ounces, so I'd expected that the labor would be difficult. But soon, I'd thought, the pain would be over. Soon I'd have Justin . . .

One final push, the feeling of that tiny new life slipping from my body, and a rush of swelling happiness.

And then had come confusion. Urgent voices, hurried hands, a sterile figure, gowned and masked, who'd whisked my baby out of the delivery room and down the echoing corridor. I'd heard the high-pitched crying, frantic, rising to a scream above the fast receding footsteps, and I'd struggled to rise, to go after my baby. "What is it?" I'd begged them. "What's wrong?"

I remembered my mother's anguished eyes, and the doctor saying Justin wasn't breathing, and me shaking my head. "But he's crying . . . I can hear him crying."

No, they'd told me gently. That was someone else's baby, not my own.

I'd refused to believe it. *This isn't him,* I'd

thought, when they'd taken me to view the little body, to let me hold him. *My baby's alive, he was crying, I heard him . . .*

The kettle rattled on the stove and whistled to the boil. Brushing my cheeks with an impatient hand, I brought myself back to the present and reached for the teapot.

My mother's voice called from the sitting room, "Need any help?"

"No," I called back, "I can manage." I said it again, very quiet but firm and determined, for my ears alone: "I can manage."

Managing Bridget was another matter. My mother might not be having the most relaxing time in Vancouver, with Granny picking battles, but I had a hunch my holidays would not be much more restful. Bridget had a certain knack for finding trouble. The drive to Wales alone was an adventure.

I didn't realize I'd been holding my breath until it came out in a sigh of pure relief, as the driver ahead of us slid his rust-riddled Ford off the roundabout's first exit.

"Bloody good job, you dozy old pillock!" Bridget called after him, uncaring that he couldn't hear. She put her foot to the floor and her sporty blue MGF sprang forward, accelerating with a force that pinned me to my seat. "Some people," she informed me, "should be taken off the road."

I bit my tongue in time.

Turning my head, I focused on the blur of passing hedges and went on playing the little silent traveling game I always played when driving with Bridget, counting the number of times we escaped certain death. I'd lost count in that near collision just outside of Bristol, but since then the score had risen once again to a respectable nineteen. Twenty, I amended, as we hurtled past the next car on a blind curve.

Not that I really expected any harm to come to us. Bridget could have walked blindfold across a minefield and come safely out the other side — her life was somehow charmed. But it did make me breathe a little easier when we came round the curve to find the road was empty.

"Not much traffic here," I remarked.

"You want to see it in the summertime. Tourists everywhere." She pulled a face. "It took me ages to get down here last July."

I looked round. "Last July?"

"Mm. James had the house then, as well, for a fortnight."

"I see. So the two of you are . . ."

Bridget glanced sideways, mischievous. "That would be telling."

"I thought you liked telling."

She laughed. "Bloody cheek. I've half a mind to become celibate, and leave you lot at Simon Holland with nothing to talk about. Is Graham still running a book on my love life?"

I assured her that he was. "But I'm afraid he's put rather long odds on James Swift."

"Poor old James." She sighed, fondly. "I met him at the London Book Fair this year, did I tell you? One of those cocktail party things, I don't remember it exactly. James took me to dinner afterwards, and . . . well, you know. He *is* a damned good-looking man, I must admit."

"But?" I prompted, and she smiled.

"Exactly. But."

"He's very much your physical type," I said, knowing how much she admired the sleek and slightly predatory look, "so I'm assuming it's not that."

"Oh no, he's prime," she said, using her trademark term of approval. "But you know me, I need a challenge. James is far too dull."

I refused to believe it. "A man who writes novels like *The Leaden Sky* can't possibly be dull."

"Cerebral, then. He thinks too much. I like a man to *act*."

Turning in my seat, I looked at her,

31

amused. "So why on earth did you agree to spend this Christmas with him?"

"Because he asked me. And I do so hate to disappoint." Shifting gears, she overtook another car and nearly clipped a cyclist, who waved his fist and shouted as he wobbled in our wake. "Besides," said Bridget, taking no notice, "James isn't the only interesting man in Angle."

I recognized her tone of voice, and knew that it spelled trouble. "Oh, Bridget."

"What?" She looked round, innocent.

"You're never thinking of making a play for some other poor sod while we're here, are you?"

"Darling." Her smile was arch. "He's not a poor sod. He's a playwright."

I rolled my eyes heavenward. "God, give me strength."

"Oh, don't be so Victorian. It's not as though I'm *married* to James, or anything."

"Well, true, but surely when you're staying with him —"

"Don't worry," Bridget said. "I'll be discreet."

"Define discreet."

"No photographs." She winked. "Besides, James will be so busy talking to you that I doubt he'll even notice what I do."

"Oh, I *see*." I smiled, catching on. "So

that's why I'm here, is it? To create a diversion while you do the dirty work."

"And maybe get yourself another client, in the process."

"Well, you're living in cloud-cuckoo-land if you think any man would find me so diverting that he'd fail to notice you."

She clucked her tongue. "You underestimate yourself."

"I'm only stating fact." Settling back in my seat, I took stock of our new surroundings. We'd reached the outskirts of a town — the hedges, flashing by, changed into houses, with a sign pointing off to a railway station on the left. "Where are we now?" I asked.

"Pembroke."

"Oh, really?" I strained forward, longing for a view of the town's famous castle, but Bridget whipped us neatly round a roundabout and down a steepish hill between the pastel houses. Here the road flattened out again, chasing a serpentine course round a strip of green common, while the town itself ran on along the rocky promontory rising to our right. The old stone walls that once had ringed medieval Pembroke still stood stoutly at the common's edge, supporting the sloping jumble of tightly packed buildings and shops perched on top. But it wasn't till we

33

came to the end of the common and turned at the road junction there that I caught my first sight of the castle.

A dark, muddy gray, it soared straight and secure from the edge of the promontory, an immovable sentry set right at the top of the high street with traffic and pavements pressed close to its walls. Impressed, I twisted in my seat to keep the view of it, trying to imagine how it would have looked five centuries ago to peasants toiling in the fields below its walls.

"Oh, for God's sake," said Bridget, and leaned on the horn. "Get a move on."

She was talking to a pedestrian this time, an old man with blowing white hair who was taking his sweet time in crossing the road. He turned his head slowly, and looked at me, smiling.

"Idiot," Bridget pronounced him. We picked up speed again, tucking round another narrow curve between old houses. I had one last glimpse of the castle from a different angle as we dipped along a river and entered a deep, quiet wood thick with fallen leaves from which the tall pale trunks of ash and poplar, birch and spindly hazel rose to close above our heads. Bridget said to me, encouragingly, "Nearly there. It's only twenty minutes' drive from here to Angle."

I'd been hoping for a coastal road, so I could see the sea, but when we emerged from the wood the road stayed stubbornly inland, bordered by steep banks that tried to hide the bright green pastures on the other side. The banks themselves were rather curious, with their stone-and-grass fronts and the high blackthorn hedges on top. I'd never seen anything like them.

"They're true Pembrokeshire banks," Bridget said, when I asked her. "I suppose they're made that way to give some shelter from the rain, or something. The weather can get fierce, down here."

It wasn't fierce today. There was only the wind, waving soft down a ripple of dead flaxen grass at the edge of the green field beside me. It might have been spring. I'd read a few brochures on Wales these past few weeks, and endured countless lectures from my Welsh assistant Lewis, so I knew the weather here was somewhat softened by the Gulf Stream. I remembered enough of the maps, too, to know that we were heading west along the Angle peninsula. To the north of us, just out of sight, would be the sheltered waters of Milford Haven. Ahead of us and to the south lay miles of protected scenic coastline, part of the long stretch of high, ragged cliffs, windswept beaches and unspoiled coves that made up the Pembrokeshire Coast National Park — a rambler's paradise, the guidebooks had proclaimed, and one of the most beautiful coasts in all Britain — the only one deemed worthy to be designated a National Park.

I'd expected to be dazzled by the scenery. Which was why, when I finally glimpsed the Milford Haven estuary a minute later, it surprised me to find the view spoiled by a sprawling oil refinery.

Bridget agreed it was awful. "But people have to work somewhere. And at least they're all kept to this bit of the Haven. Once you get round the tip of the peninsula, you'd never even know that they were here. James hates them, though," she told me. "He's as bad as your brother, the way he goes on."

I marked that down as a point in his favor. "Does he have family down here?"

"Who, James? No, I don't think so. Why?"

"I only wondered. His mother's Welsh, as I recall."

Bridget smiled. "Been swotting up on James Swift, have you?"

"Well . . ."

"Then you know more than I do. I've

never really asked him anything about —
oh, bloody hell!" she burst out, braking to a
sudden stop.

My seat belt snapped me smartly back to
stare in some amazement at the cause of
our near accident. A waddling row of ducks,
unhurried, filed across the road as Bridget
left the engine idling.

"They do this every bloody time I'm on
this road," she complained. "I swear they
recognize the car."

She was probably right, I decided. The
lead duck certainly seemed more intent on
irritating Bridget than on anything else. He
reached the other side, pecked once or twice
without enthusiasm at the hedgerow, then,
turning, led the whole troupe back again,
toward the safety of their pond. He looked
up rather smugly as he passed, and Bridget
called him something rude.

I laughed. "I thought you liked ducks."

"Oh, I do," she told me, sweetly. "I love
ducks. Lying on their backs in orange
sauce." The last bird scuttled nervously
aside as Bridget rammed the gear stick up
again and the MGF sprang forward. "I
daren't run them over, though. My publicist
would have a fit. 'Children's author kills
defenseless duckling,' " she mimicked the
headlines. "It would never do."

The road curved and narrowed again till the banks closed in upon us and the blackthorn scraped the car at either side, making it all but impossible to see round the bends or maneuver to avoid oncoming cars, but Bridget, ever confident, plowed bravely on, refusing to reduce her speed. I closed my eyes, and didn't open them until she said, in cheerful tones, "There's Angle."

We were turning now, at the top of a tall hill, preparing to start our descent to the village. Below us, the sea circled round the blunt point of the land, biting in at both ends of the straight line of paved road that cut through the narrowest part of the peninsula, running like a ribbon from one large rounded bay to the other. Along that ribbon I could see the speckled squares of cottages, and rising from their backs were narrow patchwork fields that climbed a hillside nearly as high as the one we were on before falling again to the icy-blue stretch of the Haven behind.

The Haven was filled with activity — two long dark gray ships that were probably tankers inched past the jetties that sprouted like claws from the opposite shore, and a handful of smaller boats wove through the wake of a giant white ferry boat headed for Ireland. The oil refinery I'd seen earlier was still a dominant feature here, sprawling off to the right, but I caught at least a glimpse of coastal splendor as we dipped toward the village.

My first impression of Angle was a brief one — a cluster of cottages painted in the pastel colors of the seaside, pale cream and lemon and soft pink and mint, their chimney pots puffing out smoke . . . the gray stone, crenellated tower of what looked to be a church . . . the little yellow Wall's ice-cream sign set outside to mark the village shop. But I didn't get a proper look. Bridget turned down a short lane through the houses and bumped round the edge of the easternmost bay, where fishing boats bobbed at their moorings in a sheltered inlet and a small stone bridge spanned the tidal estuary that cleft its way across the pebbled shore. Leaving the village behind us, we rolled up and over the bridge and the gates of a long, lovely house rose to welcome us.

It had, as Bridget mentioned, been three houses once — I could still make out the divisions on the front facade. And the ruined tower she had promised me was even better than I had imagined. Square-walled and impressively intact, it stood like a stern gray sentry at the far end of the house, while a few large crows wheeled round its upper reaches, lending atmosphere. The house and the tower would both have been fully at home on the moors — windswept and lonely, with the curlews screaming overhead. But they were equally impressive here, a comfortable stone's throw from this sleeping seaside village, with the reed-choked tidal estuary making a kind of a moat between the tower and the deeply shadowed churchyard opposite.

What a wonderful place for a writer to work, I thought.

Bridget, following my gaze to the cozily smoking chimney at the far end of the house, misunderstood completely. "Don't worry," she assured me. "The fires are just for show. James wouldn't stay in a place that didn't have central heating."

A man had straightened from the front garden at the sound of our approaching car — a tall man in jeans and a heavy ribbed sweater, his dark golden hair slightly longer than I remembered it from his television appearances. He raised his hand in a wave of greeting and came across to meet us.

It wasn't until he drew level with my open window that I realized he wasn't James Swift.

"Hello," he said cheerfully, bending down to rest his elbows on the car. "You're early."

Bridget arched an eyebrow. "And you would be . . . ?"

"Christopher." He shot her a boyish grin. "I'm afraid James isn't here at the moment, but if you want to bring your car round the back, I'll get you settled in."

He stood upright again and, turning, led the way along the drive, while Bridget took her foot off the brake to follow. "Well, this is interesting," she said slowly. "A brother, do you think?"

"That would be my guess. They look so much alike."

"They do, indeed."

I flicked her a wary glance, but her expression showed curiosity, and nothing more. "Bridget . . ."

"Mm?"

"This local man you've set your sights on . . . he's a playwright, you said?"

"That's right."

"Anyone I'd know?"

"Ah," she said, with a smile. "Now, that *would* be telling."

"Oh, come on."

But standing firm, she shook her head. "You'll find out soon enough," she promised. "All good things come to those who wait."

CHAPTER 4

An ancient bridge, and a more ancient
    tower,
A farmhouse that is sheltered by its
    wall . . .
        — W. B. Yeats, "My House,"
    from "Meditations in Time of Civil War"

It was a bit of a squeeze to coax the MGF through the narrow gap between the ancient tower and the high stone wall at the lawn's edge, but Bridget managed it with confidence, swinging the car round to follow the drive up the side of the house. We were on an uphill slope now, rising gently to a level with the upstairs windows, while the house appeared to sink into the earth beside us.

Ahead, I saw a row of three large sheds, the middle one blocked by a muddy-wheeled tractor, but before I could ask the obvious question, Bridget stepped in to explain.

"It's not just a name, Castle Farm — it's a real working farm, owned by James's Uncle Ralph and Auntie Pam. They're not really family, you know, just old friends of his mother; he's known them for years. Their daughter's up in Yorkshire, somewhere, and whenever they visit her James minds the house while Owen — he's a local man, another farmer — minds the animals."

I didn't need to ask what animals she meant. I could see the metal roofs of cowsheds nestled in a hollow just behind the house, and the fields of pastureland above us on the hillside held a scattering of woolly sheep, watching our approach with idle interest. A marmalade cat scampered out of the way as Bridget parked between a gray Rover and a sleek silver Mercedes at the top of the drive, on a level bit of grass beside the tractor.

Christopher caught up with us a moment later, stretching out his hand for Bridget's suitcase. "Here, let me take that for you. Mind how you go," he warned, as we turned to double back on foot along the drive, toward the house. "We had some rain at lunchtime, and it's still a little slippery."

I'd forgotten how quickly the weather could change, on the coast. There was no sign of rain now, nor cloud; only the sun glaring down from a blinding blue sky. The brisk wind had teeth and I turned my collar to it, hefting my own small suitcase and falling into step behind Bridget and Christopher.

Castle Farm looked deceptively smaller, from this angle. The middle of the three joined houses jutted backward from its neighbors, forming one wall of a half-sunken courtyard, sheltered by high earthen banks sloping down from the elbow-curved drive, screened by ash trees and one lovely lilac. It was into this courtyard that Christopher led us. My feet slipped on the flagstone walk, and I shifted my grip on the suitcase to counterbalance, waiting until I was sure of my step before raising my head again to admire this compact gardener's paradise, where every level place and cranny bloomed with pots of greenery and flowers that had somehow held their own against the cold, and a lone leaf still danced at the top of the graceful viburnum that hugged the side wall. Someone, I thought, loved this house a great deal, to have taken such pains with the landscaping.

I followed Christopher and Bridget through the maze of flowerpots, heading for the white-painted porch that protected the house's rear entrance. There were two more cats here — a great hulking tabby that watched us with oddly intelligent eyes, and a tiny pale gray one curled up on a window ledge.

Bridget bent to stroke the larger one. "Hello, Big Boy."

Christopher turned. "Oh, that's right, you've been here before, haven't you? You'll know all about the cats. Aunt Pam's got seven of them now. Elen's been taking care of them, and feeding them, but they still like to wait round the door here, in hope."

The little gray cat meowed sharply and leaped to my shoulders in one fluid movement.

Too late, Christopher warned me, "He does like to jump, that one. Here, let me help." The cat, once settled, wasn't easy to dislodge. It took a few tries but he finally came clear with a small tearing sound, like Velcro.

I raised my head, and caught the crisply pleasant scent of coal smoke. "Now there's something you don't smell in London too often."

"What? Oh, the fire." Christopher nodded, depositing the cat beside the door. "Yes, I like a roaring fire, myself. James isn't so keen. But Uncle Ralph said I could use all the coal that I liked, and Uncle Ralph," he told us, "is the King of Castle Farm. He outranks James."

Bridget raised an eyebrow. "You're James's brother, I take it?"

"Got it in one," he congratulated her, holding the door open. "I'm not so talented nor famous, I'm afraid, but I am much better looking." He said that lightly, jokingly, with a smile meant to charm, and Bridget smiled back.

Like mirror images, I thought, each trying to beguile the other. But Christopher had already spoiled his chances. Bridget never went for men who were so openly flirtatious. She preferred the ones who snubbed her, who afforded her some challenge. I might have tipped him off, but given that he'd been so quick to carry Bridget's suitcase, leaving me to lug my own across the slippery flagstones, I didn't feel inclined to offer any help to Christopher Swift.

Instead I sidled past him, through the doorway, and into a light-filled porch that ran between the end house and the middle one like a long narrow passage, with wooden doors at either end. The lovely, faintly musty, homely old-house smell assailed me.

"You want the door on the right," he instructed us.

We stepped up and into a spacious, sunny

yellow kitchen that looked as though it might have been two rooms, once. They'd been able to remove the wall, but not the fireplace. It stood firm in its redbrick surround at the room's center point, with great arches to each side of it through which I saw beyond into the sitting area, where a stylish blue sofa and chairs ringed a small television. The kitchen furniture was plainer — a scrubbed pine table hugged the wall beside me, near the door, and to my left an old Welsh dresser held an orderly display of cream-colored crockery. I was almost disappointed to see the modern dark green cooker and American-style fridge — I'd half hoped for an Aga and icebox.

Still, there was a fire in the fireplace, and the sweet sharp smell of coal, and flowered curtains tied well back to let in the afternoon sun.

"You'll have to excuse the mess," Christopher said, pushing plates and cups back from the edge of the work top. "We had a bit of a crisis last night, with Elen and Stevie, and we haven't caught up with the cleaning. Your beds are made up, though — we did manage that."

"Elen's here?" Bridget said that too sharply. She flicked me a strange, apprehensive glance. "I thought she was going to

47

Bristol."

"She was. But she had a dream, or some damned thing, that told her she should stay." Christopher shrugged, leading us through into another narrow passageway. "You know how Elen is."

Unable to contain my curiosity, I asked, "Who's Elen?"

"Uncle Ralph's tenant. She rents the big house at the other end, the East House." We were in the front hall, now, with doors to either side of us and a set of ancient-looking double doors opening out to the sunlit front porch with its checkerboard flooring of red and gray tiles. Climbing the wide flight of stairs to the upper floor and bedrooms, Christopher explained that the East House was still a self-contained unit. "Uncle Ralph meant to knock it together with these," he said, waving his hand to include the two joined houses we were in, "but after Elen and Tony moved in — Tony was her husband, friendly chap, he died the summer before last — after they moved in, Uncle Ralph sort of put his plans on hold. And now that Elen's on her own with the baby . . . well, I don't think there'll be any renovations for a while."

My head came up. "She has a baby?"

"Yes, a little boy. Stevie. He's not a year

48

old yet. You'll hear him," he promised. "He's teething."

My body stiffened slightly, my legs growing heavier, feet dragging up the final few stairs. I felt Bridget watching my face as Christopher came to a stop on the landing, swinging the nearest door wide to reveal a large, high-ceilinged room with a four-poster bed. "You're in here," he informed me, "and, Bridget, you're down at the end of the passage, next to James . . ."

"The Cleopatra room? I know the one. I can give Lyn the rest of the tour," she said, sending him a brilliant smile. "I don't suppose you'd be a dear and put the kettle on? I could murder for a cup of tea."

She came into the room with me, standing just inside the doorway while I let my case drop with a bounce to the mattress and took a look round. The room was restful, painted soft pale cream with sea-green carpets and green hangings on the bed. And the bed itself was absolutely splendid — a true antique, its posts carved and rubbed smooth with years of polishing, like those I'd seen in the royal bedchambers at Hampton Court. I was trailing my fingers down one heavy bedpost when Bridget spoke, behind me.

"Look, I didn't think she'd be here, or I

would have told you earlier, you know, about the baby." Bridget hadn't been my client then, five years ago. My employers at Simon Holland had been rather concerned, as a matter of fact, when I'd signed her, since representing a children's writer necessarily meant coming into contact with children themselves, at events and book signings, but I'd managed to convince them that it didn't bother me to be near children. Only babies.

I'd never mentioned Justin's death to Bridget, that I remembered. But ours was an incestuous business. She would have heard the rumors.

She went on, "If it's going to be a problem for you . . ."

"I'll be fine." I set a smile on my face and turned to show her just how fine I was. "Stop worrying."

Relieved, she came forward. "It's quite the room, isn't it? I told James you'd like it, because of the view."

Since it was a corner room, with one large window facing front and another in the end wall right beside the dainty fireplace, I wasn't sure which view she meant. I chose the front one, drawing back one panel of the deep green velvet curtains.

The ruined castle tower, tall and somber,

dominated everything. It seemed quite close enough to touch, a few short yards away across the lawn, the gaping blackness of its slitted windows staring back at me like human eyes — not sinister, but wary. Perched atop the crumbled crenellations, an enormous crow sullenly gazed at the boats in the bay, head sunk low. Beyond the tower and the crow, I saw the line of the village itself — the gray square tower of the church, a lower building, with a playing field beside it, that I took to be the school, and a row of huddled roofs that stretched along the road and out of sight, with narrow fields behind.

In summer, Angle likely came alive with families down on holiday, with caravans and barking dogs and children still wet from the beach and sticky with ice lollies. But now winter had come and the village was sleeping. I saw only one car rolling drowsily down through the houses.

"Best view in the house," Bridget said, at my shoulder. "I thought you'd like having the tower so close. I remember how much you enjoyed dragging me through all those ruins in France." She frowned. "I don't think I could sleep with that thing looking in on me, personally. I'd have nightmares."

I'd have nightmares anyway, tower or no, but I didn't tell her that. Instead I lied and

51

said, "Yes, well, I don't have your imagination, do I? So I don't have to worry." Moving back to the bed, I unzipped my suitcase and began to unpack its unexciting contents — a few sweaters, a pair of jeans, plain black trousers, woolly socks . . .

"God, I do envy you," Bridget said. "You always pack so sensibly."

"Years of practice." I'd only brought one dress — a simple black velvet thing, sleeveless with a scoop neck, that I hung now in the wardrobe before sorting the rest of my clothes into drawers. "I'm not a patch on my mother, though. She used to go on holiday with a tiny little flight bag, and she'd somehow manage to create a different outfit every day."

Bridget, who had sat on the edge of my bed to watch, laced her fingers round her knees and grinned. "Your mother is a frightening sort of woman, isn't she? Like Mary Poppins. Is there anything she *can't* do?"

Offhand, I couldn't think of anything. I pushed the sock drawer shut and straightened, dusting my hands on my jeans.

"There," I said, "that's that lot taken care of."

"You've forgotten something." Bridget pointed to the bulging Jiffy bag still taking up a corner of my suitcase.

"Oh, that's all right, it can stay there. I had Lewis go through the office shelves and choose some books that I could have on hand for Christmas presents, since I didn't know exactly who would be here."

She reached for the packet, her upward glance dry. "So tell me again that you're not like your mother."

"I'm not, really. And you can stop poking that, your present and James's are still in the car."

She pulled a face and upended the Jiffy bag, spilling its contents out onto the bed. "I'm surprised you let Lewis pick these for you. He has peculiar tastes, as I recall."

I smiled. My assistant was the only man I'd ever met who could resist Bridget's charms — he did it with ease, as a matter of fact, the result being Bridget had always regarded him rather distrustfully. "Look," she said, holding a book up in evidence, "here's one in some bloody foreign language, even."

I looked at the cover, and smiled. "That's Welsh, I expect. Trust Lewis. What else did he put in there?"

She flipped through the titles and called them by category. "Mystery, mystery, poetry, some historical nonfiction thing, that one about trekking through Africa . . . oh, and bless his heart, he's put in one of mine, as well." She turned it over. "God, why did you let me use that photo? I look hideous."

It was her first book in the Llandrah series. Lewis, efficient as usual, had provided gifts to suit all ages, even those barely old enough to read. Not wanting to think of the baby next door, I looked away quickly. "Right then, I'll just go wash up, if you'll point me to the bathroom."

"Out the door and to your left. But don't be too long, will you?" she called after me. "I really am dying for tea."

Downstairs, Christopher had set out biscuits on the kitchen table with our teacups, and a rather tempting plate of cold ham sandwiches. "You can thank James for those," he told us, nodding at the sandwiches. "He thought you might be hungry."

"Darling James," said Bridget, tucking in. "Where did you say he was?"

"I didn't." Christopher leaned back against the doorjamb. "He's gone up to the Hall, actually. Shooting pheasants."

Bridget looked surprised. "But James doesn't like guns."

"True. But then he's not the type to disappoint the local gentry. He's not as rude as I am. I declined the invitation," he explained, helping himself to a biscuit. "Blasting birds out of the sky isn't my idea of an afternoon's fun. And with James about, it's just as likely to be me that gets blasted, instead of the pheasants."

The resemblance between the brothers really was quite striking, I thought, looking at him. They shared the same blue eyes, the same dark golden hair that my mother had once termed "British blond," the same angular jaw and the same dashing smile that displayed teeth so perfectly straight one could hardly believe they were natural. But Christopher, I decided, was the younger by at least five years.

His eyes were still on Bridget, assessing her, trying to charm.

"When James told me he'd invited a fellow writer for the holidays," he said, "I must admit I didn't think he meant someone like you."

She smiled. "You were expecting tweeds and brogues, then, were you?"

"Not really. Some tall, gaunt creature dressed in black, with granny glasses and a fringe, perhaps."

"Sorry to disappoint."

"Not at all." He turned to me. "You're going to think me awfully rude, I know, but I'm afraid I've forgotten your name."

I was used to that, in Bridget's company. "It's Lyn. Lyn Ravenshaw."

"My agent," Bridget added. "Although I suppose she doesn't fit your image of a literary agent, either."

"On the contrary." He looked me up and down. "She looks exactly as an agent ought to look."

I sipped my tea, amused. "Is that a good thing or a bad thing?"

But he'd already returned his attention to my more entrancing client. "You write children's books, James said. That must be fun."

"I'm not sure any form of writing can be called 'fun,' " said Bridget. "Fulfilling, yes. Enjoyable, yes. Bloody hard work, definitely." She took another sandwich to replace the one she'd eaten. "I take it you don't write, yourself?"

Christopher shook his head. "No, I'm not as clever as my brother. Can't even scribble a sentence."

"So what do you do?"

"Antiques," he said. "I have a shop in Bath."

She glanced up, intrigued. "*Do* you?" She'd always had a weakness for antiques. But Christopher, not knowing this, failed to take full advantage of his opportunity.

Instead he shrugged and played the matter down.

"Not nearly as exciting as a writer's life, I shouldn't think. I feel quite dull, compared with you lot."

Watching him smile, I had a suspicion that Christopher Swift never thought himself dull. His ego would never have permitted it.

To me, he said, "You and I are the odd ones out, you know. There seem to be more writers down here in Angle than locals."

I saw a chance to satisfy my earlier curiosity. "Yes, Bridget did say you had a playwright here, as well, but I didn't catch the name . . ."

"Was that a car?" asked Bridget, tipping her head to listen.

Christopher stopped, and listened, too. "I don't hear anything."

"My mistake."

"Now what were you asking . . . ?"

"The playwright," I prompted him, ignoring Bridget.

"Oh right." He nodded, picking up the thread of conversation. "Well, you'll have heard the name, of course — he's rather more famous than my brother, and a good thing too, because old James is vain enough already —"

A new voice interrupted from the back

door; a cultured male voice, instantly identifiable. "That's slander, that is." He let the kitchen door swing closed again behind him as he came into the warmth, his blue eyes finding Bridget first, then Christopher, and finally coming to rest on me. "Miss Ravenshaw, I presume." The familiar smile flashed, as James Swift came across to greet me, offering a hand streaked with red from the afternoon's shooting. "Don't mind the blood," he said. "I've just committed murder."

Chapter 5

And after that, she set herself to gain
Him, the most famous man of all those
  times . . .
— Alfred, Lord Tennyson, "Merlin and Vivien"

I had heard others talk about the magnetism of the man, but even having been fore-warned, I fell victim to it now, myself. He was shorter than his brother, and stockier, with the same handsome features less care-fully drawn, as though they'd been formed by a hastier hand. That didn't surprise me. James Swift's appetites — for food, for drink, for women — were legendary, and now that he was nearing forty he'd begun to pay the price of self-indulgence, the once-sharp lines of jaw and cheekbone thickening and growing faintly softer, heavier. He must have seen the change himself, because he'd grown a beard since I'd last seen him interviewed on television — a closely trimmed dark beard that made a rakish contrast to the waving lion's mane of golden hair that touched his collar at the back.

He tossed that hair now, casually, and smiled, and gave me back my hand. "You don't look fierce at all," he said. Then, over my shoulder, he told Bridget: "My love, I can't battle with this one. I might do her damage."

"Don't you believe it," said Bridget. Grinning, she reached for another sandwich and drew one leg up underneath her on the chair. "She scares my publisher to death, you know. The only reason he gives me those obscene advances is because he's terrified of saying 'no' to Lyn. He did it once, in the beginning," she revealed, with a sympathetic shake of her head, "and he's never been the same man since."

"You don't say." James Swift took a second, more piercing look at my innocent face before bending to the sink to wash his hands. "Bridget's told you, I'd imagine, that I've fallen out with Ivor."

I nodded. "Yes, she did mention you weren't entirely happy."

"Is that how she said it? She puts things so politely." Turning off the taps, he moved to dry his hands on the tea towel. "The truth is that we nearly came to blows last time we met, but then I don't need to tell you what Ivor's like," he said, turning to face me. "You worked for him, didn't you?"

Yes, I had worked for the great Ivor Whitcomb. Ivor was the Goliath of the London literary scene — an older agent, powerful, abrasive, and a man who'd frightened *me* to death when I'd first come to work for him. He'd all but engineered my marriage. Martin Blake had been his blue-eyed boy, his favorite client, and in Ivor's eyes I had become the one responsible for Martin's self-indulgences, his early death. If I had been a better wife to Martin, he'd once told me, Martin would have been at home that night, instead of driving home from God knows where so drunk he couldn't see the road. I hadn't let the accusations bother me — Ivor was simply the sort of boss that one endured and, after all, his pay was good. But I could never forgive him for the things he'd said my first day back, just after losing Justin. How he'd said it was my fault for being thoughtless, for not giving up my riding like Martin had told me to. Not a word of consolation, not the smallest show of sympathy. I'd posted out my CVs that afternoon.

I looked at James now, and answered him. "That's right. I was with Ivor three years, before Simon Holland."

Bridget smiled. "Lyn thinks that it's unethical to try to sign you up, James, while you're still on Ivor's list."

"Really?" The beard gave his smile a roguish edge. "Unethical, maybe. Impossible, no. Are there any sandwiches left?"

Christopher, who'd been leaning indolently in his doorway, fading with the ease of long habit into the wings while his brother made his entrance, now brought himself forward again, not challenging for center stage, but staying in the circle of the spotlight. "Didn't they feed you up at the Hall?" he asked, pushing the sandwiches nearer to James. "Or doesn't one feed hunters?"

"Dulls the instinct, do you mean?" His brother smiled. "No, actually they fed us rather well, but that was hours ago. I've walked the whole of the estate, since then. At least," he qualified his statement, stretching his back, "it feels as if I have."

"You're out of shape, that's all," said Bridget, cheerfully. "It's like I told you — you can't sit all day and scribble and expect to keep in trim. You have to exercise."

"You don't," he countered.

"Yes, but then I have a rather high metabolism." Shrugging, she helped herself to the biscuits. "Energy to spare. And I write all my books while pacing back and forth across my sitting room, I'm never still. Whereas you," she told him, watching while he took the chair beside her, "sit there like a lump, for hours on end. It can't be healthy."

"Writers, my dear girl, are made to die young. All the famous ones do. Which reminds me," he said, "who were all of you discussing when I came in? This person who's rather more famous than me?"

"Gareth." Christopher straightened away from the door frame, and reached for a biscuit. "Lyn was asking me about him."

My brain, always loving a puzzle, latched on to the clue. He was talking about the playwright, of course. Bridget's playwright. And Christopher had hinted I would recognize the name. Now, who did I know that was famous, named Gareth? My memory switched on, searching backward . . .

James Swift passed a hand across his bearded jaw, as though the feel of it were new. "Of course, I do dispute the fact that Gareth's better known than me. After all, he hasn't written anything since *Red Dragon Rising,* and that was seven years ago."

I had to swallow, hard, to keep from choking on my tea. *"Red Dragon Rising?"*

"Yes. You do remember it?" His voice was

dry. "I've never met a person yet who hasn't seen the blasted thing."

That was hardly surprising. The play had hit the West End like a whirlwind, laying waste to all its competition. I'd seen it first with Martin, and the two of us had sat completely spellbound through the spectacle — a violent and poetic tale of Owen Glendower's, or, as we learned to say, Owain Glyn Dŵr's fifteenth-century rebellion, with dialogue so beautiful that, even now, whole passages stayed with me, haunted me, clung to my memory like ivy to stone. I'd gone back to watch the same production four times, on my own, and had marveled, like everyone else, at the talent of the self-contained young Welshman who had written it, Gareth Gwyn Morgan.

An ordinary-looking man, as I recalled. I couldn't quite picture his face, but he hadn't been handsome, or brooding, or wildly passionate. And he'd shown little interest in publicity. While the critics had raved, and the West End, electric with anticipation, had waited for Morgan's next masterpiece, the man himself, in imitation of the hero of his play, had slipped from London like a shadow, eluding any journalist who tried to follow.

And then, a few years later, when the play

64

was adapted into an equally lyrical film that turned heads at Cannes, there had been another ripple of excitement, like an earthquake's aftershock, and word had been passed round that Gareth Gwyn Morgan would surface again. But he hadn't, and after a few halfhearted tries to run the man to ground, the newspapers, defeated, had lost interest.

I myself had formed an image of the playwright as a modern day Glyn Dŵr, moving stealthily, unseen, among the wild Welsh northern hills. It came as a decided shock to learn that he was living here, in Angle.

"And how on earth," I asked Bridget, "did you manage not to mention this? You're horrible at keeping secrets."

"True. And I can't say I haven't been tempted to tip off a few of the tabloids, you know, and use the money for a nice long holiday in Greece."

James laughed. "You'd never make it to the airport, darling. They're very protective of Gareth, down here."

I looked at him. "But surely . . . I mean, this must be a popular place, in the summer. You'd think someone would have spotted him by now."

James didn't think it likely. "Gareth hasn't

got the sort of face that people spot."

"Like yours, you mean," said Bridget, giving him a playful shove.

"Well, quite. I couldn't hide if I wanted to; it'd be a bloody waste of time to try. Besides," he said, laying one hand over Bridget's, "I'm sure I'd be missed."

Not by Bridget, I thought. Not so long as there was bigger, more exciting game to hunt. Knowing her as well as I did, I had only to look at her face to know that she'd already met the mysterious Gareth Gwyn Morgan, and that he'd shown no interest in her. There was nothing she loved better than a challenge.

Veiling her eyes with her lashes, she looked at James demurely. "But of course I'd miss you, darling." She squeezed his hand and gave it back to him. "And so would Lyn. She loves your work. You should have heard the names she called the Booker judges, last year."

"Really?" He looked gratified. "Mind you, I don't put much stock in prizes, really."

Bridget pointed out that the only people who said that were the ones who didn't win. Yawning, she stretched and checked her watch. "I'm absolutely knackered. All that driving. Have I time, do you think, for a bath and a bit of a nap?"

James arched an eyebrow. "Time?"

"Before dinner."

"Oh, God." His eyes rolled. "It begins."

"Well, I have to be fed, darling."

"Every five minutes?"

She smiled. "Don't exaggerate. Do I or don't I have time before dinner?"

"You take as much time as you like," he invited her. "We're just going down to the pub."

"Right, then. I'm off upstairs."

Christopher followed her out of the room with his eyes, and again I thought how much he was like Bridget. I could almost see the wheels at work, deciding what approach could best be used to make the conquest.

James saw it, too. "Hands off, little brother."

"There's no harm in looking." Helping himself to the last cold ham sandwich, he pushed back his chair and stood. "I think I'll go lie down a while, myself. I didn't get much sleep last night, with all the goings-on."

Whistling, he went out and James brought his gaze round to mine, apparently feeling the need to explain. "We were both up quite late, I'm not sure if he told you . . ."

"He did say that there'd been a crisis, yes."

"Crisis." The word amused James. "I suppose you could call it that. Elen, my Uncle Ralph's tenant next door, is a bit off her nut. She heard some sort of noise in her son's room last night and she went all hysterical, thought that some creature was coming to get him. We had to call Owen to quiet her down. That's my uncle's friend, Owen, from down in the village. You'll meet him tomorrow, he sees to the farm when my uncle's away. He'll probably try to recruit you," he warned, "for his whist drive."

"I can't play whist."

"Just as well. So then," he said, with a smile, "would you like to make the pitch for Simon Holland now, or shall I take you for a walk around the farm and introduce you to the sheep?"

"A walk sounds lovely."

It was clearly not the answer he'd expected — he'd been leaning back more comfortably into his chair, arms folded, preparing himself for conversation. My reply brought his movement to a halt. "Oh right. Right, of course. Let me just fetch my jacket, then." Rolling to his feet, he eyed me with interest. "Bridget told the truth, I see, about your code of ethics."

It wasn't ethics, I could have told him. I

68

wouldn't have felt the least bit guilty stealing a client from Ivor Whitcomb, but I'd been sitting in a car all day and I was longing for a chance to stretch my legs, to breathe the country air and cleanse my weary mind and body of the hustle and hassles of London. Talking shop right now would be the worst thing I could do, I thought. I wanted reviving.

And I'd always been rather fond of sheep.

The cluster of ewes kept a respectful distance on their side of the fence, heads lifting now and then to watch us, soft breath steaming in the crisp air of the dying afternoon. We were losing the light, and the setting sun had tinged the clouds a golden rose that glowed against the cold flat blue of dusk.

James, beside me, propped his elbows on the fence rail and resumed his guided tour. "You know, you're standing on the only freehold farm in all of Angle."

"Really? Who owns all the others, then?"

"The family at the Hall, where I went shooting. They own everything — the Hall, the village, everything. Have done for nearly two centuries. One of their ancestors went off to fight the South African Wars, that's why some of the houses in Angle look sprung from the colonies. Neo-Natalian, they call it, that flat-topped design. And the Globe Inn" — he pointed behind us to the half-obscured outline of a colonnaded building in the village street — "that's the best example. Pure Johannesburg."

I looked across the narrow, feudal fields of rich red earth and verdant pasture sloping gently down from either side to form the shallow valley of the village, thinking how furious my brother Patrick would have been to know one family owned all this. He hated the concept of massive estates.

"Castle Farm," James went on, "was the old Rectorial Glebe land, you know, till it came up for auction in the twenties and Uncle Ralph's father managed to outbid the local gentry. There wasn't much to the property, back then, it was really just the tower and the dovecote and the ruins of a house, but Uncle Ralph's dad fixed things up again and added on the East House."

I turned to look down at the long, unbroken building with its dun-colored pebble-dash walls. "So the part that we're in is the oldest, then."

"Yes. No one knows how old, exactly, though we know there was an inn here in Elizabethan times."

Squinting a little, I studied the westernmost end of the house, comparing the heavy stone walls to the shape of the tower. "The tower's much older than that, surely?"

"Norman," he said with a nod. "There's an old legend goes with the tower, you know, that says in those days there were three sisters, all of whom inherited their father's estate, but none of whom wanted to live with the others. So one built a house where the Hall now stands, one built the castle — that's the castle there," he put in, pointing back again toward the village, "or at least the ruins of it, behind the post office, there isn't much left. And the third sister built this square tower, to live in."

"But nobody knows who the sisters were?"

"I doubt they ever existed, myself. I should think it more likely the tower belonged to some great Norman nobleman. Ordinary people," he said, with authority, "didn't have dovecotes."

We were standing by the dovecote, now, not more than ten yards distant from the gray stone dome-capped turret with its wooden door ajar. The sheep grazed round it, unimpressed by its obvious age, and the tabby cat dozed in the doorway. I smiled. "I'll have to take a picture of this, for a friend of ours — Bridget's former illustrator, actually. She has a thing for dovecotes."

"So does Christopher," said James. "My brother, if he could, would make it a hanging offense to tear down any building that predates the war. Still, he does come by it honestly, I suppose. Our mother loves old things."

He straightened away from the fence, and tearing myself from the dull-eyed ewes I turned to follow him, back along the curving drive that ran alongside the house. We'd come full circle round the property, and the tower, at the bottom of the drive, seemed to be waiting for us.

I felt small in its shadow. Even in its ruined state, the stone walls rose some thirty feet straight up, to scrape the sky with jagged fingers darkly stained with moss. It was a narrow structure, hard and angular, save for the turret-like curve at one corner that probably sheltered a stairwell inside.

Reaching out, I ran my hand caressingly over the cold stones as we walked past. "Is it safe to go up?" I asked, always keen to explore a ruin.

"Yes, I think so. Uncle Ralph should have a key somewhere, I'll take a look tomorrow."

It was too late to go up the tower anyway. The light had nearly gone. My trailing fingers snagged on something sharp, and I pulled my hand back, breaking contact with the tower wall.

"Come on," said James, "it's getting cold. Let's go and have a drink."

CHAPTER 6

In faith, he is a worthy gentleman,
Exceedingly well read, and profited
In strange concealments . . .
— William Shakespeare, *Henry IV, Part One*

We went in through the front door, through
the white-painted porch with the checkerboard floor. It smelled sharply of cut wood
and coal dust and damp quarry tile.

"If you're ever in the mood to light a fire,
you'll find the things you need in here," said
James, lifting the hinged lid of a long
wooden box fitted snugly underneath the
porch's window. "There's a shovel there, for
the coal — every room has its own scuttle,
which you need to heft about, I'm afraid —
and that little box holds sticks for kindling.
Firelighters and newspapers are in the hall
cupboard. Only don't burn the local papers," he warned me. "I save those, for
research."

I nodded, shrugged my jacket off, and waited a decent interval before following up on his last comment. "Is your new book set in Angle, then?"

"Not Angle, specifically — I couldn't stand the lawsuits. No, I've taken the rather more cowardly path of inventing my own coastal village." Moving into the hall, he pushed open the nearest door and stood aside to let me enter first. "I've been thinking that I ought to go one better, and invent my own damn county. The Thomas Hardy touch, you know. Though anyone with half a brain will recognize the Milford Haven references, no matter what I do."

This room, I thought as I went in, was clearly where he did his writing. In the center of the carpet, a rosewood table, spindle-legged, strained to support a tilting stack of books and magazines at one end, and a slick laptop computer at the other. An elegant mantelpiece on the wall behind had also been converted to a temporary bookshelf, and the fireplace grate was mounded high with cinders, as though someone had set light to it and then become distracted, leaving the coals to slowly choke on their own ashes.

My own bedroom, I judged, must be directly overhead, and the windows here offered the same sort of views, of the fields to the west, and the walled lawn and drive to the front. And the tower. It looked quite forlorn in the fast-fading light.

James crossed to draw the wine-red velvet curtains. "It always makes me think of old detective novels, this room does. A murderer could hide behind these curtains and you'd never see him."

I saw what he meant. The walls were built so thickly that the windows cut deep wells into the plastered stone, and the front window formed a bay in which a man could easily have stood. He could easily have *sat* there, I amended the thought, in an overstuffed armchair, and still have stayed hidden.

The curtains drawn, James switched on a pair of chairside lamps, and in the warmer light I felt a tug of recognition. "You've written about this room, surely? In *The Leaden Sky*. It's Bernard's study."

His startled upward glance told me I'd scored full points. "How the devil did you spot that?"

"You did a brilliant job describing it. Right down to the one missing brick on the hearth, and the chair where the dog always slept." I pointed to the armchair in the corner, and he smiled.

"Do you always remember books in such detail?"

"Normally, I don't remember them at all — not even ones by my own authors. I've read so many books, published and otherwise, that I almost never can recall the plots and characters, only how the story made me feel when I was reading. Some people, you know, can write beautiful prose, but they never do touch your emotions."

He came round to stand behind his desk, his expression intrigued. "And how do my books make you feel?"

"Uncomfortable." I tipped my head and thought a moment, seeking to explain. "Not in a bad way, but . . . it's rather like reading Marx, if you know what I mean. You're raised to see the world one way, and then Marx comes along and says: 'No, that's all wrong. You must look at it *this* way,' and you suddenly feel quite off balance. Uncomfortable."

"Yes." His eyes warmed.

"I still forget your plots, though," I confessed, with a smile. "And your characters."

"You remembered Bernard."

"I remembered Bernard's study. Not at all the same thing. It's only that your descriptions are so very visual, I tend to store them up like snapshots. I couldn't tell you what

77

Bernard was doing, for example — only that this was his room."

"How curious." He looked at me. "I, on the other hand, remember everything I've ever read. And the more appalling the writing, the more it seems to stick in my memory."

"Yes, well, that would be deadly for an agent," I said. "With all the typescripts that I have to read each week, it's sometimes better to forget."

He agreed it must be trying. "Have a seat, wherever you can find one, won't you? I'm afraid I'm rather messy when I'm writing."

I felt more privileged to be in the midst of James Swift's mess than in the spotless sitting room of someone with less talent. Just the thought that I was actually here now, in his writing room, and talking to him, gave me a secretive thrill. Shifting a slippery pile of newspapers from a comfortable-looking wing chair I sat, while James turned with a frown to the drinks cabinet. "Would you like a glass of sherry? I'm afraid we've only got Amontillado, nothing sweet."

"That's fine. I prefer a dry sherry."

He poured one for himself, as well, and settled himself at his writing table, angling his chair round to face me. "So tell me, Miss Ravenshaw . . ."

"Lyn."

"Lyn. Are there ethical restrictions on an author asking questions of an agent?"

I smiled. "I'm not aware of any."

"Good. Then may I ask how long you've worked for Simon Holland?"

"Four years." Like an angler who feels the first tug on his line, I leaned back in my wing chair and waited.

"And how many authors do you represent?"

I made a mental count. "Twelve."

"Anyone I'd know?"

"Well, there's Bridget, of course, and Edgar Salazar, and Dorian Peake, and . . ."

He raised his eyebrows, interrupting. "Christ, I can't imagine those three sharing a cab, let alone an agent. You must have eclectic tastes."

I lifted a shoulder. "I like what I like."

"And you've been Bridget's agent how long?"

"Four years, also. Since I came to Simon Holland."

"Ah." He raised his glass in a mock salute. "So you have stamina, as well. She's quite a handful, isn't she? Though, to be fair," he said, "I imagine Ivor would say the same of me."

That set me thinking. "May I ask *you* a

79

question?"

"Certainly."

"Why don't you want to stay with Ivor?"

"Because he wants to interfere."

"In what way?"

James sat back, one elbow resting on the table's polished edge. "It bothers him that my books aren't successful, in commercial terms. Not that he doesn't like my writing style — he does. But lately he's begun to make suggestions. What I ought to write, you know, and where it should be set, that sort of thing. No one," he said, "tells me what to write."

I recognized the stubborn tone, the stamp of a true writer. And I took his side wholeheartedly. Originality was not a team pursuit, and any story worth the telling grew in solitude.

Above us, the floor creaked and James, glancing up, drained his sherry glass, ending our interview. Not that I minded. The bait was still there at the end of my line and I knew that he'd come back to take it again.

He smiled. "I'd best go change my clothes," he said. "That's Bridget waking up, and you know what she's like if she's not fed on schedule."

"A pint of prawns," read Bridget from the

menu, relishing the words. "That does sound heavenly. Or should I have the breaded mushrooms?"

James, returning from the cigarette machine with a packet of Silk Cut, lit one and stretched himself back in his chair. "Have them both," he suggested. "I've seen you eat, darling. I'm sure you can do it."

There was something odd about his behavior toward her this evening, or at least, it struck *me* as being odd, having seen them together earlier. Then, he'd been affectionate and plainly pleased to see her; now he seemed almost deliberately indifferent.

I shrugged it off as being none of my business, and studied the menu. I'd been tempted by the prawns as well, but a quick glance at the sweets list convinced me to trade off my starter for a sticky toffee pudding afterward. Having settled on the breaded plaice with jacket potato for my main course, I set the menu down and turned my attention to the objects hanging round me on the warmly yellow walls of the Hibernia Inn's cozy lounge.

A long polished shotgun had been mounted over the entrance door in the corner, and a sabre hung above the door to the kitchen, just opposite where I was sitting. There were other trophies as well — a military helmet cased in glass and a ship's sextant, which were mounted proudly on either side of a full-color aerial photograph of Angle, graced the wall across from me, as did a giant ship's wheel, gleaming brass on wood, ringed round by smaller photographs of what appeared to be lifeboats.

On the massive stone fireplace filling one end of the lounge another sword and scabbard hung beside a wood-and-leather bellows, and two old framed parchment handbills exhorted me to rally round the "Royal Tars of Old England" and join the King's Navy.

My favorite decorative touch, though, was without doubt the tidy collection of sailor's caps clinging like stemless mushrooms to the ceiling, behind the bar, each one emblazoned with the name of its own ship. And under them, the landlord kept a friendly eye on all three rooms: the lounge, the public bar, and near the back, a smaller games room from which issued the faint repeated thunk-thunk-thunk of someone playing darts.

It was early yet, and our table of four was the only one waiting for service. The landlord had time to chat.

He reminded me a little of my father, with his dark mustache and laughing eyes. "Now, let me guess," he said to James. "The steak and chips."

"With salad."

"Four specials a night, we have," the landlord said, shaking his head as he noted the order, "and you never want to try them."

Christopher grinned. "He's a creature of habit, you know. Always has been. But *I'll* have the tikka masala." He set the list of specials down, and nodded upward, at the ceiling. "I like the decorations, by the way."

"Thanks. The girls did that." The landlord looked up, too, at the ropes of colored tinsel looped along the wooden beams and spotlights. It glittered on the walls, as well, and ran along the valances above the curtained windows at our backs. And beside us in the corner by the fireplace a small tree, weighted down with fairy lights, twinkled cheerfully against the night outside. "They did a good job, didn't they?"

Christopher agreed they'd done a smashing job. "We aren't having a tree, this year. My brother Ebenezer, here, thinks it a waste of money."

"James!" Bridget turned on him, her eyes reproachful. "Of course we must have a tree. You can't have Christmas without a tree."

"We'll see," he said.

The landlord smiled. "Well, you've plenty of time yet, to talk him round."

He was quite right. Christmas wasn't until Friday next — a full week away. I reveled in the fact. I'd taken a lot of stick from my colleagues for being given such a long holiday, but Bridget was one of our agency's star clients, and when she'd told my boss she wanted me to spend the full fortnight in Angle, I'd known there wouldn't be an argument. Just as I knew now, from the look in her eyes, that we would have a Christmas tree at Castle Farm before the sun went down tomorrow.

James, who either hadn't noticed Bridget's look or didn't know its meaning, calmly hitched the ashtray closer and wished good bloody luck to anyone who tried to talk him round to doing something that he didn't want to do.

"He can always be bribed with brandy," Christopher revealed. He glanced at the landlord. "Has Gareth been in?"

"Not yet. He'll be up at the Point, I'd imagine. They were having some sort of training exercises for the lifeboat today, and they usually go to the Point after that."

Bridget glanced over. "I didn't know Gareth had anything to do with the lifeboat."

"Yes, well," said James, "he's much more

civic-minded than the rest of us." I caught the faintest edge in that before he turned to me, all charm. "Sorry, forgetting my manners. Of course you won't know what the Point is, will you?"

"Oh, she doesn't need to know that," said the landlord with a grin, but James told me anyway.

"It's the other village pub, the older pub, just up behind our house along the bay. Supposedly their fire was kept alight for . . . what, three hundred years?"

The landlord nodded. "Shame they couldn't keep it going. But it's nice up there, you want to go and see it," he advised me, "for the atmosphere. But only for the atmosphere." He winked. "I don't want to give away all of my business."

Christopher reminded him the Point was only open at the weekend anyway, in winter. "Just let me know if Gareth does come in, though, won't you? I've a message to give him, from Elen."

Bridget's gaze lifted from the menu. "Why would Elen be sending him messages?"

"Because Gareth," said James, "is the girl's knight protector."

The landlord grinned. "There's some would say he's got a guilty conscience. Little Stevie doesn't look much like his daddy, if you take my meaning."

"Oh, come on," Bridget said. "He looks even less like Gareth. And besides, she's much too young for him."

The three men exchanged glances and looked away quickly, straight-faced.

"Yes, you're probably right," said the landlord, avoiding her eyes. "It's only gossip. Now then, what can I bring you?"

As always, Bridget's order was the longest one to take. I saw the landlord's eyebrows rise, and watched his gaze sweep over her small figure twice, as though he wondered where the food would fit. But he tactfully said nothing.

When he'd left us, James leaned back and blew a thoughtful smoke ring up toward the tinseled beams. "Gareth and Elen. Now there's a combination I'd not thought of," he admitted. "I suppose she's rather pretty, in her way, but really, in her mental state, it almost seems indecent."

Bridget looked at him. "I thought you hated gossip."

"Oh, I do. I'm just intrigued."

"Well, I'd be willing," she informed him, "to bet ten pounds that it's all talk."

His eyes slid sideways, to study her face. "Why all this interest in Gareth? I thought you didn't like him."

"Darling." Her smile was sweet. "Everyone's entitled to some privacy."

Which was, I knew, one of her famous nonanswers, that might be interpreted any number of ways. She always gave nonanswers to avoid the complications of an outright lie. Having known Bridget as long as I had, I'd become rather skilled at the solving of riddles, and I took her statement to mean that her feelings about Gareth Gwyn Morgan were private, but James didn't read it that deeply.

"Yes, I suppose you're right," he said. "Still, I'll have to take a closer look at Elen's son, I think."

"Good luck." Bridget's tone was acid. "She'll never let you near him. She went after me, remember, when I tried to pick him up last summer?"

James assured her he hadn't forgotten. "How could I? You made quite a scene."

"Well, she was being an idiot. Trying my patience. It wasn't as though I was hurting the child."

Christopher shrugged. "She's a little protective of Stevie, that's all."

"A *little* protective?"

James stubbed out his cigarette, cutting in smoothly. "But we must be boring Lyn, with all of this. Surely we can find a more interesting topic to talk about."

I wasn't bored, in fact, but I recognized the look on James Swift's face. Martin had looked like that, too, when the talk at a party had focused for too long on somebody else. Like one of my father's more difficult roses, his ego would wither unless you fussed over it constantly. Writers, I knew, could be hard work, that way.

Still, I'd come here for a reason, and I'd known that spending Christmas in the company of writers would demand a bit of tact. Lowering my wineglass, I showed my most attentive face to James and, with a smoothness born of practice, said, "So tell me, how did you get started writing?"

"You did that rather well," said Bridget later, as we turned off the village street, setting our backs to the silent Globe Inn with its amber light burning high up on its long colonnaded facade. The light didn't follow us far down the pitch-dark gravel lane that led to Castle Farm. Christopher and James, not hampered by high heels, were strolling some few yards ahead of us, two indistinct shadows that my eyesight couldn't separate.

I stumbled on a rut, and grabbed at Bridget's sleeve to steady myself. "Did what rather well?"

"You know. Distracted James."

"Just doing my job, as requested," I told her. "Though the man would have had to be blind not to notice you watching that door."

"Was I really so obvious?"

"Yes."

"Oh." She frowned for a moment, then shrugged it away. "Well, it didn't much matter, he never came in. Gareth, I mean. He must still be up at the Point."

I looked at the rough lane ahead, and the shivering darkness. I never could see well, at night. I knew there were pastures sloping uphill to our left, and straight ahead I saw the long black outline of what must be Castle Farm, but really the only thing I saw with any clarity was the enormous oil refinery across the bay, a web of dull and misted lights that hovered in the starless sky. The other pub, so James had said, lay somewhere round that corner, past the farm. My heart sank. "You're not planning to drag me up there for a nightcap, or anything, are you?"

"God no, not tonight. I can't drive in this state, and I don't fancy walking any further than I have to. No man," she said, "is worth sore feet."

I thought her very wise, and said as much.

"Besides," I said, "he might have left the Point by now and just gone home. It's getting late."

"Darling, he's a playwright," she reminded me, as if that meant he had to keep late hours. "And anyway, he's not at home. That's his cottage there, the one without a light on."

I looked where she was pointing, at the curve of lane behind us, but I only saw a spiny clump of hedge and the suggestion of a roof. As I turned back my heel slipped again on the hard rolling stones and I righted myself with an effort. "We should have brought a torch."

"I didn't think," said Bridget. "I always forget how dark it gets, out here. But James has torches at the house, I know. He keeps one in his writing room, in case the power goes off." She turned her head toward me. "And speaking of his writing room, I must say I'm surprised at you."

"Why's that?"

"With all that talk at dinner tonight, you didn't once ask him about his new book."

"Is that wrong?"

"Well, it's very restrained for you, that's all." Her voice smiled. "I just wondered if maybe you weren't feeling well . . ."

"Very funny. I *am* on holiday, you know."

"Agents," she informed me, "don't take holidays."

"No?"

"It's a known fact. You don't switch off. Oh, hell," she broke off suddenly. "I've stepped in something squishy."

"Never mind," I said. "We're nearly there."

Ahead of us, the two pale shadows that were Christopher and James had stopped beside the gate, to wait for us. The tower rose up blackly at their backs, and Bridget, looking at it, shuddered.

"God, I'm glad *my* windows don't look out on that," she said. "I wouldn't sleep."

Walking with her, silently, I wondered what she'd say if she knew just how much I'd give to spend a single night not sleeping.

CHAPTER 7

Or if she slept she dream'd
An awful dream . . .
— Alfred, Lord Tennyson, "Guinevere"

Justin was crying.

I heard it again, rising over the harsh wind that swept through the wasteland — a small sound, but one that I couldn't mistake. He was too far away, I thought. Too far. I stumbled and fell to my knees on the endless road, feeling the sting of the sharp scattered stones. And then something brushed past me, a cold thing as black as the night, and I saw it was the serpent, grown enormous from swallowing the river, and I knew that it was after Justin now, that it was following his cries and it would find him.

"No." I struggled to my feet and started after it, watching that hideous tail slither off in the darkness and knowing I'd never be able to catch it. Beneath me the ground heaved and yawned and I screamed as I pitched headlong into the chasm . . .

I didn't hear the sound that woke me.

One minute I was falling and the next my eyes were open, blinking dimly in confusion at the canopy above me and the heavy draperies twisted round the bedposts at my feet. They looked like two cowled women, standing silent, watching me, and for a moment I felt something close to fear, but then I shook the foolish feeling off impatiently.

Rolling onto my side, I turned my back to the imagined eyes and burrowed in the blankets, curled against the cold that crept between my sheets despite the fire that flickered on the hearth, not far away. The fire . . .

I raised my head to stare at it, to make quite certain it was real. It couldn't have been burning long — the flames were just now taking hold, their blue-edged tongues of red and gold stretched upward by the violent draft that drew them up the flue.

Warily, I pulled myself up to a sitting position against the soft pillows and looked slowly round from the door, its brass bolt firmly fastened on the inside, to the windows that looked out on the sleeping church and village. Through the rippled glass the tower gazed benignly down upon me, and below its walls the estuary glimmered in the dim uncertain moonlight. I was looking at the water when the curtains at the window fluttered gently and became a gown that rustled as its wearer took a step toward my bed.

"Be not afraid," a soft voice said. "It is but me."

And I wasn't afraid. It was then that I knew that I wasn't awake after all, but still dreaming.

The woman came forward and I saw her clearly by firelight. She was young, and quite slender, and dressed all in blue, her calm features framed by a tightly stretched wimple that gave her a saintly appearance.

I took a closer look, and shook my head. "I'm sorry, I don't know you."

"Yes, you do." She stretched one hand toward me, and I saw the small child clinging to her sleeve. A blue-eyed boy of four or five, with tumbled golden curls. "My son," she said. "My only child. I beg you guard his life."

"Who, me? But —"

"Please, you must. They mean him harm. They mean to take him from me." She took the boy's hand in her own and held it out, imploringly. "Please."

The boy looked up in silence, small and

trusting, and I shrank into my pillows. "I can't," I told her, wishing there were some way to explain. "I'm truly sorry, but I can't."

"Then he is lost." Sad-eyed, she turned and slowly led her son away, through walls that melted in the gloom and shifted shape, becoming trees and moonlit fields and one dark road that wound off in the distance.

I'm dreaming, I thought. *This is only a dream.* Through the heavy thick mist swirling inside my mind I could just feel the coolness of linen pressed close to my cheek, and I focused on that, bringing all of my concentration to bear on the one simple act of opening my eyes. It took several tries and a great deal of effort, but at length my weighted eyelids moved.

I lay still for a moment, blinking dimly in confusion at the canopy above me and the heavy draperies twisted round the bedposts at my feet. I felt no creeping cold, I saw no fire . . . and there was no one in the room but me.

But I thought I heard, far off, a child crying in the darkness.

CHAPTER 8

Then when he had filled the air with so many and so great complaints, new fury seized him and he departed secretly, and fled to the woods not wishing to be seen as he fled.
— Geoffrey of Monmouth, *Vita Merlini*

The crows were gathering above the tower.

They rose behind the house and skimmed the roof slates in a beating, chattering mass that broke and swelled and closed again in flawless tight formation. Dropping to the tower walls, they clutched a moment at the ancient stones, then loosed their grip and soared and wheeled like blackened bits of dust trapped in a whirlwind. Wherever one settled, another one took to the air, crying harshly, as though there were some limit to the weight the walls would bear.

Pulling the front door shut behind me, I took a few steps on the wet grass and turned to squint up at the close-curtained windows, amazed that anyone could sleep through this cacophony of crows. As my gaze fell again I saw something I hadn't before — a stone face mounted in the peak above the door. Eyes closed, serene, its nose sheared off and flattened over lips that, although straight, appeared to smile, the long face looked more male than female. I studied it a moment, and I had the oddest feeling that those closed eyes somehow saw me, too.

Even when I'd turned and started walking, I had the sense of being watched. I squared my shoulders, setting my face to the sea-scented breeze blowing in from the Haven and the moon-shaped bay. Since the nightmares had started, I'd got in the habit of taking a walk after waking, to clear my thoughts.

And this morning they wanted more clearing than usual.

The dream had been the same for five years, always the same, the only variation being how long I spent searching through the wasteland for my son. It was, as nightmares went, familiar, and I understood its meaning. But last night it seemed my subconscious had chosen to add a new twist. Psychology wasn't my forte, but I'd read enough books on dreams and dream analysis to know the images and symbols came from somewhere. And I remembered reading something to the effect that a shift in one's dreams was a thing of significance, signaling some sort of change in the life of the dreamer.

The only change I knew of was the change in my surroundings since I'd come down here from London, and I didn't see how that could have a negative effect. Even daybreak seemed more peaceful here, with the sun still slowly climbing in the soft transparent sky, and my breath making mist in the air, and my crunching footsteps sounding crisply on the gravel drive. Pushing the woman in blue and her golden-haired child from my mind, I walked on.

One of the cats came to join me — the little gray cat that had jumped onto my shoulders yesterday. He kept to heel for several yards, but wasn't keen to leave the property and abandoned me at the gate. Here the drive angled down and became an unpaved road, and the road, in its turn, split itself into two — one part chasing over the little stone bridge that led up the back way to the village, while the other part carried along at the edge of the water, winding steadily uphill until it vanished round a bend in the shoreline.

I'd been across the bridge already, in the car with Bridget, and I didn't fancy walking through the village, so I chose the coastal route instead, savoring the solitude. The road was rutted deep and soft from recent rain — I had to watch my feet to see I didn't turn an ankle — but I had a closer view here of the fishing boats that bobbed against the bar, ropes creaking as they strained against the tide. And behind them, on the farther shore, a dark green regiment of trees stood solemnly along the curving waterline, to guard the eastern boundary of the village.

As I rounded the corner, the bay, washed with ripples, stretched wide to meet the bluer Haven, and the breeze blew more expansively. I breathed it in and walked a little faster, past the handful of houses asleep at the roadside; past the narrow pungent strip of beach where coils of darkly shining seaweed marked the progress of the tides; to where the road abruptly ended in the car park of a small white building sign-posted "The Point House." This was the pub, I thought, that everyone had been talking about last night — the one that only opened at weekends. It certainly wasn't open now. The only signs of life came from the line of laundry hung to dry behind the silent building, and the three Welsh Black cows in the next fenced field over, heads turned to watch me.

I stopped walking and stared back at them, considering my options.

A stile bridged the rail fence at the corner of the car park, underneath a wooden sign that pointed me encouragingly up the posted coast path. But the path crossed the field, and the cows barred my way. No, I corrected myself, peering more closely, not cows. Bullocks.

"Blast," I said. It wasn't that I was afraid of bullocks, really. They didn't have the nastiness of bulls. But they had enough residual testosterone, I'd found, to make them apt to flex their muscles when they thought they could intimidate. And since I was only a puny human being, and a female one at that, I didn't much fancy my chances of making them move.

Still, I gave it a try. "Oy!" I shouted, doing my best to sound fierce. Waving my arms above my head, I drew in a lungful of air and tried again, full volume: "Oy!"

The three black heads stayed motionless, save for the twitching of one ear.

"Smug bastards," I accused them. "If you had an ounce of chivalry you'd —"

The nearest bullock interrupted with a sound between a bellow and a snort, and as

I watched the three of them spun round and lumbered up the pasture to the farther fence. A moment later I saw what had prompted their move. A tiny blur of white and brown was trotting down the coast path from the opposite direction. Ignoring the bullocks completely, it came across the bottom of the pasture, bouncing through the long grass like an oversized hare with a small wagging tail. It looked like a Jack Russell terrier, short-limbed and sturdy, but its hair was much longer than any Jack Russell's I'd seen, standing all out on end like the hair of some wild mad scientist.

I crouched to greet the dog as it squirmed underneath the fence rail. "Hello, scrapper," I said. "Where did you spring from?"

The dog sat back to grin at me, dark button eyes dancing with mischief. I rumpled its ears and my fingers touched leather, set deep in the tangle of hair. It was wearing a collar. "Morgan." I read the brass tag dangling at the dog's throat. "You're a boy, then, are you, Morgan? Are you a boy?" I never had been able to work out why people always said things twice to animals, especially since we were unlikely to receive an answer anyway, but I was just as guilty as the rest. "Go on, Morgan. Go on, lead the way."

I stood, and let the little dog surge on ahead, across the field, while I hopped the stile, keeping an eye on the wary bullocks. I needn't have worried. They kept close to the fence as my newfound friend darted back and forth around my heels, circling and urging me on.

"I'm coming," I promised, and with a sharp woof he was off again, leading me up the climbing path that hugged the edges of the fields, while to the right of us a mass of gorse and bramble tumbled steeply down the cliffside to the Haven. It had been years since I had walked a coastal path, and I'd forgotten how incredible it felt to be so high above everything, to look down and see gulls wheeling under me while on the blue sunlit water the tankers and small boats moved leisurely round one another, completely unaware of my existence. Absorbed in watching them, I barely glanced at the lifeboat station when we passed above it. The little dog sniffed round the top of the steps leading down to the lifeboat, but finding nothing to his interest, led me on.

Some braver souls — or sheep, perhaps — had trampled little paths that sprouted off from time to time and disappeared into the thickening gorse, winding down toward the water, but as I'd always had a healthy respect for the dangers of cliffs I kept my own feet firmly on the main path, only stepping to the grass to round the places where the soft red clay grew muddy, so I wouldn't slip.

Ahead of me a screen of leafless trees, pale sycamores, rose up to take the place of gorse and bramble, plunging boldly to meet the water swirling white against the rocks, and an old shed, rather run-down and abandoned, stood in silence by the path. I hesitated, looking from the trees to the shed with its gaping smashed windows and rusted tin roof, feeling that twinge of misgiving that I always felt when entering a lonely place. But the dog had already squeezed under the next stile and, unaffected by the change of atmosphere, stood wagging on the other side. I shook my hesitation off and followed him. After all, I reminded myself, as the trees closed around us on both sides and the air grew heavy with the smells of the damp ground, littered thick with campion and foxglove and brown ferns withering between green clumps of wild garlic — after all, this *was* a public path, and even this late in the year, there must be ramblers trekking up and down it all the time, especially on a Saturday. If something happened to me here, I cheered myself, at least my body wouldn't languish undiscovered.

The dog perked up his ears and stopped. Sniffed the air.

"What's the matter, Morgan?" But I had heard the footsteps, too. The squelching steps of someone coming down the muddy path. Tucking my hands in my pockets, I turned my gaze deliberately away to watch the glinting water of the Haven flash between the sycamores, trying hard to look carefree as I walked on. I only caught a glimpse of the man as he came through the trees — a dark man, not tall, wearing denims and boots. The dog, head bent low, started forward to investigate, and I whistled for him sharply. "Morgan! Come here, boy!"

The man stopped short, and blocked the narrow path. He watched the little dog approach.

"It's all right," I told him. "He's perfectly friendly." Snapping my fingers, I made my tone firmer. "Come on, Morgan, do as you're told."

Folding his arms, the man lifted his eyebrows and shot me a withering glance. "His name's Chance," he informed me, in a rough-edged Welsh-accented voice that held no trace of humor. "And just for the record, I don't often come when I'm called."

I recognized him, then. Not his face, so much, as his voice and his movements, the way he was holding his head. And the name on the dog's collar, of course. "Sorry," I said. "I read the tag, you see, and just assumed . . ."

Gareth Gwyn Morgan said shortly, "Well, now you know differently."

It was the patronizing tone, I think, that set my teeth on edge. I never had liked being spoken to as if I'd only half a brain. Clenching my fists in my pockets, I lifted my chin. "Most people, Mr. Morgan, put the dog's name on the collar, not their own, so you needn't act so damned offended."

His dark glance flicked me, unimpressed, and without a word he whistled for the dog and started walking round me. I felt my eyebrows rising and irrationally I looked toward the trees, seeking a witness to his rude behavior.

I couldn't hold my tongue. "And a bloody good day to you, too." Turning sharply on my heel, I set my back to him and carried on the way that I'd been heading, up the path. Bloody writers, I cursed silently. And I'd thought *Bridget* was difficult . . .

I felt his gaze burning a hole in my shoulder blades, and his voice followed after me, clipped and unfriendly. "You're a fool to go that way. The coast path's no place for a woman alone."

He whistled for the dog again, and I heard the crackle of bramble and twigs as he started away, and unable to help it I stopped and spun round.

"As an exit line, that lacks a certain logic, don't you think?"

He paused. "What?"

"Well, you can't say I shouldn't be out here alone and then *leave* me alone. That just doesn't make sense," I told him, drawing satisfaction from his tightly exhaled breath. "I'd have expected better dialogue from someone with your talent."

He slowly turned to study me, and I saw his eyes harden; grow wary. "And what the devil would you know of my talent?"

"Quite a lot, as it happens. I *was* looking forward to meeting you, but —"

"Christ," he broke in, ill-tempered, "what rag is it this time? You won't bloody listen, the lot of you, will you? You're wasting my time and your own, coming here. I don't give interviews."

"Very wise of you," I said. "One reads enough unpleasant things, these days."

And then, because I always liked to have the last word in an argument, I wheeled again and walked away along the muddy path, hoping that my rigid back looked properly disdainful.

"Well, of course you didn't like him." Bridget buttered her toast with the superior air of a fictional detective who'd outwitted Scotland Yard. "It's the name thing, you know."

I lowered my coffee cup, frowning. "What name thing?"

"Well, think now. What's your name?"

"Lyn."

"Your full name."

"Lynette."

"And he's Gareth." She reached for the marmalade, smugly. "Arthurian legend, remember? Lynette went to Camelot to find a brave knight who could rescue her sister, only instead of getting Lancelot she ended up with Gareth."

"Oh right," I said, as memory stirred. "She gave him proper hell, as I recall."

"Mm. They hated each other. So you see, you can hardly expect to get on with my Gareth."

"Because of the name thing."

"Exactly."

"And was there anyone who *did* get on with Gareth, in the legend?"

"Lynette's sister," said Bridget. "The one

he went to rescue. They fell madly in love with each other."

"Ah, well, there you are, then. I don't have a sister."

"Neither do I, which means that you and I are sort of sisters by default, doesn't it? So Gareth has to fall in love with me."

I knew better than to try to sort that one through before I'd had my second cup of coffee. "I suppose that there's some planet, somewhere," I told her, "where all of your theories make sense." Yawning, I stretched and looked around the sunlit kitchen. "Are we the only ones up?"

"Well, I haven't a clue about Christopher, but James was still snoring when I came downstairs. He's a night owl, is James. I don't know that I've ever seen him mobile before noon."

"That does sound appealing."

"What?"

"Sleeping till noon."

Bridget smiled. "Don't get any ideas. You're coming with me, on a top secret mission." Lifting the lid of the teapot, she checked the color of its contents before pouring her first cup. "I've already talked to Owen, and he said he'd be happy to help us."

Owen, I remembered, was the man taking

care of the sheep and the cows and the farm. I looked at her, faintly suspicious. "To help us do what?"

"You'll see."

"Bridget —"

"It's nothing illegal," she promised. "You needn't look so disapproving. Owen's much too honest to commit to something truly underhanded."

"Mm," I said, reserving judgment.

"You'll like Owen. He drives a van," she added, as though that were somehow relevant.

I'd known Bridget long enough to learn her thoughts were rarely random. "And do we *need* a van," I asked, "for this secret mission of yours?"

"You'll see." Checking her wristwatch, she sugared her tea. "At any rate, we have another half an hour before we're supposed to meet him. Time enough for one more round of toast," she told me, happily.

I would never know where Bridget put it all. She seemed to be continually eating, yet her waistline stayed dishearteningly tiny. I had only to look at a rasher of bacon, myself, and my trousers felt instantly one size too small.

They felt rather tight now, as I pushed

back my chair. "Let me just go and change, then."

"What for?"

"Well, I can't go like this. I've been walking through mud." I twisted one leg round to show her the dark splattered hem. "And I only ever wear this sweater walking, it's all frayed at the bottom."

"It's fine," said Bridget, firmly. "No one will see you, we're not going far."

"Yes, well, the last time you said that we ended up at that garden party with all those photographers from *Hello!* and *Private Eye* milling about, remember? And I'd rather not be flashed around the nation in this sweater."

"Oh, ye of little faith." She sighed. "All right, then, change it if you must, but don't be too long, will you? And for God's sake, don't wake James."

CHAPTER 9

Now, worn with much weeping,
she is not what she was . . .
— Geoffrey of Monmouth, *Vita Merlini*

I liked Owen on sight. He was an older man, gray-haired and ruddy-faced, with a solid, square build and big capable hands and crinkled gray eyes that seemed to find the world amusing. I felt rather less fond of his van. Compact and red, wanting only the words "Royal Mail" on its sides, it had not been designed with its passengers' comfort in mind, and my seat in the back felt decidedly wedged. My only consolation was that Bridget wasn't driving, and she *had* said we weren't going very far.

As we rolled through the east gates of Castle Farm, down to the bay, Bridget leaned to look up through the windscreen. "I do hope it won't rain." The morning had grown milder since I'd come back from my walk, and the wind had carried clouds in from the sea. They gently bounced off one another; clung and stuck and thickened, softening the sunlight till there were no shadows left.

Owen looked, too, with a more expert eye. "There's no rain in those clouds. Not for now, anyway." He took the road over the bridge, tooting his horn at a young woman walking ahead of us, pushing a pram. I looked quickly aside at the sight of the pram, so I only got a glimpse of her, a small form dressed in brilliant blue with masses of bright curly hair.

Bridget turned in her seat as we bumped our way up to the main village street. "That was Elen."

"Have you met her, yet?" asked Owen.

"No, I . . ."

"Lovely girl," he pronounced her. "She's what we used to call a 'flower child,' a true free spirit. Never has a spiteful word for anyone." Turning into the empty village street, he went the short distance along to the hedged road signposted to Pembroke and turned again, shaking his head. "She hasn't had an easy life, that little one. You know she lost her husband?"

"Yes."

"Lyn's a widow, too," said Bridget, using

me as proof that Elen's hardships weren't unique.

Owen looked to me for confirmation. "Are you? I'm so sorry. You'll know how the poor girl feels, then. She and Tony . . . well, they made a handsome couple. So in love. It's always a shame when the young die," he said.

Bridget, quick to take advantage of the opportunity to gossip, said, "He died before Stevie was born, didn't he?"

Owen nodded. "Elen didn't even know that she was pregnant, at the time. When she found out . . . well, I think it was the only thing that kept her going all last winter, knowing she was carrying his child."

From Bridget's expression, I knew she was remembering the comments we had heard last night about the baby's parentage. Knowing she was capable of saying something tactless and that Owen, who appeared quite fond of Elen, wouldn't like it, I tried to gently guide the conversation off that topic, asking Owen whether Elen had family in Angle, to help her.

"No, not anymore. There was only her mother, and she died a while ago. Cancer," he told me. "And Tony's people, they live way up north somewhere. Didn't even come for the funeral. They didn't approve of his marrying Elen, you see, so they just cut him off. Very cold."

Cold indeed. I couldn't imagine a family that did that. After all, my parents hadn't been keen on my marrying Martin, but they'd always treated him with courtesy.

Owen shrugged. "Elen sent them a notice, when Stevie was born, but they sent it right back. Said he wasn't their grandson. Imagine."

Bridget refused to be sidetracked. "Still, she isn't completely alone, is she? I mean, I'm told Gareth takes care of her and the baby."

"Well, Gareth was good friends with Tony, wasn't he?" Owen's tone implied the fact was common knowledge. "And I know he still feels guilty, that he wasn't around to stop Tony from going to Freshwater West. It was dangerous weather for angling that day, with that storm coming in. Those waves came out of nowhere — they figure one knocked Tony clear off the rocks. It was hours before they recovered his body."

"I can't see how it would have made a difference, Gareth being there," said Bridget. "You can't protect somebody from a wave."

Owen agreed. "But guilt's an awful thing, you know. Just sits and twists inside you. Twists a person's mind, it does."

I knew exactly what it did — I'd lived with it these past five years, wondering if Ivor's accusation might be right, if my riding had somehow done damage to Justin, or if it was some medication I'd taken, or maybe that one glass of wine at the publishers' party . . . Gareth Gwyn Morgan, I thought, didn't know what guilt was. He wanted to try walking round in my shoes.

Owen seemed to hold the man in high esteem, though. He smiled as he said, "Besides, if Gareth wants to think a thing, you're wasting breath to argue. He's a stubborn man."

I could have thought of quite another adjective. Instead, I bit my tongue and took an interest in the scenery. We were nearly at Pembroke now, approaching the lovely green wood on its outskirts.

"There's a house for a book, now," said Owen, nodding at an old home coming into view just out my window. It stood some distance back from the road at the edge of the wood, darkly brooding. "My mother used to have to come past here by horse and trap, when she was young. It scared her half to death, that house. She always told us it was haunted."

I didn't blame her. I should have found it easy to believe in haunted places here, myself. As we dipped and twisted through the silent wood, where pale sycamores and spindly hazel trees rose like ghosts themselves from the thick russet carpet of dead fallen leaves, I fancied that I felt a hundred eyes that followed us, and seemed to catch at times a flash of strange elusive movement at the corner of my eye. By the time we reached the place where the stream widened out and the castle loomed up in the foreground I wouldn't have been at all surprised to see medieval sentries on the battlements, or shades of some Welsh prince's army massing round it, laying siege.

But there was only the castle. I watched it rather wistfully as we approached, but knowing Bridget didn't share my fondness for historic sites I doubted she'd have made it the target of this morning's "secret mission." I was right. Owen drove straight on past, through the pastel-painted shops of Pembroke and out the other side of town. At the next village he took a turning south. We'd just come through a rather nasty S-bend, with a little church set off among the trees to the right, when my curiosity became unbearable.

I looked at Bridget, questioning. "Should I have packed a lunch?"

She only laughed and kept the secret, and

I had to wait till Owen, moments later, turned us neatly off the road into a bustling car park. "Here we are," he announced.

I looked up at the building, read the sign, and smiled, finally catching on.

"I should have bloody known," I said, to Bridget.

James lit a cigarette and lounged against the open doorway of the dining room, blinking in the slow deliberate fashion of a man who had awakened to discover that an elephant was sitting on his bed. "And where," he asked, "did *that* come from?"

"Manorbier Garden Center." Bridget sat back on her heels, all innocence, careful not to crush the strings of fairy lights she'd stretched across the carpet.

He inhaled smoke and nodded, looking up the full height of the tall Norwegian spruce, to the place where its tip touched the ceiling. "What, they just dropped one by, then, did they?"

His sarcasm was lost on Bridget. "No, of course not. Owen took us over there this morning, in his van."

"Ah."

"You simply cannot have a proper Christmas," Bridget said, "without a Christmas tree."

She had a point, I thought. And she *had* picked a smashing tree. It rose a full nine feet and let its branches drop in perfect, bushy tiers that spread to fill the space between the end wall windows. This was the first time I'd been in the formal dining room, a long, high-ceilinged room that jutted out into the garden from the rear wall of the middle house. Pale pink roses softly climbed the wallpaper, and twined around the heavy ivory curtains that were drawn back, now, to let the daylight in. The richly polished walnut table, chairs, and sideboard held court at the far end of the room, leaving our end free to be a sort of sitting area. And when we'd pushed the pink armchairs and footstools aside, sliding them back to the walls, they'd framed the perfect space in which to set our tree.

"Could you have got one any bigger, do you think?" asked James, still looking up.

Bridget shrugged. "Owen said we ought to have a large one, with these ceilings."

"Well, if Owen said it, who am I to argue?" He yawned, and rubbed his neck. "I don't suppose there's coffee left?"

"Darling," she told him, "it *is* one o'clock. If there is coffee left, I don't think that you'd want it."

He considered this and, saying nothing,

turned and wandered off again along the passage. Bridget grinned.

"He's always grumbly, when he first wakes up," she told me. "Here, plug that in, I want to test this lot."

I watched the fairy lights blink on to mark a tiny airport runway down the carpet. "How many of these did you buy, anyway?"

"Three boxes of a hundred. Don't tell James," she advised, "or he'll spend the night watching the electric meter spinning."

I promised not to tell. And the tree did look lovely, with all of those lights, though it took us an hour to string them round to Bridget's satisfaction. "Oh, damn," she said. "The ornaments. I must have left them in Owen's van, he'll have taken them home. Wait here, I'll run over to his house and fetch them."

Happy to obey, I sank into the nearest armchair and massaged my pricked and stinging hands. With Bridget gone, the house sighed into silence. If I hadn't known that James was somewhere — working in his writing room, no doubt — I would have thought myself alone.

I yawned. The fairy lights grew softer, blurring into tiny stars that spun against the darkness as my eyelids drooped. Only a minute, I promised myself. I'd only keep

119

my eyes closed for a minute. But it was several minutes later when the quick approaching footsteps brought my head up with a guilty start. I blinked, and tried to think of some excuse to make to Bridget.

But it wasn't Bridget.

The blue-robed woman came across the carpet and her long gown whispered to a stop beside my chair. Viewed this close, in daylight, I could see she was not beautiful, but still her young, fine-featured face held strength and dignity, and the shadows of great sorrow. Not a face, I thought, that one would soon forget. She fixed her soft, reproachful eyes on me, and drew a sighing breath, and spoke. "Will not you do me this one service?"

I found my own voice. "Look, I'm sorry, but —"

Wordlessly, she raised her hand and once again the little boy appeared, his small face more imploring now, and wet with recent tears. My own son might have looked like that, if he had lived — a child of five, with golden hair. I felt my own eyes fill, and looked away.

"You are his only hope," the woman said. "His last hope. They will take him from me."

"Why?" I asked. "Why would they do that?

Why would anybody want to harm this boy?"

"Because my son was born beneath the banner of the Dragon Kings, and men in these dark times fear Merlin's prophecy." She paused, half turned her head to listen. "The time grows late. They will soon come. Please . . . take him, hide him, keep him safe."

But I couldn't keep him safe — that was the problem. I'd failed to keep my own son safe; how could I take responsibility for someone else's? I shook my head. "You don't know what you're asking."

"You are the person he has chosen."

As if to make his own appeal, the boy took one step closer, arms outstretched, but even as I watched him he began to fade like warm breath in the winter air, growing ever paler, insubstantial.

His mother turned sad eyes on me. "Too late." She sighed. "Too late."

And then she started fading, too, and I believe I held my own hand out and called for her to wait, and then the colors of the dream began to run and I was running too, tears streaming down my face.

My eyes came open slowly. I looked around the empty room and knew I was alone, that I had been alone the whole time, that the woman and her child had been illusions. *It was all a dream,* I told myself. *You know it never happened.*

But I went on crying, anyway. The tears, at least, were real.

CHAPTER 10

I met a lady in the meads,
Full beautiful — a faery's child,
Her hair was long, her foot was light,
And her eyes were wild.
— John Keats, "La Belle Dame Sans Merci"

"The prophecies of Merlin?" James's eyes, above the computer, still held that dream-like look of writerly preoccupation, for all he'd said I wasn't interrupting anything. He leaned back in his chair and tried to focus on my question. "The prophecies of Merlin," he repeated. "Well, I —"

"There's no point asking James about a thing like that," said Bridget, coming in to join us. "He's got the world's worst memory, haven't you, darling?" She'd been upstairs in the bath and the scent of soap and lavender clung to her, delicate. Twisting her damp hair into a makeshift ponytail, she pushed up the sleeves of her sweater and crossed to the coal scuttle, turning to look at me over her shoulder. "What's got you interested in Merlin?"

I'd been hoping no one would ask me that. I could hardly tell the truth — that I'd dreamed of a woman who'd told me men feared Merlin's prophecies. As a reason, that sounded ridiculous even to me, and I couldn't afford to have James think me mad. But I'd dreamed of that same woman twice now, and that troubled me, and I had thought that perhaps if I could break this new dream into its component parts and learn what each part meant, at least I'd feel more in control. I tried to come up with another excuse. "Actually," I said to Bridget, "it started with you going on about Arthur this morning."

She frowned, picking up one of the discarded pages of James's typescript that littered the carpet and wadding it to stuff between the coals. "I don't remember saying anything about Arthur. Only Gareth."

"But you mentioned Arthur" — I held firm — "and that reminded me of Lewis. My assistant," I told James. "He's Welsh, you see, and always insisting that Arthur's Welsh, too, and not English. And Lewis once said that all Welshmen should know Merlin's prophecies." Which was also true, I thought, pleased at my memory for digging that up at this moment. I could clearly remember him saying that, now, during one of his lectures to me on Welsh history. No doubt that's why it had worked its way into my subconscious mind, and my dream. I relaxed. "But it's really not important. If you don't know —"

"I'm afraid that I don't." James frowned faintly, watching Bridget as though something she'd just said had set him thinking. And then I saw his face clear and his gaze came back to me. "You know, you really ought to ask our neighbor, Mr. Morgan. He remembers all that rubbish. I could introduce you, if you like."

"No thanks. We've met."

"You have?"

"This morning, on the coast path. He mistook me for a journalist."

"Oh dear." He smiled. "And you're still in one piece?"

Bridget told him not to worry. "I've seen Lyn take down men twice Gareth's size." She struck a match and touched it to the paper, then sat back to watch it burn. "There, now, keep your fingers crossed that those sticks catch, this time . . . that's done it." Satisfied, she stood and brushed her sooty fingers on her jeans. "Honestly, James, you ought to use this fireplace more often. It gives the room a certain ambience."

He swiveled in his chair. "Yes, well, I already do have a tree dropping needles all over my dining room — that's all the ambience I need. Besides, the very point of central heating is to save us all the fuss of *building* fires in the fireplace."

"Don't be daft. You cannot have a proper Christmas," Bridget said, "without a fire."

"Christ." James sought assistance from the ceiling. "Not another of your Christmas things. What's next? A Yule log blazing in the hall and ten lords leaping round my writing room?"

"I thought the eight maids milking might be easier to do. We do have cows."

"We do, indeed." He looked at me. "You've been her agent *how* long?"

"Four years."

"You should be sainted." He turned again and, shutting down his laptop, pushed it further down the table so he could rest an elbow on the place where it had been. "I suppose I'd best give up the thought of working, while you're here. I find the company of women too distracting."

I shared his smile, and settled back. "Do you write every day?"

"Not every day, no. Sundays are my days

of rest, and sometimes when the story isn't flowing I do give myself a holiday."

Bridget took the chair across from mine. "In other words, he hardly works at all. That's why it takes him so damn long to write a book."

He took her teasing lightly. "That, my darling, is what separates the writer from the hack — the time we spend in crafting every sentence to perfection."

"Give over, you pretentious git," she said, and plumped the cushions at her back. Lacing her fingers across her stomach, she stretched her feet toward the fire and yawned. "So, how much have you done today?"

"Four paragraphs." He felt for his cigarettes and lit one. "Rather a good day, for this book. It's coming more slowly than the others did, for some reason. Ivor," he told me, "would say it's my setting. He doesn't approve of my writing a book set in Wales — Scotland's easier to sell, he says."

I very nearly told him what I thought of Ivor's viewpoint, but I caught myself in time. Instead I said: "I'm sure whatever you choose to write will be brilliant."

Someone groaned in the hallway. "Oh, please," said Christopher, putting his head round the half-open door, "don't *feed* his ego. It's quite large enough, as it is."

James turned. "And where have you been hiding?"

"Pembroke Dock. Elen had some shopping to do and she couldn't find Gareth, so I drove her in." Crossing to the fire, he gave the coals a cheerful stir. "Have I missed anything?"

"There's a forest sprouting in the dining room," James said, "but other than that . . ."

"My God." His brother looked amazed. "Don't tell me that you've gone and bought a Christmas tree?"

"Of course I didn't buy it. It was here when I woke up."

"I see. Well done," said Christopher, to Bridget. "You've accomplished the impossible." He glanced round, and the sight of me seemed to remind him of something, because he immediately began patting down his jacket pockets. "Oh right, I forgot, there's a letter that came for you . . . ah, here it is."

I silently groaned when I saw the intertwined green *S* and *H* of the Simon Holland agency printed on the slim envelope.

Bridget was instantly curious. "How did the agency get this address?"

"I left it with Lewis."

James frowned and looked at his brother.

128

"When did that come? In this morning's post?"

"Yes."

"And it's taken you this long to give it to her?"

"Well, I met the postman on my way out, didn't I? So I put this in my pocket. And I've only just got back."

James thought that rather inconsiderate. "It might be something important."

"I doubt it," I said, not wanting them to argue. "The agency would ring me in a crisis." And to prove how unimportant the letter probably was, I set it to one side, unopened.

Christopher, who hadn't appeared to be bothered by conscience in the first place, took no notice. He was already thinking of something else. "We didn't have anything planned for this evening, did we?"

James narrowed his eyes. "Why?"

"Elen has invited us to dinner."

"I don't know that I'm up to macaroni cheese . . ."

"Spaghetti Bolognese," his brother corrected him. "Gareth's coming too, and that's his favorite meal, apparently."

Which rather decided the matter, for Bridget.

It wasn't until a few hours later, when I

was sitting in her bedroom waiting patiently and watching while she shuffled through the hangers in her wardrobe, that it suddenly occurred to her I might not be so keen to go to Elen's. Turning, she sent me a dubious glance. "You are all right with this, aren't you? I mean, with there being a baby and everything . . ."

I assured her I'd be fine. "It doesn't bother me to see a baby, Bridget."

"Good." Openly relieved, she turned her attention back to the wardrobe. "Be honest, now. Which one would you choose?"

I tipped my head, considering. "The turquoise one, I think."

"You're right. The black's too sexy for spaghetti, isn't it? Too bad," she said. "It makes me look like I've lost half a stone."

If Bridget slimmed at all, I thought, she'd simply disappear. As it was, she hardly took up any space in the gigantic mirror hung beside the bed. Trying on the turquoise dress, she twirled before her own reflection, critically.

I'd shared this ritual before. I knew enough to keep my own face bland and not say anything — the most innocent comment or change of expression could send Bridget back to the wardrobe. Instead, I looked around the bedroom, larger than my own, with Chippendale-style furniture in some dark wood that glowed against the golden damask paper on the walls. The whole room had been done in shades of gold and Nile-blue, as rich as an Egyptian tomb, and the canopied bed was so soft that it seemed to engulf me in satins and silk. I sighed. "I guess James likes you best."

"What?" She glanced round sharply. "Oh, because of the room, you mean? Yes, isn't it lovely? Not the sort of thing you'd expect to find in a farmhouse, really, but James's uncle has some gorgeous furniture. Most of it, I'm told, he bought from Elen."

I lifted my eyebrows. "From Elen next door? Really?"

"Mm. It's what she does, you know. She works from home, restoring furniture and selling it. James says his Uncle Ralph keeps her in business."

Christopher, meeting us downstairs, confirmed this. "Elen wouldn't let him reduce the rent when Tony died, so he started buying furniture instead, to help her out. He has his work cut out for him," was Christopher's opinion. "Elen and Tony spent all of their spare time at auction, you know — that green shed at the top of the drive is still packed to the rafters with what they brought home. She'll be years working

131

through all of that."

Bridget was clearly intrigued. "Really? A shed full of furniture? I'd love to have a peek at that."

James, coming into the front hall to join us, told her that shouldn't prove too difficult. "Elen's always forgetting to padlock the shed." I noticed he himself didn't bother locking the front door behind us as we left, but then we were, after all, only going next door.

The evening air had sharpened, and I pulled my collar tighter as I followed the others across the front lawn to the East House. It blended nicely with the older buildings, though I could tell it had been added in this century. And when Christopher gave a brief knock at the door and then opened it, calling "hello" with the casual air of a man who was sure of his welcome, we entered a porch full of bright colored tile and floral stained glass, pure art deco. The large and gracious entry hall beyond it made our hostess, when she finally appeared, look somewhat small and lost.

But then, she was small to begin with.

I doubted Elen Vaughan would reach my chin. She had that lovely, fragile look some women keep past girlhood, and I felt half afraid that I would break her hand by grasping it too hard. Owen had been right about her "flower child" look, only I would have called it "New Ager" — the silver-ringed fingers and long crystal pendant and masses of fair curls tied back with a lavender scarf. Her peasant-style blouse was not unlike the ones I'd worn in my own childhood — fashion came right round again, my mother always said — and the crinkled cotton skirt that brushed her ankles had a row of tiny bells that dangled from the waistband, making music when she moved. She couldn't, I thought, have been much more than twenty. Over our handshake her blue eyes studied me as frankly as a child's, and when she smiled I thought I knew what made Gareth Gwyn Morgan and Owen and Christopher feel so compelled to take care of her.

James alone seemed immune. "And of course," he said, continuing the introductions, "you remember Bridget."

"Yes." The doll-like blue gaze drifted past me, and the smile wavered. "How are you?"

It was not, I thought, the most enthusiastic greeting, but Bridget didn't seem to take offense. "Fine," she said, and looked round. "The baby's not up, then, I take it?" She seemed rather pleased by the fact.

Elen lost what remained of her smile, growing wary. "He's sleeping."

A deep voice spoke out of the dimness behind her. "And the person that wakes him will have me to deal with. It took me an hour to settle him down." Gareth Gwyn Morgan strolled forward to join us, relaxed in dark trousers and polo neck, holding a drink in one hand. He looked slightly less threatening, here, than he had on the coast path that morning, but I still couldn't class him as friendly. One of the cats had come with him and he gave it a nudge with his foot that sent it scurrying back down the corridor. He nodded at James, and at Christopher; let his gaze linger on Bridget . . .

"Why, Gareth," she said, "what a pleasure to see you again. I believe you've already met Lyn."

He looked at me, expressionless. "We haven't had a proper introduction."

"Lyn Ravenshaw." Accepting the challenge, I met his eyes squarely and held out my hand. "I work for Simon Holland."

I fancied his gaze altered over our handshake, but the change was imperceptible. "I should have known."

"I'm sorry?"

"Your executive director's a persistent bugger, I will give him that. I've told him time and time again that I don't want to sign, but he won't give up."

The ego of the man, I thought. First he'd thought me a reporter, chasing for an interview, and now he apparently thought I'd been sent to seduce him to join Simon Holland. I smiled my sweetest smile, and set him straight. "I hate to disappoint you, Mr. Morgan, but I didn't come down here because of you."

James draped an arm round my shoulders, defending my honor. "She came because of me. Although she's Bridget's agent, actually. Is that a drink?"

"Your agent? Is she really?" Gareth slanted a laconic look at Bridget, seeking confirmation. "You want to take much better care of her then, and not let her go walking the coast path alone."

"Oh, Lyn can take care of herself," Bridget told him. "I could tell you some stories . . ."

I cut her off smartly. "You do and I'll raise your commission."

"You see?" Bridget laughed. "Tough as nails."

James, still with his arm round me, eyed Gareth's glass. "What is that, Scotch?"

"Apple juice. But never fear, I'm sure that we can find you something stronger."

Elen recovered herself. "I have sherry," she offered, "and Scotch. Gareth, could you . . . ?"

"Of course." Taking charge, he led us through into the dining room while Elen retreated again down the corridor, presumably to check on the food. I was glad of the chance to move, to slip free of James's brotherly hold. He was just being friendly, I knew, but Bridget didn't like to share, and I couldn't afford to offend either of them. I deliberately hung back to let them both go in ahead of me, then followed after Christopher.

This dining room appeared, if possible, even larger than the one next door, with an art deco fireplace and a soaring seating alcove filled with windows at the front. At the opposite end of the room, where a second door stood open to a dimly lit passage — the kitchen passage, I deduced — the wall was all but hidden by a huge glass-fronted china cabinet.

"Wow," said Bridget, looking at that cabinet, "this I like."

"It's not for sale," said Gareth, shortly. Then, as an afterthought, he showed us the bottles and glasses laid out on the sideboard and said, "I'll let you help yourselves to drinks."

I chose the sherry, and retreated to the far side of the room where I absorbed myself in studying a wall display of photographs. A wedding portrait had been given pride of place, and seeing Elen, proud and laughing, circled by her husband's arms, I felt a prick of sympathy. He looked so young, I thought. So young and full of life, his broad smile brighter than the summer sunlight gleaming on his golden hair.

"You've found the shrine, I see," said James, moving up behind me. I thought it a surprisingly callous comment for a man who wrote with such sensitivity about other people's lives, but then perhaps James hadn't lost a loved one, yet. Still, he was right — this was a shrine. It only wanted candles and some incense. Every photo showed the same young man — sometimes alone, sometimes with others, always smiling. And, with the one exception of the wedding portrait, always the same age, as though the record of his life had been confined to one brief summer.

"I'm surprised she kept this one." James pointed to a picture at one edge of the arrangement, an inexpert shot of Tony Vaughan in angler's gear, his face all but obscured by the hood of his bright orange raincoat. "He looked like that the day he died. I shouldn't think she'd want to be reminded."

"Were you here the day he died?" I asked

him, glad of the excuse to look away from all those photographs.

"I was. I'd only just begun to get the germ of the idea for the book, so I came down to poke about, to do some research. Not the best of timing, really. I arrived the Sunday morning, and that night they brought the body in. Elen," he informed me, "went quite mad. There was some talk, you know, of putting her in hospital."

"In hospital? Was she as bad as that?"

"My dear girl, she was barking. Seeing demons in her bedroom. The doctors were worried she'd do herself harm."

I frowned. "And now?"

"Supposedly, she's better now." He shrugged. "I'm no psychiatrist, I wouldn't know. But there are some who think young Stevie would be better off in care."

I thought about this later, watching Elen slice the bread. In her small hand the long knife somehow looked more dangerous, as a Doberman might look on the end of a lead being held by a child — one didn't get the sense that she was fully in control.

"So," said James, "I take it all was quiet last night? No more sounds from Stevie's room?"

Gareth answered for her and his voice, I thought, held a warning for James. "No."

138

Elen, oblivious to the interplay between the men, said, "Gareth put a new lock on the window for me, too, so Stevie will be safe now."

Safe from what, I didn't know, and didn't want to ask. The less we talked of babies, the more comfortable I'd be. Head down, I concentrated on my food — an easy thing to do, since it was excellent. Barking she might be, but Elen could certainly cook. Her sauce, unlike mine, didn't come from a jar, nor had any of the marinated vegetables she'd heaped onto the Technicolor plate of antipasti. And the bread, from its warm yeasty smell and texture, must also have been freshly baked.

Christopher, who apparently not only shared Bridget's penchant for flirting but also her appetite, finished his first helping faster than anyone. He looked expectantly at Elen. "Is there more?"

"Yes, of course . . ."

"It's all right, I can get it." He rose, plate in hand, and headed for the kitchen while Elen told the rest of us, "There's more of everything. I always make too much."

"With Bridget and my brother here, you won't have any leftovers," James promised her. He poured himself another glass of wine and glanced at Gareth. "Oh, I nearly forgot — Lyn was asking me earlier. How much do you know about the prophecies of Merlin?"

"The prophecies?" His frown, I thought, looked faintly diabolical. "A fair amount. I have the book, at home."

"What book?" asked James.

"Geoffrey of Monmouth's *History of the British Kings.* The prophecies are part of that. It's rather hard-going twelfth-century prose, and the prophecies themselves don't make much sense, they're more like riddles."

"There you are, then," Bridget said, to me. "You should borrow the book."

I studied the man seated opposite. "I don't imagine Mr. Morgan likes to loan his books."

Our eyes locked, while he weighed the challenge. "No, you're right," he said, at last. "I don't. You'll have to read it where it lies." I caught the smugness in his smile, and knew he knew I'd rather die than visit him at home. "You can come tomorrow morning, if you like."

"Good," said James. "That's all arranged, then. Anyone for wine?"

Gareth declined the offer. "Why," he asked me, "do you want to know about the prophecies?"

I didn't have a chance to answer. From

the floor above a sound rose sharply, unexpectedly, demanding our attention.

Elen's baby was awake, and crying for his mother.

CHAPTER 11

For if there ever come a grief to me
I cry my cry in silence, and have done.
None knows it . . .
— Alfred, Lord Tennyson, "Guinevere"

I reached for my wineglass to hide the effect that the sound was producing. *Please stop,* I begged silently. *Oh, please stop crying.* My fingers clenched convulsively around the glass's fragile stem and snapped it as I drank.

"Oh, blast!" I leaped too late. The dark red wine spilled down my left side to my lap, an ugly spreading stain.

"White wine," said Bridget quickly. "I remember reading somewhere if you pour white wine on top of red, the stain won't set. Do you have any, Elen?"

"No, I'm afraid I —"

James cut in to say there ought to be a bottle or two in his Uncle Ralph's dining room. "Look in the drinks cabinet, under the window."

I stood, grateful for the opportunity to leave the room, to leave the house, to leave the crying baby.

"Shall I come with you?" asked Bridget.

I shook my head. "No." Overhead the crying rose again in volume, grew more piercing and persistent, and my hand shook as I set my napkin down beside my plate. "No, I'll be fine. I'll be back in a minute." I managed to walk, very calmly, from the dining room, my footsteps firm and even on the flooring, like a soldier making an honorable retreat. I didn't start running until I reached the lawn.

In the front porch of the larger house, I pulled the door shut and leaned against it, steadying my breathing. The crying couldn't reach me here — I only heard the rattle of the windowpanes above the covered coal box, and the scuttle of a bit of leaf across the checkered floor. Relieved, I closed my eyes and felt my heartbeat settle. There, I thought, that's better. I can manage.

Upstairs, I changed clothes and spent some minutes in the bathroom, pressing the cold dripping flannel to my cheeks until the face in the mirror looked less flushed and more like my own. I was letting the water run out of the wash basin when I heard a faint creak from the landing outside.

I half turned my head. "Is that you, Bridget?"

No one replied.

Reaching for a towel, I blotted my face dry and opened the door, peering out. "Hello?"

No one was there.

But when I went downstairs a minute later, carrying my red-stained blouse, I found Bridget in the kitchen, making a systematic search of the cupboards. "You were taking so long," she explained. "I just thought I'd come see if you needed a hand. You've got the blouse, have you? Good. We can use the washing-up bowl, it should be clean enough."

"You weren't just upstairs, were you?"

"No. Why?"

"I thought I heard something."

"Well, you know old houses. They're always . . . ah, here we are." Triumphant, she held up a bottle of white wine.

I looked at the label. "Oh, Bridget, we shouldn't use that one."

"Why not?"

"It's Bordeaux, that's why not. What we want is a table wine, not so expensive . . ."

But she was already applying the corkscrew. "Wine," she said firmly, "is wine." She stuffed my blouse into the tub and upended the bottle, her gaze sliding sideways to study my face. "It wasn't because of the baby, was it?"

"Sorry?"

"That this happened," she elaborated, nodding at the sodden blouse, now bleeding streams of pink. "Because if the baby *is* bothering you, then I want you to tell me. I really didn't think that he would be here, honestly I didn't, and I don't want you having a miserable Christmas."

"I won't have a miserable Christmas," I promised her.

She tipped back the bottle in time to save some of the wine. "Good. Then let's have a glass each of this and get back to the party. I'll need you to keep James diverted," she said with a wink, "while I'm talking to Gareth."

I fought the need to sleep.

It wasn't that I was afraid to face the dream, but after this evening at Elen's — with Stevie crying on and off upstairs and Gareth jabbing at me all night with his pointed little comments about Londoners and agents — after all that, my nerves felt quite raw and exposed, and the last thing I

145

needed to see was the blue woman coming toward me with child in tow.

Instead I propped my pillows firmly up against the headboard and began to read. I didn't often read for pleasure, but in a bookcase in the dining room downstairs I'd found a paperback copy of Wilkie Collins's *The Woman in White,* a long-forgotten favorite and the perfect book for keeping me awake.

I'd never managed to unveil the trick of Wilkie Collins's prose. It was, on the surface, as heavy and labored as one would expect from the pen of a stalwart Victorian, laced with descriptions of trivial things, the sentences strung out with commas and colons until they became full-page paragraphs. But underneath the ornate style lay *something,* some force that compelled me along like a hand at my back, and I found it impossible, once I had started, to put his books down.

It was light when I finished.

Not full light, but rather the flat gray suggestion of dawn that precedes it. The moon, fighting hard to hold on to its reign of the sky, had dug in its heels at the edge of the tower and hung there, a glimmering disc of pure white. The little morning star was there as well, looking down on me, watching and

146

waiting. It looked small and cold, and my limbs felt an answering chill. By now I had gone beyond tired, to that fuzzy-edged, cobwebby level of consciousness that falls between sleeping and waking and makes doing either impossible. But the ache in my legs called for movement.

I dressed and went downstairs with the thought of making tea, but trying to move quietly around that sleeping house proved to be difficult — each floorboard had its own small voice, the cupboard hinges creaked, and when I turned the taps the water thundered through the pipes so forcefully it seemed to shake the walls. It was safer, I thought, to forget about tea. I put the kettle down again and went to fetch my coat.

Outside, at least, I didn't run the risk of waking anyone. If I stayed off the gravel and kept to the grass, my footsteps made no noise.

At the foot of the drive I turned west this time, setting my back to the tower and the reed-filled estuary to follow the curve of the lane that would lead me out onto the main village street. We had taken this lane coming home from the pub, Friday night, but I hadn't yet walked it in daylight. Not that it was daylight now — the sun was little more than a faint spreading stain of pink above the bay behind me. Still, the chilled blue dawn gave light enough to see by.

To my left a faintly worn footpath struck a course across the rough grass, through a kissing gate set in the old rail fence, to a small, tidy park with a playground for children. I felt a small tug deep inside at the sight of the dangling baby swings and I quickly turned to look the other way, to where the still-green pasture sloped uphill to meet the plowed and narrow fields of reddish soil. They looked like potato fields, to me, but I wasn't certain. I must, I thought, remember to ask Owen what they grew down here, in Angle; what crops would thrive so close beside the sea.

A mingled scent of salt and seaweed, not unpleasant, clung damply to the morning breeze that touched my upturned face, and I closed my eyes a moment, breathing deep. The air itself was like a tonic, cleansing all the grime and weariness of city life away, and in my ears the rush and murmur of the waves against the shore sang like the soothing calm refrain of some old song, forgotten once, and now remembered, haunting in my mind. I filled my lungs again, absorbed in the sensation. So absorbed, in fact, that by the time I heard the sound I could do little to react.

It was a strange sound, soft and snuffing, like a small pig rooting in the wet grass at my feet. I opened my eyes and looked down. The wiry little terrier, more brown than white now, splattered with mud, tilted up his fox-like face and laughed at me, his stump of a tail fiercely wagging. I quickly glanced in all directions, but could see no sign of Gareth Gwyn Morgan. The dog was apparently walking alone.

"Good morning, Chance." I greeted him, and bent to scratch the perked-up ears. "Where's your nasty master, then? Where is he?"

The dog angled his head to the right, then the left, as all dogs do when trying to make sense of speech. Giving up with an uncannily human shrug, he turned in the lane and looked back, expectant.

"Yes, well, I was heading that way to begin with," I told him. "You're welcome to come if you like."

He didn't really keep to heel. His little legs moving a mile a minute, he bounced before me like a blind man's cane, investigating everything. As we rounded the corner, just yards from the street, he veered suddenly left and went straight into someone's back garden, to sniff round their dust-bins.

"Chance!" I hissed, trying not to wake the neighborhood. "Get out of that!"

It had about as much effect as tugging on a giant's sleeve. Ignoring me, he moved a little further round the bins, clearly intrigued by whatever he smelled.

"Chance, for heaven's sake." I stopped and stood, uncertain, while the windows of the pink cottage attached to the garden gazed down on me in silent accusation. "Come *on,*" I urged the dog, and when he shrugged me off a second time I gathered up my courage and went after him.

It was not, I decided, the most equal of struggles. For something so short-legged and muscle-bound, the dog could move like lightning, and he seemed to view the whole thing as a jolly sort of game — three circles round the dustbins, then a pause, and round again the other way, tail wagging with such energy I feared it might fall off. When I tried to head him off he dodged, and knocked one bin over with a dreadful clatter.

It rolled, but to my great relief, the lid stayed on. "You're lucky," I informed the terrier, who didn't look at all contrite as he watched me bend to chase the rolling dust-bin. I'd nearly got it upright when the back door of the cottage opened. Chance woofed and scarpered, leaving me alone to face my fate, but before I could turn round a dry voice stopped me.

"There's a man comes on Tuesdays to deal with those, thanks all the same."

I hung my head. "Oh, bloody hell." In a burst of frustration, I wrestled the dustbin back into place and wheeled to face Gareth Gwyn Morgan.

He stood square in the doorway, arms folded, stone-faced. "Are you sure you're not a journalist? That's just the sort of thing that lot go in for, searching people's rubbish."

I set my teeth, refusing to give him the satisfaction of a reply. Instead I merely sent him what I hoped was a defiant look, and turning on my heel, prepared to leave. Behind me, Chance whined sharply and I heard the heavy conflict in his master's exhaled breath.

"Miss Ravenshaw."

I stopped, not looking back, and he continued.

"Would you like to come inside?"

It seemed so unlike him to offer that my head moved of its own accord. I stared at him. "Inside your house?"

"That's where I keep my books," he said.

151

"And you were rather keen, as I recall, to read the prophecies of Merlin."

"The prophecies . . ."

"I did tell you that this morning was convenient," he went on, his gaze flicking upward to scan the spreading pinkish stain that warmed the dawning sky. "And this is definitely morning."

He was daring me again, I thought, and his next words confirmed it. His dark eyes deliberately free from expression, he curved his mouth into the ghost of a smile. "Or are you too afraid to spend an hour in my company?"

I raised a steady eyebrow. "And why would I be afraid?"

"Why indeed?" he asked, and stood aside, inviting me to step across the threshold.

CHAPTER 12

Sometimes he angers me
With telling me of the moldwarp and the
   ant,
Of the dreamer Merlin and his prophecies,
And of a dragon . . .
   — William Shakespeare, *Henry IV, Part I*

The plastered stone walls of the cottage breathed cold down the back of my neck as I came through the door.

"You'll want to leave your jacket on," was Gareth's curt advice. "I'm not as civilized as your friend Swift, I don't have central heating. And the Aga's decided to be a right bastard this morning."

I tended to think of an Aga as something one found in a Home Counties kitchen, expensive and gleaming, its color selected to match one's collection of Le Creuset pots, but here in Gareth's square and spartan kitchen, the cooker had no such pretensions. It looked ancient, for one thing — its solid, cream-enameled bulk wedged in the nook where the old hearth had been, black stovepipe disappearing up the chimney. The rectangular stove lid had been levered upright on its hinges to expose an iron hob that years of use had reddened round the edge, and at the front, to the right of the ovens, the fire box stood open, with its cover removed and a few wads of paper stuffed into the smoldering coals. From the piles of cold ash and spent matches that littered the brick hearth, it appeared that he'd been battling with the Aga for some time.

"And you, my lad," he told the little dog, who'd bent to sniff the ashes, "can keep your big nose out of that. I've no desire to spend my morning cleaning up your mess."

After my own experience with the dustbins, I couldn't help smiling. "What kind of a dog is he, anyway?"

"The bloody-minded kind," he said. "A long-haired Jack."

"A Jack Russell terrier? Really? I didn't know they could have long hair."

As if to prove the point, Chance gave his body an allover shake so his wiry white hair stood out in all directions, making him look more like a mad scientist than ever, before he padded past us on his stubby legs to peer with hopeful eyes into his food dish.

"The walking stomach," Gareth said. "You've had your breakfast, Chance, there's nothing for you there. Why don't you show the lady where we keep the books?"

At that last word, the dog perked his ears up and cocked his head sideways, then gave an acquiescing woof and trotted back across the kitchen, past the narrow bare oak table to a partly open door. The room beyond had, I imagined, been intended as a dining room, but Gareth Morgan didn't look the type to entertain. Instead, the dark walls had been hidden behind an assortment of bookcases, most of them old, some with glass doors, some painted, all crammed with a varied collection of volumes. Underneath the only window, facing out on the back garden, an impressive rolltop desk and chair provided what appeared to be the only place to sit, and I didn't need to see the scribbled paper, open books, and scattered pens to know that this was where the playwright worked.

Gareth walked over to switch on the desk lamp, dispersing the studious shadows.

For a moment it occurred to me I really didn't need to read the book of Merlin's prophecies — I already knew how they'd worked their way into my dream. It was all

Lewis's fault, for giving me so many lectures on bloody Welsh history, I thought. Small wonder my subconscious had picked up the phrase. But still, there remained one small part of the dream that I couldn't explain, and I'd become something of a fanatic when it came to interpreting dreams. I liked to know where every symbol came from, what it meant.

Gareth flipped his papers upside down and turned the chair toward me. "Have a seat."

I sat, exhaling an experimental breath to see if it made mist. My nose felt numb with cold. Thrusting my hands deeper into my pockets, I pressed them to my knees and watched while Gareth, looking quite comfortably warm in a thick Irish sweater and black denim jeans, bent to scan a bookshelf.

He was not, I admitted, a bad-looking man. Not a handsome one, in the traditional sense — he would need to be taller for that, and less angry, his features more even. But as he looked now, leaning forward in profile, the crisp black hair flopped on his eyebrow to soften his frown, I could understand why Bridget thought him "prime."

"Here it is," he said. "Geoffrey of Monmouth." He pulled a small volume from one of the bottom shelves. It had been through the wars, that book. The spine was torn, and the pages had started to shift and come loose from their binding. Gareth turned them with care as he straightened. "It's not the most trustworthy history of Britain, but good for its time. He's the one who goes on about Troy."

"Troy?"

"Mm. Brutus the Trojan," he said, more specifically. "Great-grandson of Aeneas, the great Trojan war hero."

"As in Virgil's *Aeneid*?"

"Exactly."

I looked at him, curious. "What does that have to do with British history?"

"Everything, if one believes Geoffrey of Monmouth. The tale goes that Brutus got tired of fighting the Greeks, and on the advice of the goddess Diana set sail with a small group of Trojans and ended up settling here. Built a new Troy where London is now, spread his seed, and became the first ruler of Britain."

"You're joking."

He shrugged, and turned another page. "It's no less strange than any other legend. I assume it's just the prophecies you're after, not the bit about Vortigern's tower."

"Whose tower?"

"Vortigern." I must have looked a blank,

because he sighed. "The British king who dug up Merlin in the first place."

"Ah. I'd better start with him, then."

"Right." He set the book in front of me and pointed to the place. "That's where it starts."

He didn't move away, as I'd expected, but stood firm by my shoulder, his frown pricking warmth down the back of my neck. I read the first sentence, and read it again . . . and a third time, but it wasn't any use. I couldn't concentrate. Not when I felt like a mouse being watched by a hawk. I set the book down; glanced up sweetly. "If I promise not to bend the pages back or mark the margins, will that set your mind at ease?"

"What?"

"Well, you don't look very trusting."

The frown became, briefly, a withering glare, but he gave me the point. At the door, he remembered one final instruction. "There's a heater in the corner, you should plug it in. I don't want Swift accusing me of giving you pneumonia."

I found the small electric fire and turned it on, gratefully, resting my feet as close as I dared to the reddening element. From the kitchen came the sounds of crackling paper, metal scraping brick and rattling coals, telling me that Gareth had resumed his battle

158

with the Aga. Chance, torn between us, turned round several times and then settled himself in the doorway, his head on his paws, trying his best to watch both rooms at once.

Free from distractions, I started to read.

I'd never known much about Merlin, beyond his most obvious role in Arthurian myth. I always pictured him as old, white bearded, dressed in wizard clothes. So it was something of a shock to find him here, in Geoffrey of Monmouth's belabored chronicle, running through the pages as a small boy, strangely fatherless, with local rumors naming him the offspring of the devil.

I read how Vortigern, a widely hated British king, had tried without success to build a tower on a hill, and had been told by his advisers that the walls would continue collapsing until the mortar had been mixed with the blood of a child who had no father. A seemingly impossible task, since even illegitimate children had fathers. By chance the king's men had found Merlin, whose mother swore no mortal man had fathered him. But when they brought the boy to Vortigern, young Merlin took control.

His sacrifice, he said, would be no help. The tower would still crumble. The problem lay much deeper — underneath a pool of water, deep within the hill, two dragons slept, and woke, and warred with one another; and their fighting shook the ground and made the tower fall.

And so, just as Joseph in the Bible had been freed for reading Pharaoh's dreams, Merlin's mystic powers saved his life. King Vortigern gave orders that the pool be drained, releasing the dragons, one white and one red. As the dragons proceeded to battle each other, the king asked the boy to explain what this meant.

His answer seemed clear enough, even to me: the white dragon stood for the Saxons, the red for the Britons. The Saxons, at first, would prevail, but the Britons would some-day arise and defeat them.

To the Welsh, that would mean that one day they — the heirs of the Britons — would challenge the English and win. But Merlin didn't stop with that. Encouraged by the king, he drew breath and launched into the prophecies proper . . . and that's where he lost me.

For all he used plain language, his words made little sense. And the visions he de-scribed were murky, thick with allegory, the sort of things old men in dusty universities might spend their lives deciphering. "A man shall embrace a lion in wine, and the dazzling brightness of gold shall blind the eyes of the beholders," Merlin told the king. "Silver shall whiten in the circumference, and torment several wine presses."

It seemed to me that Merlin had been embracing a few things in wine, himself. He sounded like my brother after several pints of lager.

"Merlin, by delivering these and many other prophecies," the book informed me, solemnly, "caused in all that were present an admiration at the ambiguity of his expressions."

That didn't surprise me. What was it the woman had said in my dream? *And men in these dark times do fear the prophecies of Merlin.* No bloody wonder. Interpreting the man's predictions would have driven anyone to drink or raving madness.

I sighed and read the pages through again, more slowly. I was searching for a reference, any reference, to the only symbol from my dream I hadn't yet resolved — the dragon kings of whom the blue-robed woman spoke. Dragons I found in abundance — red dragons, white dragons, dragons of gold. But no dragon kings.

From the kitchen came the grating squeak and clang of a door being shut on the Aga.

Gareth's footsteps crossed the hard floor, and I heard him running water through the taps. The water stopped. He paused. And then his measured tread came back again, toward the open doorway of the room where I sat reading.

"I'm making tea," his voice announced.

I chose to accept that, in spite of the phrasing, as some sort of offer. "I'd love a cup. Thank you."

His hospitality didn't extend, though, to delivery. He merely called me when the kettle boiled. The Aga had reluctantly begun to warm the kitchen. As I stood by the table and sugared my tea, I felt the spreading heat against my legs.

"I see you won your battle," I remarked.

"I always do." He raised his own chipped mug of tea and leaned against the work top. "You're making sense of Merlin, then?" he asked me, in a voice that knew full well I wouldn't be.

I should have lied. I should have said I found the reading easy. But the hot tea and the Aga's warmth had made me sluggish, and it seemed a great deal simpler to admit that I hadn't the faintest idea what Merlin was on about. "Mind you, that hardly matters, since he hasn't said a word about the dragon kings."

"The what?"

"That's the prophecy I'm after," I explained. "Something to do with a child born under the dragon kings' banner, whatever that —"

"Why?" His tone cut like a knife blade, and I hesitated.

"Sorry?"

"It's a straightforwards question. Why do you want to know?"

Some instinct warned me that my answer was important, but he didn't look the sort of man to be impressed by dreams. "It's for one of my authors," I lied.

"Not for Bridget?"

"God, no. She'd have asked you herself." That, at least, was the truth, and I saw him acknowledge it, the small muscle twitching again at the side of his mouth. He raised his mug and drank, his dark eyes quietly assessing me.

At length, he said, "I should think it's the poems of Merlin you want, not the prophecies."

"Merlin wrote poems?"

"Well, that rather depends on how much you believe. Like the Gospels." He shifted his shoulders to rest with more comfort against the hard work top. "There's a little green book on my desk, in the back left-hand corner. You bring that in here, and I'll find you your poem."

I grappled with that order for a moment, but in the end my curiosity proved stronger than my pride. I fetched the book.

He searched the pages quickly and methodically, as one who knew exactly what he wanted. It didn't take him long to find the place. "Read that," he said, and handed me the poem.

"*Afallenau?*" I twisted my tongue round the title.

He corrected my pronunciation, softening the *f* into a *v* and turning the double *l* into an unfamiliar sound, as though he'd put his tongue against his teeth to say an *l,* then blown hard instead. "It's Welsh for 'Appletrees.' "

"Ah." I read the first few lines and frowned. "It's definitely Merlin."

"What?"

"He likes to be obscure. Oh, wait a minute, here's something . . . 'I prophesy the unvarnished truth — the rising of a child in the secluded South.' No mention of kings, though."

"Try reading further on, towards the end."

I found it in the eighth verse.

" 'A tale that will come to pass,' " I slowly read the lines aloud. " 'A staff of gold, signifying bravery, will be given by the glorious Dragon Kings. The graceful one will vanquish the profaner. Before the child, bright and bold, the Saesons shall fall, and bards will flourish.' "

He nodded. "That's the one."

"So the Dragon Kings would be . . . ?"

"The ancient line of British kings, who claimed descent from Brutus."

"Brutus the Trojan again."

"That's right."

"But he's mythical, surely."

"Most legends," said Gareth, "are rooted in myth. And legends live longer than truth."

I considered this, reading the verse through a second time and frowning as I realized that this couldn't possibly have influenced my dream — I'd never read the poems of Merlin, never knew that they existed. Even Lewis hadn't mentioned them, in all his talk of Wales. But the words had come from somewhere. "And the Saesons are . . . who? The Saxons?"

He nodded. "The English, in general."

So this really was just the red dragon again, rising up to defeat the white dragon of England. Except that this poem predicted the Welsh would be led by a child.

Gareth watched me. "Who is he?"

"I'm sorry?"

"This author of yours. The one who's too lazy to do his own research."

"Oh." I shrugged. "You wouldn't know him."

"Try me. What's his name?"

My racing mind hit on a name that I knew wouldn't register — that of my assistant.

Gareth arched a brow. "But that's a Welsh name."

"Well, yes, I believe he was born in Caernarfon . . ."

"He should be ashamed of himself, then. Every Welshman should know Merlin's prophecies. They're a part of the *brut,* the old underground poems that fueled Welsh resistance."

I'd been smiling to hear him echoing Lewis's own sentiments, but at the word "resistance" something clicked in my brain, and I suddenly remembered where else I'd heard of Merlin's prophecies. "Of course, you did use them in *Red Dragon Rising,* didn't you? That scene in the church, before Owain Glyn Dŵr begins his rebellion — he mentions the prophecies then."

"You have a good memory," said Gareth.

"Well, I did see the play a few times." I remembered now, clearly, the power of that one brief scene, when the rebel Welsh leader confronted his destiny — I even felt sure that he'd used the words "dragon kings."

"Do you have a copy of it here?"

He shook his head. "I never read things once they're finished. The urge to revise never ends."

"Oh."

"But you're right about Owain mentioning the prophecies. In real life, he used them quite freely to fuel his rebellion. A very clever man," was Gareth's personal assessment of the legendary rebel, "and in many ways the greatest hero Wales has yet produced. There's a local tradition that claims he was born here in Pembrokeshire, not far from Wolfscastle, where I grew up."

"Is that why you wrote about him?"

"Partly. But it would be hard to be Welsh and not feel a connection to Owain, no matter where he was born. He was to Wales what William Wallace was to Scotland, only more than that. To the people who followed him, Owain Glyn Dŵr was Arthur returned, as the prophecy promised. He was never betrayed," Gareth said, leaning back. "That's a bloody rare thing, in our history. In anyone's history. Even Wallace was sold by the Scots, in the end."

I nodded and glanced at the book in my hand. "So the child Merlin mentions in this poem, then . . . is that Arthur, or Owain, or . . . ?"

"Both, in a way." He shrugged. "The birth of the divine child — *y mab darogan,* or the son of prophecy — is a cornerstone of Celtic myth. Take Arthur, for example — he's conceived by magic, raised by strangers, that's the classic archetype. And Arthur, you'll remember, didn't die. Neither did Owain. The bards sang no eulogies over him, gave him no grave." He paused, and turned his gaze toward the window to the gently rising fields, and his accented voice became something like music, like one of the speeches he wrote for the stage. "We don't let any of them die, in Wales — Merlin and Arthur and Owain — we keep them close by and asleep in the hills, to be wakened if ever we need them."

I felt the magic of his words, and something more — a sense of solid permanence and peace, deep peace, that flowed between the land and Gareth, drew me in its circle. But the mood only lasted a moment. Turning back, he said, "Now if you've finished, I've got work I should be doing." And all poetry forgotten, he crossed over to the Aga to refill his mug of tea.

CHAPTER 13

For so must all things excellent begin.
— Edmund Spenser, *The Faerie Queene*

"I never trust a man who doesn't drink." James flipped a frying egg and turned his head to light a cigarette. He wasn't drinking tea, himself — he'd poured a generous measure of liqueur into his coffee.

Bridget, at the table, asked: "Why *doesn't* Gareth drink? I've always wondered."

It was Christopher who answered her. Rocking his chair on its two back legs, he clasped his hands behind his head and slanted her a knowing look. "Because, my dear, the man's an alcoholic."

"Never."

"Mm. Though I suppose, to be perfectly truthful, he's really a . . . what do they call it? Oh yes, a recovering alcoholic. Condemned to drink squash for the rest of his life."

James glanced up from his eggs again, clearly intrigued. "Is he really? I wasn't aware."

"Well, it's not common knowledge."

"And you heard it from . . . ?"

"Elen."

"Ah. I really should tell the girl . . ."

"Tell her what?" Christopher asked.

James smiled faintly. "That you can't keep a secret, of course."

Christopher said something rude about secrets and let his chair drop again, yawning. "I hardly think any of *us* will run off to the *News of the World*. And besides, Bridget asked me."

Bridget, who'd been lost in thought, surfaced at the sound of her name. "What? Oh yes, well, I wondered. There's usually a reason, isn't there, why someone doesn't drink, and Gareth didn't strike me as the health-mad type." Buttering a slice of toast, she topped it with one of her own eggs and reached for the pepper mill. "Anyway, Lyn, I'm very angry with you for not waking me this morning. I'd have loved to see the inside of that cottage."

"He's done a lot to it," said James. He tipped his eggs out of the frying pan onto a plate and sat down at the table to join us. "The upstairs, I'm told, is quite unrecogniz-

170

able. Auntie Frances would be pleased."

Bridget looked up, curious. "And who is Auntie Frances, now? That's not your Uncle Ralph's wife's name."

"Quite right," he said. "That's Auntie Pam. No, Auntie Frances would be . . . what, Chris? Uncle Ralph's aunt?"

Christopher confessed that he'd lost track of the connection. "She's likely related to everyone, here in the village. No matter how long Gareth lives in that place, or how many improvements he makes, it will always be called Auntie Frances's cottage."

Bridget smiled. "I do miss living in a village."

"I'm afraid I can't quite picture you in one," said James. "You must have caused a scandal."

"Heaps of scandals. But that's half the fun, and anyway, a writer is expected to be odd."

I couldn't help but smile myself, remembering the two years she'd spent living in her little house in Hampshire. Her neighbors, I thought, were probably still undergoing therapy.

"So Lyn," she said, "do tell. What does it look like?"

"Gareth's cottage?" I shrugged. "It looks

like you'd expect an old cottage to look. You know."

She sighed. "You'd never make a spy."

"Well, Bridget, have a heart. I only saw two rooms."

"I am amazed," said James, "that you saw anything at all. My own eyes would never be open that early."

They were barely open now. I watched him narrow them against the upward drift of smoke from his freshly lit cigarette. A man like James, I thought, who concerned himself with interior lives, with a grittier world of clubs and pubs and city streets at midnight — he just wouldn't understand the pleasure in my morning walks, the joy of breathing air that felt alive, of seeing everything laid out before me, clean and new, the way it must have been the day the world began.

Unable to explain, I simply said: "I've always been a morning person."

"Six o'clock, my dear girl, isn't morning. It's the middle of the night."

Christopher smiled and tipped his chair back again, looking at me. "It's good luck that Gareth was already up."

"I didn't go round there to see him," I said, not wanting anyone to get the wrong idea. "I was just walking by, and I stopped for a minute to play with his dog, and he came to the back door, and asked me inside."

I could see Bridget's wheels working. "I wonder," she mused, "whether Gareth is up early every day?"

"Oh, I should think so," said Christopher. "That's when he writes. At least, Elen says —"

"Elen," James said, "says a lot to you, doesn't she?"

"Yes, I suppose that she does." Christopher lifted his chin, and a look passed between the two brothers — an odd sort of challenge. James backed away first, turning smoothly to me.

"So, did you manage a peek at the masterpiece? Gareth's new play," he explained, when I looked at him blankly.

"I didn't even know that he was writing one."

"Good Lord, I'd have thought that an agent could smell work in progress," he said. "Like a bloodhound. It must have been there on his desk."

"Unless he had it hidden." Bridget rose to rinse her plate. "He's a very private person, darling."

He hadn't hidden it, though. I remembered the neat stack of handwritten pages

I'd seen on his desk — the ones he'd turned over before I sat down. "What's the new play about?"

"I don't know," James said. "That's why I asked."

Once again, Christopher showed off his insider's knowledge. "It's another historical, apparently."

"Ah." James stubbed out his cigarette. "There you are, then."

Christopher's mouth curved. "I shouldn't dismiss it so lightly. He did rather well with his last one."

I might have pressed him for details, only just then we were interrupted by the sound of a cheerful bass-baritone voice singing "White Christmas." James, feigning shock, peered out into the garden. "God help us, it's Englebert Humperdinck."

The singing was switched to a spirited whistle as Owen came in through the back door, his boots caked with muck from the cowshed. "What the devil are all of you doing indoors on a glorious morning like this?" was his greeting.

"Finishing breakfast," said James.

"At a quarter past ten? Bloody scandal." He shook his head, turning to me. "You've been out though, I hear, lovely."

Bridget nudged me. "See? That's village

life for you. Everyone peeking through windows."

Owen grinned. "I aren't peeking through nothing. Gareth told me. I met him just now, coming back from his ride."

"Gareth rides?" I felt a little twinge, and heard the wistful note that crept into my voice. The last time I'd been on a horse I'd been carrying Justin, a few months before he'd been born. I'd competed in dressage in those days, and loved it. I'd owned my own horse. But I'd sold her a month after Justin had died. After what Ivor had said, I hadn't been able to look at her without wondering, and even though my doctor had done his best to assure me that being on horseback hadn't been a factor in Justin's death, I'd felt enough lingering guilt to take most of the joy out of riding.

Still, I missed it. I missed the smell of horses, and the feel of them beneath me, and I couldn't help but feel a little envious of Gareth.

Owen nodded. "You'll have passed by his mare on your way to the Hib."

"That's the pub we ate dinner in," Bridget explained. "The Hibernia."

"There's a paddock," said Owen, "this side of the road, just before you reach the Hib. That's where Gareth keeps Sovereign.

She'll come to the fence if you call her. Just don't feed her," he warned me, "or Gareth will never forgive you."

James stifled a yawn and remembered his manners. "A cup of tea, Owen?"

He checked his watch. "No, I can't stay. I've got to run back and get cleaned up for church. I just dropped in to ask you to lunch."

That got Bridget's attention. "Lunch?"

James shook his head. "Darling, honestly. You've just finished breakfast."

"But, James, a Sunday lunch . . . it will be a *real* Sunday lunch, won't it, Owen?"

"With all the trimmings. Come at half past twelve," he offered, "and we'll have a drink beforehand."

Which rather clinched the deal, for James. "All right, then. Very kind of you and Dilys to invite us."

Owen grinned. "If you knew my Dilys, boy, you'd know that's not an invitation. It's an order."

Bridget popped her head around my bedroom door. "We still have an hour or so before lunch. Did you want to come look at the horse?"

"Mm." I nodded, not looking up. "Just give me a minute."

Like a little girl, impatient for an outing, she swung herself round with one hand on the doorjamb and entered my room, dragging her feet as she came to investigate what I was doing. "What's that?"

I shifted my seat on the edge of the bed before answering, seeking the support of the bedpost. "It's a letter from the agency."

"Not the one that came yesterday morning? You've only just opened it?"

"Well, it *was* from the office. And I am on holiday."

"What does it say?"

I read the letter through a third time, to make absolutely certain. "It seems that I've been offered a directorship."

"And high time, too. Congratulations."

I shook my head. "I said that I'd been offered one. I haven't got it, yet."

Bridget's sigh spoke volumes. She had never had much patience with the agency's executive directors. "What, do you have to swim the Channel first?"

Which came so very near the mark, I couldn't help but smile. "I have to sign a certain client."

"James?" She relaxed. "Well then, there isn't any problem, is there? James is on the brink, you know. He only wants a push."

"Bridget."

177

"Oh, I know. You're not the pushing type. I'm only saying that you shouldn't have a problem getting James to sign. He's rather taken with you."

I caught the tiny change in her tone, and glanced up. "What?"

"Well, everything he says is Lyn this and Lyn that, now. You've even got him getting up for breakfast, for heaven's sake, and he never —"

"Bridget," I cut her off, in protest, "I'm not interested in James. And he's not interested in me, not in the slightest."

"No?"

"I'd know," I assured her.

She weighed this and accepted it. "You're right, I'm being stupid. Now come on, we're running out of time. Let's go and see the horse."

I sighed, and carefully folded the letter along its sharp creases, and slipped it back into its envelope. However good the offer from my agency, I didn't have a hope of ever claiming this directorship — they'd set the bar too high. I'd sign James for them, happily. But I would not, for any price, go after Gareth.

Someone, evidently, had been sharp enough to spot the connection between the playwright and the holiday address that I had left with my assistant. And Gareth hadn't lied when he'd accused my agency of not taking no for an answer. The letter they had sent was single-minded.

Well, if they wanted him so badly, I decided, they could come down here themselves. Talented the man might be, but I, for one, had no intention of trying to woo him.

Bridget had other ideas. As we walked down the lane to the village, a few minutes later, she went up on tiptoe to peer into Gareth's back garden. "Is he home, do you think?"

"How should I know?"

We rounded the corner. She sighed. "No, his car's not there. Damn."

I sent her a dry look. "I thought you were dragging me out here to show me his *horse.*"

"Quite right. I know how you love horses." Her bounce returning, she turned and led me up the quiet street toward the pub. Just past the bus shelter and phone box, a narrow fenced paddock stretched greenly away from the roadside, and I stopped to lean my elbows on the five-barred gate.

"I don't see her."

"She's probably up in the back corner there, behind the shed." Climbing with confidence onto the gate's bottom rung, she gave a sharp whistle. Bridget whistled like a boy — it nearly split my ears.

But it caught the mare's attention.

"There, you see?" said Bridget proudly, rocking backward on the gate. "That's Sovereign, now."

I watched the horse emerging from behind the shed, a lovely coal-black mare with one white stocking and a white race slashing boldly down her forehead. "She's enormous," I said. And she was, for a mare, standing easily sixteen hands tall; sixteen two, maybe. In spite of her size she came forward with uncommon grace, and her dark liquid eyes held a gentle intelligence.

"Pretty, though, isn't she?" Bridget leaned forward and held out a carrot she'd fished from her pocket. "Come on, girl. Come look what I've brought you."

"I thought you weren't supposed to feed her."

"*You* weren't. Owen didn't say anything to me." She held the carrot higher and the mare crossed the soft grass obligingly, sniffing the air. A few feet from the gate she stopped, planting her feet and extending her neck to investigate. Encouraged by her eyes, I reached one hand to stroke her questing nose, and felt the soft warm puff of breath against my fingers.

"Oh, you beautiful thing," I said, sliding my free hand up under her forelock to scratch round the base of her ears. They twitched at the sound of my voice. Twitched again as a faint squeaking of wheels approached along the curb. A child's bike, I thought at first. But no, this sound was different, with a springiness I couldn't place . . .

"You shouldn't do that," Elen's voice warned. "Gareth doesn't like it."

I turned. She'd stopped the pram between us, and her baby, who'd been sleeping, started fussing at the sudden lack of movement. It wasn't proper crying, really — more like a halfhearted sputtering, but I found myself pressing my back to the gate.

Sovereign, munching a piece of the carrot, didn't seem to mind the noise. She watched with mild eyes as Elen tried again. "Gareth really doesn't like it."

"Oh, it's only a carrot." Bridget wrinkled her nose and climbed down from the gate, wiping her hand on the leg of her jeans. "And anyway, he isn't here now, is he?"

The baby, impatient with waiting, broke into a howl and grasped at the side of the pram, as though urging it to move. At eight months of age, Stevie Vaughan made a solid little bundle in his hooded coat and mittens. But even in a temper, nose running, his face red and mottled from crying, he still looked a beautiful baby, with curling fair hair and blue eyes ringed with spiky dark lashes.

Pulling himself up on wobbly legs to reach out for his mother, he tottered, unsteady, then tipped to one side and went over the edge of the pram.

I reacted from instinct.

I couldn't remember, afterward, how I came to catch him. We were all three of us reaching for him, holding out our hands to stop his fall toward the pavement, and then suddenly my hands were full, and I was holding him, an unexpected weight that huddled warm against my breast, his tiny fingers clutching at my shirt.

Elen straightened to stare at me, eyes wide with wonder, as though she'd just had an epiphany. "You . . ." The word was the barest of whispers.

The baby moved, warm in my arms, and his soft hair, sweet-smelling, brushed under my chin. I felt a chill between my shoulder blades, a blade of ice that barely missed my heart, and in reflex I pushed him away from me, holding him out to his mother. "Here, he's too heavy for me."

She took him, unoffended, and tucked

him back into his pram. Stevie wriggled a protest and reached his mittened hands toward me, and Elen bit her lower lip. The smile she showed me trembled just a little, but it radiated happiness. "I knew you'd come," she told me. "Margaret promised me you'd come."

And then she turned and started off again along the road, before I could reply.

CHAPTER 14

Why dost thou fix thine eye
So deeply on that book?
— William Rowley, *The Birth of Merlin*

"She's not right in the head." Owen's wife uncorked the sherry and began to pour it out, her mouth tightening. "I sometimes think our Angle men have lost their sense. It's all 'poor Elen this, poor Elen that,' but no one spares a thought for little Stevie, and it's him that's going to suffer."

Owen's Dilys was, indeed, a formidable woman. Short, round and sturdy, her chest puffed before her, she put me in mind of a little Napoleon, stoutly determined to marshal her troops. We had only just arrived, but she already had us organized in chairs around her sitting room, knees down, heads up, backs ramrod straight, like children in a Sunday school.

The Sunday school impression was made

stronger by the sitting room itself. From the crisply pleated curtains to the glass-topped coffee table, everything appeared to have been starched and polished into submission. Even the plants stood erect in their pots at the window, not daring to droop or display a dead flower. The homely smell of chicken slowly roasting in the oven seemed quite out of place in here. Almost as out of place as Owen, who even in his Sunday best looked anything but formal.

He sat balanced on an armless chair, feet braced against the carpet so he wouldn't slide straight off the slippery chintz upholstery. But like the plants, I thought, he wouldn't dare complain. This room belonged to Dilys, not to him. And she was, as I had quickly learned, a woman of opinions.

"It's all these so-called experts who deserve the blame. Psychologists." She spat the word. "Saying how you shouldn't take a baby from his mother. Well, that's nonsense. *I* say, if the mother's mad, you take that baby, so you do, and give him to a couple who can bring the boy up proper."

As she started passing round the glasses, Christopher, beside me on the sofa, broke formation, leaning back against the cushions with a vaguely idle air. "Elen isn't mad."

I took my sherry meekly, with a murmured word of thanks, and ducked neatly out of Dilys's line of fire.

"And what would you call it, then, when a girl goes round the village telling everyone there's a dragon trying to steal her child? You call that normal?"

Owen sighed. "Now, Dilys . . ."

"No, I simply can't allow that." She shook her dark head, passing judgment. "A dragon. Just imagine. She's a danger to that boy, and no mistake. A good job you were there to catch him when he fell," she said, to me.

I'd been trying not to think about it. "Really, it was nothing."

Bridget admitted that *she'd* been impressed. "Anyone would have thought you were keeping goal for England, the way you dived after that baby. I've never seen anything like it."

Dilys said, "Yes, well, I do hope that Elen was properly grateful."

"She didn't say thank you, though, did she?" Bridget looked to me for confirmation. "She only said she'd known that you would come, whatever that means."

"Ah," said James, with knowing eyes. "That's it then, she's pegged you as Stevie's protector."

My dream flashed before me. I stared at him. "What?"

"Madness," Dilys said, standing very straight and righteous. "Don't you take any notice, my dear. You've come down for a holiday. Don't let that foolish girl spoil it. Really," she said, with a shake of her head, "I can't think what possessed that boy Tony to marry her. She's always been peculiar. Such an unattractive child, she was — all hair and bony knees — no friends to speak of. And her mother was just the same, wasn't she, Owen?"

Owen stirred in his chair and remarked that, as he recalled it, Elen's mother had had many friends.

"*Male* friends, yes. She had plenty of those." Dilys sniffed. "She loved stirring things up, that one, causing a scandal. Always chasing after someone's husband."

Owen frowned. "Now then, you know that's —"

"Any decent woman," Dilys cut him off, "would have died of shame to have a baby out of wedlock, but not her. I can still see her pushing that pram round the village, as though it were a thing to be proud of. It's no wonder her daughter turned out like she did."

Christopher took a deliberate sip of sherry.

"How is *your* son doing, these days, Dilys? Married again, I hear."

"Yes, that's right."

"That would make this . . . what? His third?"

Owen answered, cheerfully. "His fourth, the little sod. It's not the marriages I mind so much, it's all the grandkids. We must have a baker's dozen of them, now. Makes for a tangle, at holidays."

"Now, Owen," said Dilys, "you know he's a very good father."

"Oh, he's good at it, I'll give you that. He makes babies like nobody's business." The older man grinned, and drained his glass of sherry in a single swallow. "Must be that place where he works, rubbing off on him."

Bridget glanced up. "Oh? And where does he work?"

"A fertility clinic, in Cardiff," said Owen. "He does all the technical work in the lab."

Christopher put it in simpler terms. "He sorts sperm."

Dilys reddened, and was opening her mouth to respond when Owen distracted her by sniffing the air. "Something's burning."

She frowned. "I don't smell anything." But her hostessing instincts could not be ignored. As she bustled out to check her oven,

Owen settled back, amused, and shook his head at Christopher.

"You'll tempt fate once too often, boy. I might not lift a finger, next time."

"Oh, I'm not afraid." Christopher slung a lazy arm along the sofa back, well pleased. "My mother's just the same, you know. All bark and no bite."

"Well, wind her up another notch — we'll see who's laughing then."

But Christopher's appetite for argument appeared to vanish when the food was served.

Her opinions notwithstanding, Owen's Dilys made a smashing Sunday lunch. I could barely see the table for the food — a platter heaped with tender chicken, thickly sliced and steaming; bowls of peas and sage and onion stuffing; roast potatoes, richly browned to crunching on the outside, that I knew would melt to nothing on the tongue; fat leeks swimming round in a savory white sauce; seasoned carrots and swedes, and two jugs of gravy to pour over everything.

"Eat," she instructed me, pushing the dish of leeks closer. "You're too thin."

I'd been called many things in my life, but "too thin" wasn't one of them. Still, I confess that I didn't raise much of a protest. At the risk of bursting zips I ate a second plateful, and a third, and chased it down with gooey chocolate pudding drizzled thick with double cream. By the time we waddled homeward, I felt rather like a pampered goose, force-fed to fullness, drowsy with contentment.

Climbing the stairs to my bedroom was out of the question, I thought. Too much effort. Instead I followed everyone else to the dim, quiet warmth of the dining room, and collapsed with a sigh into one of the comfy pink chairs by the window, tipping my head back to watch the lights twinkle and dance in the fragrant fairyland of Bridget's Christmas tree.

"It's a wonder that Owen's not twenty-five stone," I remarked, with a yawn.

Christopher, who'd managed somehow to retain the energy to saunter round the room, glanced over his shoulder and grinned. "He works it all off, between his farm and this one. But you're right, if he ever retires, he's in trouble." Pausing by the bookcase where I'd found the Wilkie Collins book, he crouched to examine its contents. "Hey, James, did you know Uncle Ralph has your books?"

"Of course he does. I gave them to him."

"Ah, well that explains it, then. I shouldn't have thought they were quite to his taste, really. Nor this," he added, prizing out a larger book and reading the title spelled out on the glossy white cover: "*The Druid's Year.* Now what the devil . . ." Flipping it open to read the flap he caught sight of an inscription and said, "Oh, it's from Gareth. That does make more sense."

Bridget recognized the name. "*The Druid's Year?* I think my friend Julia illustrated that — is her name on the cover? Julia Beckett?"

Christopher checked. "Yes, it is. She's a friend of yours, really? She's terribly good."

"I know. She illustrated all my early books. Here, toss that over, will you?"

I'd have recognized Julia's work from the cover alone, from the rich use of color and the almost fussy amount of detail that were her trademarks. The book itself appeared to be a calendar of days, detailing the seasons and the rituals and feast days of the mystical religion that had brought a sense of order to the ancient Celtic world. Bridget immediately turned to the month of June, looking for her birthday, while Christopher gave his attention back to the bookcase.

"I'd think this comes from Gareth as well," he said, holding up a slim red volume.

James turned, and squinted. "What is that, his play?"

"Mm." Christopher straightened, and

flipped a few pages. "Lots of good juicy battle scenes, you know, in this one. Manly stuff."

I stretched my hand out, curious. "May I please see that, for a moment?"

Christopher passed it to James, who was nearer; he tossed it to me in a flutter of pages. "Here, catch," James said. "What do you want it for?"

"Oh, just testing my memory." I skipped to the end of the first act, in search of that one speech by Owain Glyn Dŵr. He *had* mentioned dragon kings, surely — that's where that small bit of my dream had been born. That's where . . .

"I thought you didn't remember what you'd read," said James. "Only how you felt about it."

"Well, yes. Unless it's poetry."

"Oh, I see," he said, and if I hadn't seen his laughing eyes I would have thought his pride was injured. "So Gareth's work is poetry, while mine is —"

"Yours is wonderful. I love the way you write. But plays read differently than novels," I said, trying to explain.

Bridget, unsticking her nose from *The Druid's Year,* arched an eyebrow. "Jealous, darling?" she asked James.

"Of Gareth? Why on earth would I be jealous?"

I prudently extricated myself from the conversation, turning the pages of *Red Dragon Rising* in search of the passage I thought I remembered . . . yes, here it was. Glyn Dŵr's voice. Gareth's words: *The blood in my veins is the blood of Cadwaladr, last of those kings who were named of the dragon . . .*

I read it through again, with satisfaction. I'd succeeded in sorting out every new thing that had entered my dream, now, except for the woman in blue — and I knew there was likely a simple explanation for her, as well.

Across from me, Bridget had turned soft and kittenish again, stretching out her feet to contemplate them. "James?"

"My love?"

"What are we going to do for Christmas lunch?"

He made a sound halfway between a groan and a laugh, his head dropping back for support from the cushions. "For God's sake, Bridget . . ."

"No, I mean, are we eating it here?"

"I don't know. I haven't really thought about it."

She considered the matter a moment, then said, "I think we should. Eat here, that is.

It's not a proper Christmas if you don't have lunch at home."

James arched an eyebrow. "Are you going to cook it?"

"I might." She wriggled deeper in her chair, and set her chin deliberately. "My potatoes never do turn out as perfectly as Dilys's, but I make a cracking bread sauce."

Christopher, who'd given up the bookcase and had wandered to one of the tall narrow windows to view the back garden, half turned to face Bridget. "Could you make chestnut stuffing? The real kind, I mean?"

"If I had the ingredients." She looked pointedly at James.

"All right." He stifled a yawn. "Perhaps we'll go to town tomorrow, and let you do your Christmas shopping."

"I have to buy your present, yet," she told him.

"Well, that settles it. We'll *definitely* go to town." He stretched, and turned to me. "You're being awfully quiet, over there."

"I'm digesting." Reluctantly, I closed the book of Gareth's play, and let the pages feather past my fingers. I'd been enjoying my rereading of it, reveling again in his exquisite use of language, in the rhythm of his words. A shame the man himself was such an unappealing character. For all I would have loved a chance to represent his talent, I had no desire to deal with *him* that closely.

"Right," said Bridget, angling her wrist to check the time, "we've got another half an hour, then we really should get ready."

"And what," asked James, "would we be getting ready for?"

"The carol service."

"Ah."

"It starts at half past four," she said, "so I should think as long as we leave here at four fifteen . . ."

"I haven't been to church in twenty years," he interrupted, leaning his head back and closing his eyes. "It's not my thing. I never could sort out when I should sit, or stand, or whirl about. Who needs the aggravation?"

Bridget didn't look prepared to let him off the hook. "It's a carol service," she repeated, firmly. "You cannot have a proper Christmas without going to a carol service."

He kept his eyes closed, peacefully, not bothering to argue.

But his weary sigh spoke volumes.

CHAPTER 15

Therefore submit thy wayes unto his will,
And do by all dew meanes thy destiny fulfill
— Edmund Spenser, *The Faerie Queene*

I found myself siding with Bridget. Not only because she was my client, and thus deserving of my loyalty, but because I rather liked the thought of sitting in a village church and listening to carols. It was Christmas, after all. I'd been so busy with my dreams and Elen's baby and my crossing swords with Gareth that I'd quite forgotten why I'd come to Angle in the first place.

My only fear was that I'd never manage to unwedge my well-fed body from the chair in time to make the service. But I did it, with some effort, and by four o'clock I'd freshened up and gone outside to wait for everybody else.

I stood by myself on the lawn for a long moment, drinking in the solitude. *This,* I thought, not morning, was the perfect hour for church — the time when all of nature seemed to pause, to contemplate the sacred.

Above me, the whole sky had turned to gold, a pure and glowing gold that bled to crimson where the dying sun had settled on the hills. The crows, still clasping to the ledges of the tower, gazed across the marshy estuary to the village, wings at rest. The churchyard faced me, cool with trees that cast deep shadows on the leaning rows of headstones, from between whose ranks the church itself soared upward, gray and graceful, rising up to God the way a flower reaches for the light. And between the farm and churchyard, where the estuary wandered past the tower's walls, the feathered reeds were singing, heads bowed to the breeze, like pale choristers tuning their voices for evensong.

The hinges of the front door creaked, and James came out to join me on the lawn.

His lighter clicked; a waft of smoke brushed past my cheek. "Remind me why I'm doing this," he said.

I couldn't help but smile. He looked so like a small boy being dragged round by his family when he'd rather have stayed home, in bed. "To keep Bridget happy," I told him.

"Oh. Right." He bent his head and rubbed

his neck and nodded. "A tiring business, keeping Bridget happy. She's high maintenance, you know, like a racing car — always wanting a new set of tires, or an oil change." Lifting the cigarette to his lips, he surveyed me through the smoke. "Now you, I suspect, would be more like a Volvo."

I laughed. "Thanks a heap."

"I meant it as a compliment."

For a moment I was half afraid that Bridget had been right about his liking me — it would have been another complication that I didn't need, this week. But nothing in his eyes displayed a more than common interest. I relaxed. "It's every woman's dream, that, to be told she's like a boring Swedish car."

"Being safe," he said, "is not the same as being boring." I had the fleeting impression he was speaking of himself, and not of me, and I studied him a moment before lifting my gaze to the weathered stone face set above the front door.

"I've been meaning to ask you what this is," I told him, and pointed. "It looks very old."

"Ah, the Gerald Stone." He tilted his head up to look at it, too. "You'll have heard of Giraldus Cambrensis, the famous Welsh chronicler?"

I had slogged through his writings in history class, years ago — Giraldus Cambrensis, or Gerald of Wales, the twelfth-century writer and monk who had served the Plantagenet kings in the turbulent times of King Richard the Lionheart. "Yes, I've heard of him."

"Well, he was born not far from here, at Manorbier. Where you went to buy the Christmas tree, actually. In his earlier clerical days he was granted the living of Angle, and this face is supposed to be his. Hence its name."

"The Gerald Stone," I repeated, looking with new eyes at the serene expression on the face, the faintly smiling features.

"No one knows who did the carving, or how old it is," said James, "but it does predate the present house."

The wind struck my upturned face, making my eyes water, and for an instant the stone features seemed to change shape, growing older, more knowing, with wise watching eyes. But when I blinked again everything looked as before.

Bridget came out through the porch door and found us like that, looking up. "What on earth are you doing?"

"I've just been showing Lyn the Gerald Stone," said James.

"How thrilling." Fastening the collar of her coat, she looked round. "Are we ready? Where's your brother?"

"He went next door, to see if Elen wants to come."

"Oh, marvelous."

"Where's your Christmas spirit, darling?" His slanting glance held dry amusement. "Peace and goodwill to all men, and all that."

Bridget smiled at him, sweetly. "I've no problem with showing goodwill to all *men* . . ."

"Brat," he called her, lightly. Turning, he stripped off his gloves and handed them to me. "Here, hold these for a minute, will you, Lyn? I can't feel a thing with them on, and I need to make sure that I've got enough coins for the offertory."

Bridget frowned. "Well, I do hope Elen doesn't come."

"It looks as though you have your wish," James answered, bringing our attention to the fact that Christopher had just come round the far side of the East House, on his own.

"She wasn't there," he told us, as he came across the lawn.

"Oh, too bad," said Bridget. "Shall we go, then?"

200

"By all means." James pitched his cigarette away and, having reassured himself as to the contents of his wallet, tucked it away and reclaimed his gloves. "I can hardly wait."

"Is that meant to be sarcastic?" she asked.

"Not at all. There's nothing I love more than sitting freezing in a church while everyone around me sings off key."

Christopher grinned. "That's nostalgia, for you, surely." To the rest of us, he said, "James was a choirboy once, you know."

His brother shot him a dangerous glance. "I knew I should have drowned you in the bath when Mother brought you home from hospital."

"You very nearly did, as I recall."

"Yes, well, I should have held you under longer."

"Now, James," said Bridget, teasing, "you're forgetting what you told me. Peace and goodwill."

"Bloody rubbish." But his mouth curved as he said it, and he fell obediently into step beside me as Bridget led us past the tower, through the gate, to where the lane began. From there we took the shortcut, down across the strip of pasture to the playground fence where, one by one, we filed through the kissing gate. Two boys were playing football round the posts that held the swings, but they barely raised their heads as we went by. On the far side of the playground, under the shade trees, a green metal gate opened out to the street.

It seemed a quicker way to reach the village, really, and I marked it down to memory, as it meant I wouldn't have to walk past Gareth's garden. His cottage lay now to my right, behind a long stone wall half buried in bright sprays of red cotoneaster. Ignoring it, I turned the other way, toward the church.

I'd always found a village church more holy than a great cathedral. I'd been married in a church like this one, near my parents' home in Kent, and when my son had died I'd had him buried there, beneath the guardian yew, with all my ancestors around him so he wouldn't be alone.

This churchyard had a yew, as well — an ancient, twisted tree that spread its darkly tangled arms above the headstones, giving shelter and protection to the silent, sleeping dead. Here and there the ivy trailed across the older graves, and faded flowers languished in the grass. The peace was tangible. I breathed it in, and sighed, and Bridget, walking at my shoulder, turned to James.

"I ought to warn you, darling, Lyn does

have a weakness for places of worship. I learned that, when we went to Paris. I think we saw every cathedral and church in the city."

"It was probably good for you," James remarked.

His brother turned. "This from a man who hasn't been to church in years."

"I'm going now."

"We can only hope that God survives the shock."

But James passed through the porch without incident. Except for the smiling young woman who handed us carol sheets, nobody seemed to take notice, and I saw no sign that God had noticed, either, let alone expired. The saints in the arched stained glass windows went on staring serenely across at each other, bathed in colored light that slanted bravely through the shadows of the nave. And even the handful of people already seated in the pews seemed more intrigued by Bridget than by James.

It was a lovely little church, filled with the rich Sunday scents of oiled wood and old stone, with rough whitewashed walls and a ribbing of dark beams supporting the arched ceiling high overhead. A few memorial tablets commemorated members of the same family — the ancestors, I guessed, of

James's friends from the Hall.

"That's right," said James, when I asked. "A pity they're not here today, I'd introduce you. They said something about going up to London for a few days, but they should be back by Christmas."

Even absent, they were very much in evidence. The stained glass window set above the pew we chose to sit in had been given in the memory of another of their name. I only glanced at the dedication as I genuflected to the altar and slid into the pew beside Christopher, kneeling out of habit for a moment's silent prayer.

When I lifted my head from my intertwined hands, my gaze unexpectedly locked with a dark and familiar one — Gareth had turned in his seat near the front of the church, one shoulder pressed to the coarse whitewashed wall, to watch my display of devotion. He was too far away for me to read his eyes; I couldn't tell what he was thinking.

Elen, sitting close beside him, bouncing Stevie on her lap, looked round as well, and smiled, and waved. James raised one hand in answer, shifting sideways on the pew until his thigh touched mine, as Bridget squeezed in on the aisle end.

"Well, there you are," said James, to Christopher. "You needn't worry about Elen, Chris. She's with her knight protector."

I wasn't altogether sure how serious Christopher's pursuit of Elen was, but if he felt any jealousy now, he hid it well. He merely looked, and nodded, and leaned back against the wooden pew, turning his attention to the carol sheet. Bridget was more vocal.

"And look, she's brought her son as well. I swear I'll never know what makes some mothers bring their babies into church."

James smiled. "Ordinarily," he said, "I would agree with you. But seeing as it's Christmas, I should think that barring babies from the church would be impolitic. If nothing else, it would completely spoil the crib."

Bridget grudgingly agreed. Twisting in her seat, she looked round with new interest. "*Is* there a crib in here, I wonder?"

There was one indeed, artistically arranged at the rear of the church, where the bell rope hung down placidly beneath the tower.

"How pretty," she said. "Mind you, that sheep on the left looks a little the worse for wear, poor thing. And Baby Jesus looks as though he's had some sort of fit . . ." She caught herself too late, and flashed a guilty

205

glance at me, the way a child does who's spoken out of turn. "Oh, Lyn, I'm sorry. I should learn to keep my mouth shut."

"It's all right."

James, excluded from the brief exchange, looked from my face to Bridget's. "What's that?"

I could sense Bridget kicking herself as she answered him. "Nothing. It's nothing."

"Well, it's obviously something, if you —"

"Trust me, James, just leave it."

"Fine." Following his brother's example, he shook out his carol sheet and settled back to study it, while Bridget sent me one more sideways look, to satisfy herself I wasn't lying.

But I had told the truth — I really felt all right. It might have been because we were in church, a place that always seemed quite separate from the world outside its walls; a place where evil, pain, and sorrow couldn't enter. Here the peace, well guarded by the golden eagle perching on the lectern, flowed round and through and over me like water, and my thoughts and feelings disengaged themselves, like weary swimmers letting go the shore to float, eyes closed, upon the current. Here I could think of Justin, without pain.

That pain had happened to another

woman, in another place than this.

I knew, of course, the feeling wouldn't last. The church might give me temporary solace, but it wasn't real. Eventually, I'd have to leave and carry on with living. But for now, it did feel wonderful to stand and join in singing all those old remembered carols that seemed lovelier, somehow, because I only heard them once a year. The cold of the church numbed my nose and pricked my fingers full of needles, and when the congregation sang the bursts of misty breath showed everywhere against the dimness, curling up toward the rafters like the incense from a censer, while a small but able children's choir led us through the melodies, their faces made angelic by the pulpit's candlelight.

For the first time since I'd come to Wales, it truly felt like Christmas.

It was a joyful feeling that expanded in my chest and left no room for self-restraint. Which might explain why, when the carol service ended and we started shuffling out into the aisle, and above the sudden crush of heads my gaze locked for a second time with Gareth's, I impishly lifted my chin a notch higher and sent him my most brilliant smile. Smiling at the devil was the best way to defeat him, so my father'd always said.

I'm not sure mine defeated Gareth, but it did surprise him. I saw his eyebrows lifting in the instant before someone stepped in front of me and blotted out my view.

"Well, well," James murmured. "Look who's here."

Elen didn't hear him. Shifting Stevie higher on her shoulder, she faced me with that same bright-eyed and happy look I'd seen that afternoon, a look laced through with secret knowledge.

"Hello," she said, turning in the aisle so that her back was to the window arched above the narrow pew where we'd been sitting. I hadn't really studied the window earlier, only the memorial dedication along its bottom edge, but now I saw it showed, appropriately enough, the Nativity. I looked at Elen, standing like a modern incarnation of the stained glass Madonna behind her, and I smiled.

"Hello."

"Stevie wanted to see you."

I rather doubted that. He was asleep, for one thing, with his hand curled in a fist around a waving lock of Elen's hair. But I was reckless still with Christmas spirit, and on impulse I indulged her. "That's very nice of him," I said, and bravely touched one finger to his hand. "Hello there, Stevie."

I'd meant it as a glancing touch, a tiny stroke, and nothing more. But Stevie's small hand spread, and reached, and curled again, and held my finger fast. A flash of warmth, like an electric shock, shot upward to my shoulder as my gaze fell for the first time on the words set in the stained glass window, underneath the blue-robed Virgin and her glowing infant: *Unto us a child is born. Unto us a son is given.*

I tried to pull away, but then some stronger instinct took control, and of their own free will my fingers closed round Stevie's little ones. The heat seared down and through me, swift as wildfire chased by wind, and as it moved I felt some small and frozen corner of my heart begin to melt.

Perhaps that was the trick of it, I thought — to face the thing I feared the most and conquer it. I felt strangely free, walking home with the others in the early evening darkness. The breeze had gathered strength. It bit through the folds of my jacket and jostled the leaves of the trees in the playground, scooting the heavy clouds over the sky so the silvery moonlight grew dimmer and flickered and vanished completely.

James rustled his way through the thick grass, ahead of me. "If I hadn't seen that myself," he confessed, "I would not have believed it. She never lets anyone touch him."

"I told you," said Bridget. "She thinks Lyn's some sort of a guardian angel."

"And where did she get that idea, I wonder?"

"From someone named Margaret, apparently." She swung through the kissing gate, thinking. "I wonder who — ?"

"God damn and blast!"

Christopher, several steps ahead, turned back at his brother's outburst. "What's the matter?"

"The cows have been through here." James raised one foot in deep disgust, as I came through the gate behind him, bringing up the rear.

"Cheer up," I said. "We're nearly home."

"Oh, I'm immensely cheered," he drawled. "Church does have that effect on me."

Beside us, Bridget laughed. "It must be something in the male chromosome. Poor Gareth didn't look too thrilled to be there, either."

"Yes, well, Gareth," James informed us, "goes to noble lengths for Elen."

Christopher turned again, shaking his

head. "It's not for Elen." The clouds above us shifted and a gleam of pale light caught his hair, his eyes. "Gareth isn't interested in Elen. What he does, he does for Stevie."

"Really?" Bridget asked. "And how do you know this?"

"I know all kinds of things." His faint smile, I thought, was deliberately secretive, and watching him, I wondered if I hadn't maybe underestimated Christopher. It took a clever man to lay the proper bait for Bridget.

His tactic worked.

Before he'd reached the tower she was walking by his side, her face tipped up beguilingly, her laughter lilting on the evening breeze.

Beside me, James sighed heavily. "I don't think I can bear it."

I glanced at him, but he was looking at his watch, and not at Bridget. In the faint illumination of the dial I saw him frown. "We still have half an hour to go till opening time."

CHAPTER 16

He shall call upon me, and I will answer
   him:
I will be with him in trouble;
I will deliver him . . .

                              — Psalms 91:15

I was falling, and flailing my arms through
the blackness . . .

And then I felt the bed beneath me, warm
and safe and solid. My eyes came open
slowly, saw the firelight dancing wildly with
the shadows on my walls. She was here, I
thought, lifting my head from my pillow.
Here, in my room. By the window.

She moved, and the curtains blew forward
and billowed around her like sails round a
masthead. "This is a good thing you have
done."

I turned my face toward her, pushing the
tangle of hair from my eyes. "What did I
do?"

She moved again. The blue gown whispered to a halt a hair's breadth from the bedpost, and the firelight warmed the curve of one pale cheek as she gazed down at me. She'd lost her air of sadness, and seemed calmer now. "It will not be forgotten."

"What won't?"

"But mark me well, you must take care tomorrow," she said gravely, "for tomorrow will be Arthur's Light, a day of special danger. You must keep your vigil well, and be not swayed by the deceiver."

"You always speak in riddles," I complained. "Why can't you just . . . ?"

"I speak the truth, as plainly as I know it, and in truth your path is perilous. That you would do this for his sake betrays the greatness of your heart, and leaves me ever in your debt."

It was a strange sensation, to be dreaming, and to know that I was dreaming, and yet to feel myself responding as though everything were real. As she turned from the bedpost, preparing to leave, I pushed back my covers and scrambled out after her. "Wait," I said, "you can't go yet. You haven't said what I'm supposed to do."

She glided on, not looking back. "Sleep now, for on the morrow you will need your strength."

It suddenly occurred to me that something was missing. "Your son," I said, frowning. "Where is he?"

But already she was at the window, and the velvet draperies reached to draw her deep into their shadows while the glass became a mirror that reflected my own image.

Mine, and someone else's.

A smaller figure stood beside me, softened by the rippled glass, the blazing fire behind him setting all of him aglow until his golden curls became a halo shining round his upturned face.

And as I caught my breath and pulled my gaze away from our reflection, looking down to meet the child's eyes, I felt his hand slip warm and trusting into mine.

Chapter 17

Then to her tower she climb'd, and took the
shield,
There kept it, and so lived in fantasy.
— Alfred, Lord Tennyson,
"Lancelot and Elaine"

Owen was mending a fence at the back of the house, by the dovecote. He heard me coming up the drive and looked round, eyebrows lifting. "What's this? I thought all you London folk kept to your beds in the morning."

"Not me." I couldn't have kept to my bed if I'd wanted to. My dream had changed shape once again, and that bothered me, and when I was bothered by something, I walked.

"Oh, that's right. You were prowling round Gareth's back garden at dawn, weren't you, yesterday?" Grinning, Owen levered the fence rail back into position and reached

215

for his hammer. "Very brave you were, too. There are some who go into that garden and never come back."

I smiled. "He buries them under the flower beds, does he?"

"Most likely." Pounding one nail in, he picked up another and gave me a once-over glance. "You'll be joining them, lovely, if you don't put on something warmer than that."

"Oh, I'm fine." Holding out one arm, I showed him a fold of my thick home-knit pullover. "See? It's perfectly warm."

"Mm." His eyes remained unconvinced, fatherly. Bending his head, he positioned the nail.

It *was* chilly this morning. The wind had changed direction overnight, and blew now steadily from the southwest, pushing before it a low smudge of sooty gray cloud that chased up the long pastures and over the Haven. Outside the cozy pullover, my hands and ears grew tingly in the sharp air and my cheeks flushed red, invigorated.

I folded my arms in contentment and stood to one side to watch Owen at work. "What's the Welsh word for fence, then?"

"Don't know. I don't speak Welsh." His upward glance twinkled. "You won't find too many who do, in this part of the country."

"Gareth does."

"He's an import."

"He said he was born here, in Pembrokeshire."

"Oh, he's a Pembrokeshire man, true enough, but he comes from the other side, north of the Landsker."

"The Landsker? What's that?"

"It's a kind of dividing line, marked by the old Norman castles and such like, that separates us in the south from our Welsh-speaking neighbors. The Normans came down here just after the Conquest," he said, with the sureness of someone who'd studied his history at school. "Came and built Pembroke Castle, and fought with the local Welsh chiefs, who were already fighting each other. The old prince who'd kept them together had died — Rhys ap Tudor, his name was — and things were a bit of a shambles. And it weren't pure Welsh, anyway, even back then. There were Vikings who'd come in the raids and then settled here, taking Welsh wives. And Vikings," said Owen, "were kin to the Normans."

"Of course." I remembered my own history lessons. " 'Norman' was really a short form for 'Norseman,' wasn't it?"

"That's right. So anyway, after a bit of a battle the Normans won out, and they brought in a boatload or two of Flemish refugees to thin the Welsh out more, and we've been different ever since. 'Little England beyond Wales,' that's us."

"Is that why the place names sound English down here?"

Owen nodded. "Some are English, some more Scandinavian. Angle, that's Norse for a hook," he said, giving the nail one last tap before testing his weight on the fence rail.

"Though with all these bilingual signs now, they've had to invent names in Welsh for some towns. Bloody foolishness, that. You can't slap a new name on a sign and change nine hundred years of history."

"So you're not really Welsh, then."

"Oh, yes I am." Straightening, Owen looked down at me proudly, his gray eyes lit deep with a warrior's fire. "I'm as Welsh as the next man, and more Welsh than some, no matter what the bloody purists say. Any fool can learn a language, that's no measure of a nation. It's your blood, your birth, that matters."

He was right, of course. An Englishman could study Welsh, and speak it like a native, but he'd always be an Englishman. Nationality went deeper than the words a person spoke.

But although he'd firmly set me straight, he was too nice a man to take offense. Stretching his shoulders, he rested one hand on his hip. "Are you off on your walk?"

"I don't think so." I squinted, assessingly, up at the clouds. "It looks too much like rain."

"Then you might as well come help me see to the cows. It'll give you a bit of excitement." He winked at me, turning, and whistled a tune as he led me away from the fence and the dovecote, making an arc round the back of the house. The whistle turned into a hum, then a full-throated song, in his pleasant bass-baritone. I recognized the Christmas tune, and smiled at the words.

"Do you think there's much chance of it?"

"What?"

"A white Christmas."

Owen laughed. "No, we might have a wet one, but never a white one. We haven't had snow here in Angle for years. They might get it in Pembroke, though — inland, away from the coast."

We'd reached the row of sheds at the head of the drive. Owen paused at the third one — the green one closest to the house — and gave the door a rattle. "There, now," he said, as the open padlock tumbled to the ground. "She's gone and done it again. With all of the things she's got stashed in this shed you would think she'd remember to lock it."

He meant Elen, I gathered. Christopher had told me that she used this shed to store the antique furniture she'd gathered and intended to restore.

Owen bent to pick the padlock up. "The cats like to follow her in here, you know, when she's fetching a piece, and she used to always worry she might leave one trapped inside, not knowing. That's why she didn't like locking the door. But now I've put the cat flap in, there shouldn't be a problem."

I looked down at the piece of rubber matting nailed across the bottom of the door. "I shouldn't think you'd want the cats walking on all of that furniture."

Owen assured me they couldn't get in on their own. Peeling up one corner of the rubber, he showed me how he'd made the flap to open out, not in, by cutting the rough-edged hole several inches smaller than the matting. It was still a fair-sized hole, and I saw why a moment later when, intrigued by Owen's fiddling with the lock, the big tabby stepped from the tangle of fuchsia and rose bushes behind us and came forward to investigate.

"Go on, Big Boy, get out of that," said Owen, nudging the creature away from the flap as he clicked the padlock firmly into place. The cat, unoffended, continued down the narrow flight of concrete steps descending to the courtyard behind Elen's house.

It looked a peaceful place. At the bottom of the steps a fig tree stretched its knobby branches clear across to rest upon the roof slates of the jutting back part of the middle house, forming an arch leading into the courtyard of sloping stone terraces hemmed in by low whitewashed walls, weeping green where the weather had loosened the mortar. The coping stones, too, had been softened with green, breaking only to make enough space for a gate at the northeastern corner. That gate — painted blue, like the drainpipes and doors at the back of the East House — led into the yard and beyond to the low line of metal-roofed cowsheds.

Owen and I took the shorter route, round the side wall of the green storage shed and down a plainer flight of steps. The yard had a comforting animal smell. I trailed after Owen, not minding the mud and manure that clung to my boots. "Can I help you with anything? Really," I said, when he looked at me, doubtful, "I do have experience mucking out horses."

"These are cows."

"Well, I know that, but . . ."

"No, they're night and day from horses, cows," said Owen, solemn faced, as we entered the calf shed, "so you'd do better to just sit down over there, and keep me company. All right?"

I sat on an old-fashioned milking stool inside the doorway, and smiled. "Are you always this difficult?"

"Well now, I'm bound to be, living with Dilys. It's eat or be eaten in our house," he told me. He picked up a pitchfork and bent to his work, and I watched him a moment in silence.

"Owen?"

"Yes, lovely?"

"Can I ask you something?"

"Apparently so."

"What Dilys said yesterday, about Elen thinking a dragon was trying to take Stevie, was that really true?"

"It was." He shook out a forkful of straw and the dust scattered upward. "My Dilys might gossip, but everything's fact."

"Why a dragon?"

"What's that?"

I frowned, and tried to speak more clearly. "I can understand her worrying. That's normal, every mother worries. And because she lost her husband, I can understand why Elen might be scared of losing Stevie, too. But I should think that she'd be worried about *people* doing harm to him, not creatures from some fairy tale."

"Ah, but Elen," Owen told me, "likes her fairy tales. She lives them. Always off in her own little world, Elen was, as a child. She was different, you know. Like her mother." His eyes, for a moment, grew soft. "Always believing in magic, and princes. Elen once told me that Tony was her Pwyll" — in his voice that came out as "Pwill" — "and that he'd saved her from unhappiness, like Pwyll had saved Rhiannon."

"Who?"

"Rhiannon."

I looked a blank, and Owen shook his head and smiled, tut-tutting at my ignorance. "And you an educated lady. That's the oldest of Welsh tales, that is. The first branch of the Mabinogi."

"Oh, the *Mabinogion.*" I was at least aware of the existence of the book of Welsh myths, though I'd never read it. "So Rhiannon was . . ."

"A princess."

"Ah."

"You'll have to read the story," he said, grinning. "I aren't going to spoil it for you.

The important part is that, in time, Prince Pwyll and Rhiannon had a son, a little baby, who was stolen by . . ."

"A dragon," I concluded for him, nodding understanding. "So that's where Elen gets it, then."

"That's right."

"But you don't think she's mad?"

"Who, Elen? No," he said, as though the very thought were quite ridiculous. "She has her fancies, sometimes, but it's just her way of coping, see. She did it as a child, to keep from crying when the other children called her names because she had no father. And she did it when her mother died, and now again with Tony. No, Elen knows what's real," he told me, certain. "She's just inherited her mother's way of seeing things, the Celtic way, that sees the past and future worlds all blended in with ours. That isn't mad, it's Welsh." He speared another clump of straw and shook it clean. "*My* mother always made me walk round fairy circles in the grass, so I wouldn't step inside and disappear. Now, that's as strange as Elen's dragon, but I grew up fine," he reasoned. "So will Stevie."

"I'm sure you're right."

"I'm always right." He looked at me and winked. "Besides, with you protecting him, how could the boy go wrong?"

"What?"

"I heard what happened in the church. She doesn't let just anybody touch that baby, lovely. You'll be stuck with playing guardian, now."

"I'm not sure I want to play guardian."

"Oh, it's only for the week." Owen's level voice made light of my objections. "You'll do fine. Just see that you don't take him up the tower."

"Why is that?"

"Because the tower," he advised me, "is where Elen's dragon lives."

CHAPTER 18

Behold, the enchanted towers . . .
A castle like a rock upon a rock . . .
— Alfred, Lord Tennyson, "The Holy Grail"

I stood in the bay of the writing room window and watched the crows settle on top of the tower, its stones dripping moisture beneath the gray sky. Those solid square walls had a secretive look; I could almost believe there was something inside.

"Is it still raining?" Bridget asked, crossing behind me.

"Not really. It seems to be clearing."

She leaned forward and looked for herself, to be certain. "Thank God. I didn't fancy being stuck indoors all day."

I couldn't resist pointing out that spending the day doing shopping in Pembroke amounted to much the same thing. "Shops do tend to be indoors."

"Well yes, I know, but it's just different.

And besides, I can't shop *properly* in rain. All that dashing about on the pavement, in puddles."

"Don't worry," I told her. "If the rain does start up again, men will be tripping all over themselves to offer you umbrellas."

"Very likely." She grinned. "Men are idiots."

"Oh? Even Gareth Gwyn Morgan?"

"All right, Gareth excepted. Though sometimes I wonder, the way he lets Elen impose on his time."

I shrugged. "He was friends with her husband."

"Mm."

"Here we go."

"No, I just think it's odd," she said, turning in boredom away from the window. "Maybe Gareth really *is* the baby's father, like Christopher says."

I let my eyes follow the flight of the crows as they rose in a whirl from the parapet. "Christopher said that?"

"Perhaps not in so many words," she admitted. "He implied it, though."

It surprised me that Bridget should fall so completely for Christopher's bald-faced attempt to seduce her. Not that I imagined he was aiming for seduction in the carnal sense — I fancied he respected James's feelings more than that — but like Bridget, he couldn't seem to help himself. I turned, now, and teased her, "You're losing your touch, if the most you could get from the man was a mere implication."

"Rat." Her eyes brimmed with laughter. "But you're right, I shall have to try harder. It's a shame I can't get him alone for an hour."

"I could try to keep James occupied this afternoon," I offered. "Would that help?"

"Well . . ."

I saw her doubtful look and sighed. "Oh, Bridget, please. My interest is professional. I don't want James's body, just his books."

"I know, I know. I'm sorry."

"Look, if this is going to be a problem . . . if you'd rather that I didn't try to sign him . . ."

"What, and see you miss your shot at a directorship? No chance," she said, and shook her head. "Of course you must represent James, don't be silly."

I didn't have the heart to tell her that the offer of a directorship had nothing to do with James — that it was Gareth my employers wanted. Not that I'd have told her, anyway. Bridget had a gift for indiscretion, and the last thing that I needed was for Gareth to find out about my letter from the agency — he'd think it vindication of his earlier suspicions, that I'd come down here in search of him, and not because of James. Not that I cared what he thought, I reminded myself. I simply didn't want the aggravation.

Bridget gathered her hair back and started to plait it. "So all right, then. When we get to Pembroke, you take James."

She might have been asking me to mind her pet spaniel. I smiled. "And where would you like me to take him?"

"Oh, anywhere, I don't know. Ask him to show you the castle, he'd like that. Like I said, I only need an hour."

I admired her confidence. Still, given odds, I'd have put my own money on Christopher. Having watched him last night, I knew that his manipulative skills were at least equal to Bridget's, and whatever he knew about Gareth Gwyn Morgan, he wasn't too likely to tell her so soon — he would spin it out artfully; give her a little bit here, and a hint of it there; keep her hungry for more.

She glanced at me. "You'll just have to make sure he doesn't suspect."

"What, James?" I raised my eyebrows. "The man who went on building sandwiches and munching crisps last night, while you

Mata Haried his brother? I shouldn't worry. He's either the most trusting man that I've met, or he's hopelessly thick when it comes to relationships."

"He's not thick," Bridget told me. "He's just self-absorbed."

"Ah."

"Most authors are, really."

"I'll try to remember that."

"*I'm* not, of course. But then, I'm not an author."

"Since when?"

"I'm a writer," she said. "There's a difference. Authors are rarefied creatures, you know, who write serious fiction."

"And writers . . . ?"

"Write books people buy," she explained, with a twinkle of mischief.

A voice from the doorway made both of us jump. "Do you know," James said lightly, "I really must stop sneaking up on you, darling. I hear the most slanderous things."

Bridget whirled, both hands holding her half-finished plait. "All right, then," she told him. "I take it all back. Your fiction's not serious."

"Thank you. That's much better." He moved in to give her a kiss as she fastened off the plait and flipped it down between her shoulders. He mustn't have been standing in the corridor too long, at least not long enough to hear me call him thick, because the smile he turned to me was rather cheerful. "Are we ready?"

"Yes, just let me fetch my raincoat." For after all, I reasoned, as I went out to look on the pegs in the hallway, some of us didn't have Bridget's allure. And if the rain began again, I couldn't count on anybody rushing up to *me* with an umbrella.

I had seen the castle twice now from the outside, but I still caught my breath as we came round the bend and the great gray walls soared from the top of the hill, keeping watch on the huddle of rooftops below, making toys of the cars that were climbing the steep road toward it.

James switched the wiper on to clear a scattering of moisture from the windscreen, and took a turning just below the high street, squeezing the Merc into a narrow, high-walled lane. "The challenge," he said, "will be finding somewhere to park."

I knew we'd have no trouble, not with Bridget in the car. She could find a spot on Soho Square, and that was saying something. As we inched along the lane we passed a string of terraced car parks and I settled back to watch as Bridget pressed

231

against her window.

"There," she said, and pointed.

James shook his head. "However do you find them?"

"It's a gift."

He neatly reversed the Merc into the space, and the wipers made one final squeak on the glass before stopping. A burst of fresh, damp air invaded the car as James opened the driver's side door. "Right then, everyone out."

Christopher, wedged in the back seat beside me, shifted one leg in experiment. "I don't think I can move, you know. You'll have to leave me here."

"Poor thing," said Bridget. Scrambling out, she pulled her own seat forward and reached back to help him. "Here, take my hand."

"I can't feel my feet."

"It's my fault, for making you ride in the back." Bridget tried to look properly remorseful. "If it wasn't for the fact that I get carsick . . ."

"It's all right." He stood and stretched awkwardly, cramped at the knees. "Not to worry. I'm sure that the blood will return."

"Oh, stop whining," said James. "Just go get me a pay and display sticker, will you? The machine's over there."

Christopher stood firm a moment, rebellious, then — being the younger brother — gave in from habit, limping away on stiff legs.

This car park, ringed with stone walls, nestled right behind the high street — I could see the huddled backs of shops and businesses, and hear the swish of unseen traffic sliding wetly past them. The wind, still thick with unshed rain, sailed leaves across the shallow puddles at my feet, and I tipped my face to feel its damp caress, turning slowly round to see the view from every angle.

The low ivied wall at the rear of the car park must once have been part of the old town's defenses. Beyond it, the ground tumbled steeply down into a valley, then climbed again, slowly, under a jumble of rooftops, to crest a small hill on the opposite side.

Bridget, at my shoulder, craned forward to study the green strip of parkland that ran through the valley directly below us. "We could have just parked on the Common, you know. There's a space there, as well."

I looked, hard. "Where?"

"Right there, by that tree. Don't you see it?"

Christopher, returning with the parking

sticker, looked at her in mild dismay. "What, we're moving the car?"

"No," said James, "we are not." To emphasize the point, he took the sticker from his brother's hand and pasted it firmly to the inside of the windscreen. "There." The door locks clicked shut as he armed the alarm. "We're good for two hours, now."

Bridget looked doubtful. "Only two?"

"Darling, it's Pembroke, not Bond Street."

I sent him a pitying glance as we walked toward the narrow brick arcade that joined the car park to the high street. "I can tell you've never shopped with Bridget."

"Why?"

"She's not exactly known for speed. I've seen her spend two hours in John Menzies alone, buying magazines."

"Oh."

Bridget linked her arm through his, and smiled winningly. "Darling," she said, as though the thought had just occurred to her, "why don't you take Lyn and show her the castle?"

"I've seen it a thousand times."

"Yes, but it's bound to be more fun than trailing after me."

"True." He glanced round at me. "Would you like to do that? Right, then. Chris, what are you doing — staying with Bridget or

234

coming with us?"

Bridget, startled, lost her smile. She hadn't thought of that.

But Christopher gave the right answer. "I'll stay. There are one or two things I should pick up, myself, while I'm here."

The arcade brought us out at the side of a florist's shop, wafting thick fragrances onto the pavement, the plastic pails set round its walls spilling over with freshly cut flowers. Above them, the windows were hidden by holly wreaths, festive with red tartan ribbon and roses or sprays of red berries.

"Ooh," said Bridget, stopping.

James, who appeared to have no patience whatsoever for window shopping, consulted his watch. "Right, we'll meet you back here at a quarter past three, then." And taking my sleeve in a purposeful grip, he steered me away, down the pavement.

Every town's high street, I thought, had a character. Some were young venture capitalists, slicked down and smart, while others were tarted up mannequins, flash without substance, relying on paint to impress the observer. And some were older women, highly bred and full of grace, who seemed to carry beauty with them as they aged. Pembroke's high street — or rather, as James corrected me, its Main Street — was a favorite aunt, lively and cheerful, with an ample lap to welcome you and arms to hug you tight.

As in Angle, all the buildings here were painted in the pastel seaside shades of salmon pink and cream and soft mint green and yellow, the row of colors adding to the general festive air. Around us the shop windows glowed with a warm light that softened the gray afternoon, and the shimmer of tinsel and twinkle of fairy lights blended with snatches of carols and Christmas songs spilling from opening doorways. On the pavement the bustle of bodies pressed close and flowed past like a chattering stream. The teenaged girl in front of me, her outrageously striped woolly hat smelling strongly of incense, stopped without warning to look in a window, and stepping around her I dodged two young women who'd paused with their pushchairs to greet one another.

"Bloody people," said James. "This is why I don't like to come shopping."

I smiled. "Well, you may find that being with me is no better. I do like to puddle around, in a castle — it drives people mad."

He didn't look worried. "I'm sure I'll survive."

Stretched like a slumbering beast at the

top of the street, Pembroke Castle watched the whirl of life and color passing underneath it, as it must have watched a thousand other market crowds of Christmases long past. The walls loomed very close now, and looking up I felt a surge of childish excitement.

"Careful!" James grabbed my arm for a second time, pulling me clear of a wooden bin heaped with pale cabbages. The pavement here narrowed, in front of the fruiterer's. Breathing the pungent mixed smells of the tropics and sharp autumn orchards, I waited with James for a break in the traffic, then made a brave dash to the opposite side for our final approach to the castle's main gate.

We paused to buy our tickets in the gift shop near the entrance. "Don't be daft," said James, when I offered to pay. "You're my guest."

So instead I invested my pounds in a guidebook — a thick and thorough-looking publication with a plan of the castle set in like a centerfold. I pulled it out, for reference, as we passed through the outer gate into the barbican.

"I assume that we're meant to go this way," I said, pointing left. "Up into the Bygate Tower, and round the walls, clockwise."

"Then let's go the other way. Live on the edge." He was mocking, of course, but from what I'd seen of James I suspected he liked leading minor rebellions. He paused underneath the portcullis, hands on hips. "The most logical place to begin is the keep, really. Start at the middle and work our way out."

I looked where he was looking, straight ahead. The castle was an ancient one, built, my guidebook told me, by a Norman earl named Roger de Montgomery. The guidebook went on to brag that when the Welsh had laid siege to the Norman invaders, a year or so afterward, Pembroke's castle had been the only one in all of southwest Wales that hadn't fallen. It was easy to see why.

Roger de Montgomery, and those who had come after him, had built the castle thick and strong and solid, double-warded. We were entering the outer ward, a level field of close-clipped green with one large square of tarmac that I guessed provided space for modern spectacles. In olden times, when danger threatened, those who labored in the fields around the castle walls could move their families here for safety, while their lord and master made his own retreat to the enormous round-walled keep within the inner ward. This massive tower, meant to stand when all the other fortified defenses had been breached, would be the final refuge of those living in the castle, and the men who'd built it knew that they might one day need its strength.

While the halls beside it crumbled from the strain of staying upright, Pembroke Castle's keep had stood through eight long centuries of tumult, and looked capable of weathering another eight with ease. It had been poked at, over time. Bits of the parapet surrounding the domed roof had tumbled down, or been removed, and when we walked round to the north side I could see the black and jagged hole that marked the first-floor entrance, stripped of all its finer facing stones. But such small scars went virtually unnoticed on a building so imposing.

"I'm not sure you should be doing that," said James, as I scampered up the flight of steps toward the gaping doorway. "Those steps might not be safe. And anyway, you can't get in that way, you have to go through here."

The steps didn't *feel* dangerous, but I didn't imagine that open defiance was something James craved in an agent, and I ought to be trying to show him how well I could listen. Reluctantly, I turned back and went through the proper entrance, a much smaller door set at ground level. It felt like walking through a tunnel — the walls of the keep must have been a good twenty feet thick — but at length it discharged us, like puny adventurers, into the cavernous space.

"You see?" James, who had seen it before, pointed up at a ragged-edged hole, streaming light. "It's a doorway to nothing, the floors have all gone."

I had tipped my head backward, struck dumb by the sight.

Originally, there would have been three or more levels here, comfortable rooms, wooden floors, warming fires that burned in the royal apartments, but all of that was lost now to the callous hand of time. What remained, though, was in some ways more impressive.

Stripped to its bare outer walls, it was like a cathedral, a great hollow soaring cathedral of stone, with a perfect domed ceiling and small arching windows that slanted pale light through the reverent gloom. From every ledge and opening long streaks of soft and mossy green dripped downward, passing shades of rust and gentle blues that stained the walls in places where the plaster had not fallen from the gray, unyielding stones.

I took a breath, inhaling dust, and fumbled for my guidebook. "Seventy-five feet," I said, in awe. "This shaft is seventy-five feet tall."

James looked at me. "You say that as though it's a challenge."

"It is." I'd always liked climbing things. Turning, I spotted the newel stair, and happily squeezed up one tight winding flight to the first narrow landing. Resting my hands on the cold metal piping that served as a guardrail, I leaned through the open arched doorway to look down at James. "Coming up?"

"No, I've done it once, thank you." He sauntered forward, moving through a shifting web of light and shadow, to see me better. By the time I reached the third and final landing, he was standing in the center of the floor. "Do warn me if you're going to fall," he said, "so I can step aside."

"You wouldn't catch me?"

"From that height? You must be mad."

I took a firm grip on the guardrail and leaned out as far as I dared, to admire the view. The dome, from this height, was a marvel of masonry, hundreds of stones set with perfect precision to form an impossible half sphere that floated above me. Absorbed, I leaned further, and felt my hand slip in the instant before something clamped round my shoulder.

"Don't worry," said Gareth, behind me. "*I'll* catch you."

CHAPTER 19

Cadwaladr's blood lineally descending,
Long hath be told of such a Prince coming,
Wherefore Friends, if that I shall not lie,
This same is the Fulfiller of the Prophecy.
— Citizens' Welcome to Henry VII
at Worcester, 1486

I nearly shot out of my skin. Only when he'd
hauled me away from the edge, when my
heart had returned to my rib cage and
everything seemed right side up, did my fear
turn to fury. I sputtered and burned like a
fuse as I whipped round to yank myself free.
"Dammit, what are you doing? You scared
me to death."

"Then we're even." He let go my shoulder
but didn't step back. He was closer to me
now than he had ever been, close enough
that I could smell the cleanness of him, the
soapy warm scent of his skin and the trace
of detergent that clung to the folds of the

shirt that he wore underneath his dark jacket of old, beaten leather that smelled of the damp, cold outdoors.

He'd been up on the roof, I thought. Feeling the chill draft that swept down the spiraling stairs just behind us, I realized that Gareth would have to have been there, concealed by the shadows and blocking the wind, when I'd climbed to this level. I would have heard him, otherwise — he couldn't have come up or down the stairs, without me hearing. So he must have been there, standing silent, watching me . . .

In the confines of the landing, with the stone walls pressing all around, this new awareness of him felt disturbing, and I had to fight back an irrational urge to leap over the edge of the guardrail and into the void.

"You'd have bloody well broken your neck," he came back at me, "falling from here."

I looked up and studied his thundercloud face with the calmness that follows a shock, seeing no reason why *he* should be angry. "I was not," I said, very sure, "going to fall. I was perfectly balanced."

"Well, the next time you balance so perfectly, see that you're not standing sixty feet up."

James called out, below us. "Lyn?"

244

"Yes?"

"Are you all right?"

"I'm fine."

"Who's that you're talking to?"

Gareth answered, arrogant. "It's me."

I heard James shuffle backward, trying to see. "Gareth?"

"Got it in one."

"What the devil are *you* doing up there?"

"I'm being bloody unappreciated, that's what."

"Sorry?"

Sighing, I raised my voice. "Never mind, James, we'll be down in a minute. I just want to look at the roof."

Gareth lifted an eyebrow. "Oh, brilliant. A fall from up there would be much more impressive."

"I'm not going to fall."

"No, you're not," he agreed, "because I'm coming with you."

From anyone else, I'd have found such concern for my welfare endearing — from Gareth, it rankled. I didn't know why. It might have had something to do with the way that he touched me, his hand holding firm to the back of my coat as I climbed to the top of the parapet. His touch didn't question its right to be there, it was simple possession. And the more I tried to break from it, the stronger it became.

"That's far enough," he said. "You can see all you need to see from here."

But in defiance I went one step higher, spreading my stance to the buffeting wind and enjoying the feel of achievement. I felt like I was standing on the prow of some great ship, with all the other towers bowed beneath me, supplicant. All round me, to both west and east, a muddy-bottomed tidal river flowed and pooled about the castle walls, the water slow and idle now, with nothing to defend.

It made a calming contrast to the hurly-burly running through the Main Street in the opposite direction, where lines of miniature cars and people jostled past the tiny shops of Pembroke.

I would have gone still higher — it appeared that from the rough-flagged inner wall walk there was some way I could climb the outer dome and reach the summit of the tower — but the hand at my back was determined.

"Good enough?" Gareth asked.

"I suppose it will have to be." Looking straight down, I examined the warren of crumbling walls to the east of the keep. "What is that?"

He glanced over. "The old halls and

chancery. Why, did you want to climb them while you're at it?"

I turned my head sideways. His eyes were unchanged, but I hadn't mistaken the thread of dry wit in his voice. "Maybe," I said.

"Then I'd best show you round them myself. Swift won't be any help, he's got no head for heights."

James, waiting at the doorway of the keep, agreed. "Oh, God no, I have no great desire to go up any building that's falling to pieces." He seemed rather pleased to see Gareth. I found that surprising. From what I'd seen so far since coming to Angle, I wouldn't have thought either man had much use for the other. "No, you two go ahead."

I held back. "I can go by myself, it's all right. I'm sure that Mr. Morgan doesn't want to waste his time."

Gareth let go my jacket and shrugged. "I'm not in any rush."

His tone was a challenge. He knew I wouldn't risk appearing rude in front of James, and with his eyes he let me know he knew it. Silently, I set my jaw. Fine then, I thought. If I couldn't stop Gareth from dogging my steps round the ruins, I could at least see that he didn't enjoy the experience.

And my methods were effective. Nearly half an hour later, as I pulled myself onto the wall of the northern hall, Gareth began to unravel. "Is it really necessary," he asked, "to go up every bloody flight of stairs you see?"

"What, getting tired?"

"No." He sounded like a little boy, complaining, and I turned to hide my smile.

"I've told you that you needn't bother trying to keep up with me. I never fall. And even if I did fall," I went on, "I don't see why that should worry you. It's not as though you like me."

He considered this a moment. "Do you know," he said, "you're absolutely right."

Surprised by the change in his tone, I looked over my shoulder. "I am?"

"Yes. The next oubliette that we pass," he said, firmly, "I'm chucking you in."

He wasn't serious, I told myself, remembering the horror of that cramped hole in the dungeon tower, where prisoners were thrown to be forgotten. I knew he wasn't serious. But he played it so brilliantly, straight-faced and sober, that I wavered a few seconds, doubting. "You wouldn't dare."

His smile was unexpected. He stood, hands on hips, planted square in the stairwell. "Are we going down, now?"

I followed him warily, not really sure how to handle a Gareth in good humor. At the bottom of the newel stair we found James, waiting patiently and smoking, looking small against the lofty arching ruins of the northern hall. He glanced at us, friendly. "Well done," he said. "The only thing left to see here is the Wogan."

"She likes to go up," Gareth told him, "not down."

But he went with me anyway, into the Wogan — a huge limestone cavern set under the hall. Carved by nature, the ceiling soared over our heads, descending into darkness at its outer edges. The great yawning mouth of the cavern was sealed by a stout wall, with windows and arrow slits over an iron-grilled water gate.

"This was used as a boat store," said Gareth.

"Was the water higher in those days?"

"Probably not."

"Then how did they get the boats up here?" I asked.

"Well, they wouldn't have carried the bloody things on their backs. I'm sure they knew enough to build a slipway."

"Oh." I looked at his silhouette, black and unyielding against the cold light creeping through the thick bars of the water gate. "Now, *this* place," I told him, "would make a great setting for drama." When he didn't dispute me, I pushed forward, braver. "I'm told that you're writing another historical?"

I watched his head turn, heard the pause. "Maybe."

"Is it set here, at Pembroke?"

"It might be."

I lifted my guidebook and leafed through the pages that detailed the castle's long history, trying to spot who his subject might be. "William Marshal?" I named the great earl who had been the right arm of the first Plantagenets, and who'd nearly outlasted the lot of them, surviving three kings and standing regent to the fourth.

"A good one, but no. Guess again."

I bent to the guidebook a second time, straining to read in the dim light. Now, who, I wondered, would appeal to Gareth? The last play he'd written had been about Owain Glyn Dŵr, a soldier, a leader, a man who had battled great odds . . .

"Henry Tudor," I said.

Gareth watched and said nothing.

"That's it," I said, "isn't it? Henry VII." The first Tudor king, born at Pembroke, who'd struggled through exile and intrigue to capture the crown in the battle of Bosworth and end England's War of the Roses by joining in marriage his own house of Lancaster with the rival house of York. He'd make a fitting hero for a Gareth Morgan play.

I closed my guidebook, very sure. Gareth, an unreadable shadow against the gray light, took a step back from the water gate, and as he turned I caught the fading corner of his smile. "We'd best get on with it," he said. "There's still a lot of castle left to see."

I didn't let him shake me off so easily. As we strolled along the pathway that would take us through the curtain wall and back into the outer ward, I looked at James, pure innocence. "Wasn't Henry VII born here?"

"Yes, in that tower, there," he said, pointing ahead to the place in the fortified wall. "His uncle, Jasper Tudor, was the Earl of Pembroke, then. It paid to be related to the King."

My history lessons flooded back. I had nearly forgotten the tale of how Katherine of Valois, the widowed Queen of Henry V, had risked her neck in secret marriage to the Welshman Owen Tudor, and had given him two sons — half brothers to the boy King Henry VI. Jasper, I thought, would have been one of those sons. And the other, the one who'd fathered Henry VII, his name

251

was . . .

"Edmund," said James, when I couldn't remember. "Edmund had the luck of marriage on his side — his wife had royal blood, as well. I think Henry's claim to the throne came from her family, somehow."

"I'd like to see the room where he was born," I said, and made a point of looking at my watch. "Perhaps we ought to go there next. We're running out of time."

Beside me, Gareth calmly turned his head and showed me, in a glance, he wasn't fooled. "I have a feeling you'll be disappointed."

James agreed. "There's nothing there to see." But he indulged me, all the same.

The ascent from the outer ward into the tower was simple and straight, and the tower itself had been fully restored — James appeared to have no problem climbing the stairs to the sturdy upper floor. It was here, he informed me, in this close round chamber, that the first Tudor king had been born. "Not the nicest of rooms," he said, looking around from the narrow rectangular windows that faced outward, over the town, to the large fireplace opposite, its reconstructed chimneypiece bearing a plaque to commemorate "the birth of Henry VII in this castle on the 28th of January 1457."

"Oh, I don't know," I countered, liking the warmth of the wooden plank floor, and the stout ceiling beams overhead. "It's really rather cozy, I think. Once you put a bed in here, and draperies . . ."

Gareth interrupted my imaginings. "Henry's mother," he told us, "was fourteen years old, with her man two months dead, and a baby that wanted to fight his way out of her. I doubt that she cared about draperies."

I thought about this, stepping back to make way for a trio of tourists who'd just tumbled in from the wall walk. Young and laughing, reddened by the cold, they peered through the windows and glanced at the fireplace, exchanging comments in a language that might have been German, then whirled past us into the dark narrow gallery linking the tower to the neighboring gatehouse.

I felt the air stir in their wake, felt it brush me, as soft as a whispering gown. Looking down, I consulted my guidebook. "Did he live here very long?"

"Who, Henry?" Gareth shrugged. "Not really. When he was four or five his Uncle Jasper lost this castle to the Yorkists, and the boy was taken too, as hostage. It happened all the time, in those days," he said, seeing the look on my face.

"How long was he held hostage?"

"Ten years or so."

It seemed barbaric, really, and I said as much. "To take a woman's child away . . ."

"I know," said Gareth.

James was less affected. "Oh, she got him back eventually. And then his uncle took him to the continent for safety, brought him back in time for Bosworth Field." He looked up at the chimneypiece. "We're meant to be descended from him, Christopher and I. Supposedly when Henry marched through on his way to do battle with Richard III, he stopped the night with a family near New Quay and took a special liking to the daughter of the house. My mother's family trace their line from Henry's little accident."

"Is that a fact?" Gareth studied him with interest.

"Mm. Mind you, I'm not sure Tudor blood is something one would want. Henry VIII with his wives, you know, and Bloody Mary . . . not the most lovable characters, were they?"

The breeze blew again, very cold, and I moved to get clear of it, colliding with the door frame and losing my grip on the guidebook. It fell to the floor in a scramble of pages. And as I bent to pick it up I saw that it had opened to the portrait of a woman, set beneath some famous former Earl of Pembroke.

The portrait — an old painting — had been photographed in black and white; I couldn't tell the color of her gown. And the woman was no longer young. But there couldn't be any mistaking that long, solemn face, nor the rings on her fingers. This was, without question, the woman in blue of my dreams.

And now, of course, now that I knew who she was, I knew just where my subconscious mind had acquired her. Only last year I had handled a book about women who had figured in the history of the Tower of London, and her portrait and story had been in that book — the story of how she'd taken her young grandson to shelter in the White Tower, while his father's troops were under siege.

I didn't think it strange that she had turned up in my dreams — at least, no stranger than the other things I'd dreamed of. But I thought it rather weird that I had found her portrait here, while I was stand-ing in this room.

Because the grandson she'd protected had grown up to be King Henry VIII. And the woman in the portrait was the Lady Margaret Beaufort, who, as a frightened girl of fourteen, with her husband dead and strangers all around her, had in this tower brought a baby boy into the world, named Henry Tudor.

CHAPTER 20

And when the dragon saw that he was
cast unto the earth, he persecuted the
woman which brought forth the man child.
— Revelation 12:13

"I'm not angry," said Bridget, arranging the overstuffed freezer to make space for one more container of ice cream. She straightened, looked round to be sure there was nothing left over, then gathered the crinkling carrier bags in a wad that she thrust in the bin. Bridget never saved anything. "I just wish that I'd known he was there."

"Well, short of running a flag up the Barbican tower, I really can't see how I could have alerted you." Cradling my mug of hot coffee, I followed her through to the warmth of the dining room, taking a chair by the glittering tree. "At any rate, I doubt that even you'd have found his company absorbing. He was in a mood."

"He's always in a mood," she said. "He broods, you know. Like Heathcliff."

"Heathcliff," I told her, "was never my type."

"No? He's certainly mine."

It was a catch-all category, I thought — Bridget's type. So long as a man didn't come when she called him, she found him attractive. "You'll have to shop faster, next time. You just missed him by minutes. James did try to persuade him to stop and have tea in the Main Street, but —"

"*James* did?"

I nodded.

"How very peculiar. He doesn't like Gareth."

"Well, you'd never have known it this afternoon. Mind you," I said, "James would probably have been friendly to anyone who'd taken me off his hands. I don't think he was quite so keen to see the castle, really."

"No?" She was only half listening now, abstracted.

I smiled and changed the subject. "So tell me, what happened with Christopher?"

I felt safe enough asking — he'd gone off upstairs for a nap before dinner, exhausted from two hours of shopping with Bridget. And James was securely holed up in his

258

writing room, well out of earshot. We might have been alone in the house.

Bridget settled herself rather grumpily. "Not much. He went all discreet on me, damn him. Although," she said, losing her frown for a moment, "he did tell me one thing of interest."

"Oh, yes?"

"Gareth gives Elen money. A check every month. Don't you think that's suggestive?"

I shrugged, and sipped my coffee. "What I want to know is why you seem so eager to prove Gareth fathered the baby. I'd have thought you'd be jealous."

"Of Elen? Be serious. No, it's the intrigue I like, Lyn. The mystery. Aren't you even the slightest bit curious?"

"No," I replied, very firmly. However much I might admire Gareth's talent, I didn't want to know his private business.

"Oh, well," Bridget said. "At least my day wasn't a washout. I did get my shopping done."

"So we're all set for Christmas lunch?"

"Mm." She considered the tree with a critical eye. "Everything but the veg. I can buy those fresh, here, from the shop in the village. And I wondered, you know, if you wouldn't mind doing that thing that you do with smoked salmon . . . ?"

"With the cream cheese and horseradish? Certainly."

She sighed. "I shall have to start slimming."

"Nobody slims over Christmas," I said. "That's why I packed all my expandable clothes." The thought of food made my stomach grumble, and I tried to judge time by the darkness outside the long windows. I gave up. "What time is it?"

"Only five thirty."

"Oh. What are we doing for supper?"

"That's supposed to be my line," she said with a smile. "I don't know what we're doing. The pub, I'd imagine. You think you can hold out till seven o'clock?"

"I'll try." Something light-colored flashed at the edge of the garden, the briefest impression of movement. "Is that Owen, outside?"

She twisted in her chair. "I don't see anyone."

The flash came again, by the viburnum. "There, going round the back way, towards Elen's." But when Bridget's gaze found the right place, there was nothing to see — just the ragged black plume of an evergreen branch blowing back and forth, back and forth, raking the gravel.

Losing interest, she looked back at me. "I

suppose it might be Owen, though I didn't think he worked this late. More likely it's one of the cats, or —"

"Shh," I said, and cocked my head to listen.

Bridget hated being shushed. I saw her frown, and shift position, drawing breath for some retort, but then she paused, and I knew she had heard it, too.

It came faintly, at first — shuffled footsteps and murmuring voices that faded in places because of the wind. Then the murmuring stopped and from out of the darkness a sweet sound began, not quite steady, and started to swell. It was singing. The voices of children, a little off key, but so simple and pure as they sang that most lovely of all children's carols, "Away in a Manger."

Bridget's face shone, beautiful. "Oh, Lyn, listen . . . carol singers! Quick, where's your wallet?"

It was typical, I thought, that she would want *my* wallet at a time like this, but she looked such a child herself that I indulged her, sorting the coins as I followed her into the shadowed back passage. "Here, is two pounds enough?"

"Thanks." She opened the door.

There were five of them, ringed round the

long slab of warm light that spilled from the wide kitchen window. Red-cheeked from the cold, they bent over their song sheets, their breaths making soft puffs of mist in the air. The oldest could not have been more than eleven. When they saw we were looking, they elbowed each other and straightened their shoulders and sang louder still. *". . . but little Lord Jesus, no crying he makes . . ."*

I looked at their small, earnest faces, and blinked back the dampness that started to well round my eyelashes. It wasn't sadness, really — just the beauty of the night, and those five voices raised together, bright with innocence.

For all I sometimes wondered at the blunders of the human race, we had, I thought, created some remarkable traditions. And caroling from door to door — what people in a more poetic time had called "the waits" — was one of those rare things that made me feel distinctly warm toward my fellow man.

Above our heads, a light came on in Christopher's room, and I knew that he was listening, too. Even James was drawn from his writing room to join us in the doorway. "What's the racket?"

"Shh," said Bridget.

They were finishing the final verse. They

ended it unevenly, as children do, some trying to go on before they caught themselves,
like train cars piling up behind a suddenly
stalled engine. At the center of the group
one little girl lifted both hands to muffle her
giggle, and another blew her nose. No
longer cherubs, only children.

As we started to applaud, the oldest boy
stepped forward, shyly, holding out a
painted tin. "We're collecting for the
church."

Bridget gave him my two pounds, and
stuck an elbow into James. "Cough it up,
Scrooge. It's Christmas."

With a sigh, he dug into his pocket and
came out with change, mostly pennies, that
clattered importantly into the tin. The boy
thanked us, politely, and rejoined his group.
I was thinking to myself how very well
behaved and organized they were, for such
small children, when a figure moved behind
them and the reason for their good behavior
stepped into the light.

"Right then, boys and girls," said Owen's
Dilys, looking rather like a military leader
in a brass-buttoned coat of dark wool that
came down to her knees. It was likely the
coat's fault, I thought, that I hadn't noticed
her there before. She blended rather well
into the shadows at the edges of the garden.

I watched her herd her charges. "Time we moved on to the next house. No, Angela dear," she instructed one well-bundled tot who had wobbled a few steps toward the big East House, "not that way. We're going down here, next, to see Mr. Morgan."

"Elen," said James, "might feel rather left out."

Dilys sniffed and replied that it couldn't be helped. "We're late as it is, aren't we, children? And the vicar has promised us cocoa and biscuits."

That galvanized the children into action. They were massing round Dilys in a chattering, excited mob, when suddenly a door slammed and the sound of running footsteps surged toward us.

"There, you see?" James bent his head to light a cigarette. "I told you that she'd be upset."

Elen burst into the garden like someone possessed, her hair blowing wild, her face deathly white. She hadn't stopped to dress the baby — he was still in his sleeping suit, wrapped in a quilt, too bewildered to cry. But his mother looked ready to burst into tears.

"Please," she gasped. "Please help. It's been after Stevie."

Dilys exhaled, tight-lipped. "Elen, for

pity's sake . . ."

"It's been in his room. Please, I heard it."

James sighed, rather heavily. "Not again," he said. From which I gathered this was something of a replay of the crisis he and Christopher had weathered the night before we came. Elen, I recalled, had heard a noise in Stevie's room on that occasion, too. James took a step back from the doorway and glanced down at me. "It's all right, Lyn, she's done this before. I'll just go ring Gareth."

On his way through the passageway into the kitchen, James tangled with Christopher, coming to investigate. "What's the matter? I thought I heard Elen . . ."

"You did." James pushed past him, and Christopher turned to Bridget. "What is it? What's happened?"

"Oh, she thinks someone's been after Stevie."

"I see." He frowned. "And has anyone looked yet, to see if she's right?"

The nursery seemed secure enough. A narrow room, high ceilinged, it had one square window facing front, one door into the corridor, and one door on the built-in cupboard set into the corner nearest me.

Stevie played quietly on the carpeted

265

floor, surrounded by a scattering of toys, trying to balance a large plastic block on the tip of his teddy bear's nose while Christopher made a great show of examining everything, poking his head in the cupboard and under the cot. "No one here," he announced.

"But I heard it," said Elen. "I heard it."

Below us a door slammed, and Gareth's voice mingled with James's down in the hall, and then heavy steps stormed up the stairs to the landing. I looked up as Gareth appeared in the doorway, breathing as though he had run the whole distance from his house to here. "What the hell's going on?" he demanded.

Distracted from his game, the baby greeted Gareth with an energetic "Da!" and banged his block against the carpet.

"It was here again," Elen said. "It came like Margaret said it would, and tried to take Stevie away."

The inscrutable dark eyes flicked sideways to Christopher; moved on to me, taking note of my presence. "I see."

"It was my fault," said Elen. "I shouldn't have left him alone. Margaret told me today would be dangerous, so I watched him. I tried to be careful, you know? But it got in anyway." Looking down, she brushed one hand across her son's fair curls, breathing out on a shuddering sigh. "I must have frightened it off, when I came to look in on him."

Christopher looked round the room. "Well, it seems all right now . . ."

"You don't believe me," Elen said, a little sadly. "Do you?" Then, when no one answered her, she pointed to the window, with its clear view of the tower rising black against the moon. "He came through there, you see? I never open Stevie's window. Never."

There was no denying it was open now, but the sash had only been raised an inch or so to let in air. No person could have scaled the outside wall and squeezed through that, I thought. From the look on Gareth's face I knew he thought the same, but still he played along with Elen's fantasy, and crossed to shut the window. "There," he said. "I can nail the thing closed, if that makes you feel better. Tony's tools are still down in the understairs cupboard, right? Right. I'll be back in a minute."

Christopher followed him downstairs and their voices blended briefly, and a moment later I could hear the clinking sound of crockery that told me somebody was in the kitchen, making tea. But Elen took no notice. Her fingers toyed with Stevie's hair, shaping one curl into a perfect circle. Watching her face, I felt suddenly thankful my own mind had managed to stay sound and strong through my grief. It must, I thought, be terrible to slip so close to madness.

"I shouldn't have left him alone," she told me. "Margaret said today was dangerous, because it's Arthur's Light."

I felt a chill between my shoulder blades. "Who's Margaret, Elen?"

"Margaret," she repeated, in a tone that took for granted I would know the woman, too. "She's the one who said you'd come to keep my Stevie safe, remember?"

"She's a friend of yours?"

"Oh, yes."

"I'd like to meet her."

"Well, I don't know if you could," she said, uncertain. "Margaret only comes to tell me things, you see, when I'm asleep, but I could ask her."

The curtains at the window caught a tiny draft and fluttered and for an instant I was back in that lonely little tower room at Pembroke Castle, staring at the portrait of the woman who had haunted my own dreams since I'd come down to Angle — Henry Tudor's mother, Margaret Beaufort. Margaret . . .

No, I thought, impossible. We couldn't both be dreaming of the same young woman. Dreams were individual, the products of a single mind, not things that could be shared.

"She has a son," said Elen, still intent on curling Stevie's hair. "Like me. His name is Harry. And the dragon tried to take him, too — because it knew, you see. It knew what Harry was. What Stevie is."

I swallowed, hard. "And what is that?"

But Elen shook her head. "I mustn't say. He told me that I mustn't say."

Terrific, I thought, as I registered the masculine pronoun — here was somebody *else* to confuse things. "Who told you?"

"Merlin."

She said it so naturally, that's what amazed me. She might have been talking of Gareth, or Christopher. *"Merlin?"* I echoed.

She nodded. "He comes to me, too. Well, his voice does — I don't really see him, because of the mist. But I hear him. I hear what he says, about Stevie, and why Stevie's here. It's because of the dragon," she told me, her voice dropping low. "The dragon knows Stevie was sent here to kill it, that's why it doesn't want him to grow up to be a man."

"Ah," I said. It seemed the only thing *to* say.

"You see," Elen said, leaning forward, confiding, "the dragon that lives in the tower is white."

I heard steps on the stairs and a voice from the landing, and Christopher came through the door of the nursery, a tray in his hands. "Here you are, I've made tea," he informed us both, cheerfully. "Tea always helps."

A stiff measure of whisky, I thought to myself, would help more.

CHAPTER 21

We are closed in, and the key is turned
On our uncertainty . . .

— W. B. Yeats,
"The Stare's Nest by My Window"

Bridget poked her head in through the dining room door an hour later. "Are you sure you're all right?"

"Mm. Just knackered." And descending slowly into madness, I added to myself, in silence. After a day like this one, all I wanted was to sit awhile and have a drink and try to sort things through.

"You're not just staying home so you'll be here if Elen needs somebody?"

"No."

"Because she's really all right on her own, you know."

"I know."

"And you heard her, she didn't want anyone. Not even Owen."

"I am not," I said, firmly, "staying home because of Elen. In fact, if I have one more glass of whisky, I very much doubt if I'd hear the girl scream, let alone be of use to her."

"Well, you know where to find us, if you change your mind."

"Are you off, then?" I asked, as she bent her head to check the contents of her handbag.

"Yes, as soon as James remembers where he left the car keys."

I smiled, and rolled my head against the cushions of the chair back. "It's only a two-minute walk to the pub."

"I'm in heels," she said, holding out one foot to show me. "And besides, driving's warmer. The wind's bloody cold out there."

"Mm." I could hear it. Since we'd come back from Elen's, a half hour ago, the weather had turned. Behind the soft folds of the curtains, the long windows shuddered and rattled with each violent gust, and the chimney had started to moan. I felt snug in my chair, with my feet tucked up into the cushions, and the whisky slowly spreading warmth through all my veins.

James called from the back door, and Bridget turned happily. "Right then, we shan't be too long."

"Be as long as you like," I invited.

I rather liked being alone in the house. After living so long in the flat on my own, it always took a bit of getting used to, having other people round. They disrupted my daily routine. It felt good to be back in control for an evening, to make the sort of meal I usually made — omelet and chips with fruit compote and custard cream biscuits and tea — and to carry it through to the cozy little sitting room that opened off the kitchen, so I could eat as I usually ate, from a tray, while watching television.

I flipped through the channels, quite comforted.

". . . never meant to marry me, did you? You . . . must be rather careful with your measurements, at this point, or the pudding will . . . return year after year to celebrate the solstice." I stopped; left it there, as the camera zoomed in on a group of young people in white robes, playing Druid. It had snowed where they were, and a talcum-soft dusting had covered the grass and the top of the lone standing stone around which they had gathered. One of the girls had a nose ring. They looked, I decided, about as convincing as Bridget would look in a nun's habit.

The deep, solemn voice of an unseen narrator continued to speak. "The ancient Celts apparently took little notice of the sun-based solstices, but modern Druids, notwithstanding, choose to celebrate Midwinter's Day as the 'Light of —' "

And then, quite unexpectedly, there was no light at all. Surprised, I sat surrounded by the sudden blackness while the wind shrieked past the windows, spitting rain against the glass. The storm had knocked the power out.

Easing carefully out of my chair so as not to spill my supper tray, I felt round the fireplace hearth for the box of big wooden matches, and used them to search the kitchen. I found a small torch nestled in the drawer that held the tea towels. Its batteries were nearly dead, but it managed to throw out a small thread of light that, at length, touched the edge of a box of plain white kitchen candles, tucked back in a cupboard. I'd known they would be somewhere. Every farmer I had ever known kept candles in the kitchen, to guard against just such emergencies.

There was even a candlestick stored alongside them — an ornate antique silver piece that held three candles. Relieved, I struck a match.

The heating had only been off a few

minutes, but already the cold was beginning to creep through the walls of the old house, and the candle flames fluttered and dipped in a draft as I turned, casting weird slanting shadows that danced at the edge of the darkness. I found enough coal in the sitting room scuttle to start a small fire, but it didn't help much. What I needed, I thought, was a blanket or rug that would help keep me warm till the heat came back on.

I felt like a character in a Hitchcock film as I carefully made my way upstairs, using the candles to show me the way and keeping one hand on the railing. The linen cupboard, I knew, was at the end of the passage — I'd seen James fetching clean sheets from it, yesterday. The handle wouldn't budge at first, but a closer look showed me the old-fashioned key in the lock. Rather odd, I thought, to lock the linen cupboard — but then, every household had its quirks. I gave the key a half turn and the door swung inward soundlessly, without the noisy protest I'd expected from its hinges.

It wasn't the cupboard I'd wanted.

I stood for a moment, confused, as the candlelight showed me a section of shelving stacked with clothes and cuddly toys. Another door stood partway open just in front of me, and through it I could hear the sound of soft and rapid breathing. I knew now where I was. I had passed into the East House and was standing in the built-in cupboard set into the corner of the nursery, Stevie's nursery, just a few feet from his cot. And if I'd wanted to, I could have snatched him up and run away, without his mother ever knowing.

It bothered me more than I cared to admit, finding that door. Not because I truly thought that anyone had sneaked into the nursery earlier, but because I knew that someone *could* have done it. And that knowledge was troubling.

I had felt an unwelcome intruder myself, standing quiet and still in the shadowy cupboard. Guiltily, I'd closed the door again and locked it firmly, checked it twice, to make quite certain little Stevie was secure. And then I'd stepped a little to the left and found the linen cupboard door — unlocked, as linen cupboards ought to be — and blindly pulled a blanket from the woodsy-scented shelves, trailing it after me back down the stairs to the sitting room.

Now, settled in my chair again, I wrapped the blanket snugly round my shoulders and tried to be rational.

So there was a door leading into the East

House. So what? No one here would have had any reason to want to harm Stevie. *So stop being foolish,* I told myself crossly. *Stop worrying.*

I turned my mind to other things. My omelet and chips had congealed on the plate, but the biscuits and fruit remained edible, and I managed to coax a second cup of still-warm tea from the pot. Sitting back, I stared at the black reflecting screen of the television, willing it to come back on and offer a diversion. Even the Druids, I thought, would be better than nothing. I'd never know, now, why the devil they had all been dancing around in the snow. Celebrating the solstice, the narrator had said. Some festival — the Light of Something . . .

And then the thought struck me. I put down my fork. "Jesus."

The dining room, with its tall windows, was already freezing cold, and the storm seemed determined to come through the glass, howling and beating its fists in a fury. I held up the candles and crossed to the bookcase, my breath making mist in the air. The book was still there, on the second shelf, waiting — *The Druid's Year.*

I pulled it out and flipped the pages, scarcely seeing Julia's exquisite illustrations. The months passed in a blur of color . . .

November . . . December . . . my fingers slowed . . . December the twenty-first.

"Alban Arthuan," the book informed me. "Believed by modern Druids to be the day that King Arthur was born and delivered, as promised, to Merlin. Sometimes called 'The Light of Arthur' . . ."

The Light of Arthur, I thought numbly. Arthur's Light.

But that wasn't the thing that disturbed me the most. The most disturbing thing, to me, was that someone had marked the page.

CHAPTER 22

Scarce had we stept on the forbidden
ground,
When the woods shook . . .

— John Dryden,
Merlin, or The British Enchanter

I was running, half stumbling, and dragging
the golden-haired child along by one hand.
It was night. All around us the mist swirled
and rose and formed strange shifting shapes
and I couldn't see anything — only the
rough trampled path at my feet. I could hear
the child's breathing, behind me, and
somewhere below us the sound of the sea.
Then from out of the mist came another
sound, terrible, shaking the ground like a
wildcat's scream.

I scooped up the boy and ran faster,
spurred on by the weight of his arms round
my neck and the feel of his small, panicked
heartbeat. He was crying, without making

noise, and the tears trickled warm down the side of my neck. I squeezed him tight. "It's all right, love, we're nearly there."

But the path appeared endless.

The creature was gaining. It screamed again, closer, and the shadow of a claw slashed through the mist. *Oh, God,* I prayed, silently, *don't let me lose him. I must keep him safe.* I was breathing in sobs, now. The path tilted up and I scrambled up with it, seeking any foothold I could find.

I passed a shape that looked like James, standing off to one side of the path, calmly smoking a cigarette. "My dear girl," his voice said, "it's hardly the end of the world."

Further up, someone else — Owen, I think — reached to take the child from me, but I didn't let go. I kept running. The ground underneath me was shuddering now, and I felt the searing heat of my pursuer's breath. And then all of a sudden the path disappeared, and I was falling into nothingness, with the roar of the sea rising swiftly to claim me. I pressed the boy closer, surrounding him, trying to shield him, my own scream as loud as the thing at our backs.

Something clamped round my shoulder.

"Don't worry," said Gareth Gwyn Morgan, "*I'll* catch you."

I opened my eyes.

I was lying, quite safe, on my bed, looking up at the ceiling. My hands had made fists round the sheets and I tried to relax them, to force them to open. Still feeling unreasoning panic I turned my head sideways and looked at the window, seeking reassurance that the dream was really over.

The bright morning sunlight had pushed through the folds of my curtains to shimmer and dance on the soft painted walls. I focused on it, calmed my mind. But still, it took a long time for my heartbeat to regain its normal rhythm.

I could hear someone banging about in the bathroom, and voices. And craving the comfort of people around me, I rose rather stiffly, and dressed, and went to find out who it was. The electricity had come on again. Outside my room on the landing the air had lost its sharpness.

In the bathroom I found Bridget perched on the edge of the tub, watching Owen, who knelt, full of purpose, half in and half out of the double-doored airing cupboard.

"Well, finally," she said, when she saw me. "I was beginning to think that you'd frozen to death in your sleep, or something."

Her voice, familiar and good-natured, helped dissolve the horror of my nightmare and I felt much more myself as I assured her I'd been fine. "I had extra blankets. I slept like a log. I don't remember hearing you come in."

"We got back quite late — after one, I should think. Everyone was being very jolly at the pub."

"Did they manage to serve you your meals, then, before the lights went out?"

"Naturally." She grinned. "If they hadn't, I'd have come home for a sandwich, storm or no storm."

Owen emerged from the cupboard, to wish me good morning.

"Good morning, yourself. What's the trouble?"

"Damned immersion heater, that's what. Everything else came back on, except this." He slapped the mustard-colored water heater with one hand and stood, with a whoofing breath of protest. "Bloody stubborn bastard," he said, but whether he meant the immersion heater or himself, I couldn't tell.

Bridget swung one long leg. "Yes, and I want my bath. I've been waiting for ages."

"Hold on," said Owen, "I'll just go downstairs now, and twiddle a switch."

Bridget waited until he was gone, and then motioned me closer, bursting to tell me something. "He was there."

I lowered my voice to match hers. "Who was where?"

"Gareth was at the Hibernia, last night. And Lyn," she confided, "I think that I've hooked him."

"Oh?"

"He bought me a drink. And you'll never guess what?" She looked from left to right, dramatically, before continuing. "He asked me to drop round to see him, this afternoon. Just on my own."

"Oh." I knew what was coming. I waited.

"So here's what I'll need you to do," she went on. "After lunch, before James gets his nose in his writing, you ask him to show you the sights."

"Any sights in particular?"

"I don't know, maybe Freshwater West, or St. Govan's. He loves to show people St. Govan's. Just ask him. Then I'll plead a headache, or something, and stay behind here."

"And what about Christopher?"

"I guess you'll have to take him with you, too."

I looked aside, and made a show of trying to remember. "I don't recall this being in the Agent's Code of Practice."

"Of course it is. It comes between 'thou

shalt do everything thy author asks' and 'thou shalt assist thy author in seducing sexy men.' "

"I see."

Owen was coming upstairs again. Bridget sat back and fell silent.

Apparently the switch twiddling had done the trick. He put his head back in the airing cupboard and a moment later the heater clicked on with a comforting hum. "There now, that's got it. Just leave that to run for an hour or so, and you'll have all the hot water you need."

"Wonderful," Bridget said. "Thanks."

Leaving her in privacy, I followed Owen back out to the landing. "You'll be late for your walk," he said, teasing.

I didn't answer him immediately — I was too absorbed in staring at the door, just past his shoulder. The door that I had opened by mistake last night . . . the one that led to little Stevie's nursery, through the cupboard. It looked just as I had left it, but for one detail: the key no longer rested in the lock. It hadn't fallen to the carpet, either. Someone had removed it.

"Is something wrong?" asked Owen.

"No." I looked quickly away from the door; forced a confident smile. "It's nothing."

■ ■ ■ ■

I pushed my pace harder and crested the hill, my lungs burning. I didn't have time for this, really — it was after eleven already and Bridget, I knew, would be done with her bath now and having a fit. She would never forgive me if I didn't get back by lunchtime to help with her plan.

But I'd needed the walk.

I had taken a different route, over the bridge and along the south shore of the bay, through the cooling green woods that surrounded the Hall. I'd barely glimpsed the Hall itself, little more than a suggestion of pale walls and privilege set deep in the trees at the end of a long curving drive, looking rather forlorn with its owners away. And when the path had split in two a little further on, with one fork keeping to the coastal route along the soft shore of the bay, I'd turned instead and headed inland, up the wider lane and past the Lodge, where a little dog had come to the edge of the garden and barked its encouragement.

It hadn't *looked* a steep hill, from the bottom, but now that I had reached the top my legs felt rather sore and I needed several breaths of air to slow my racing heart.

I moved on more slowly, not paying attention. Normally, walking was good for my mind. Not today, though — my thoughts were a jumble. Part of me wanted to side with the others, and say Elen's story was madness; but part of me couldn't be sure.

Either James or Christopher could easily have entered Stevie's room last night. I couldn't think why they'd have wanted to — certainly not to harm Stevie. If anyone wanted to harm him, I felt fairly sure they'd have done it by now. The only thing that came to mind was that maybe they liked to make poor Elen panic, liked to play upon her paranoia. It would have been a rotten thing to do, but I knew they could have done it, all the same. And the more I thought about that door, the more I felt convinced that someone *had* gone into the nursery. Why else, I wondered, would the key be in the lock last night, and not this morning?

And the marked page in *The Druid's Year* could hardly be coincidence. Which meant the culprit must have known that yesterday would be the one day Elen worried most that Stevie would be stolen — the day another "chosen child," King Arthur, had been taken from his mother.

I frowned, thinking of Gareth and his talk

about the mythical divine child as I turned a second time to follow the signposted footpath that cut westward through the wood.

It was peaceful, here — green and deliciously quiet, the fallen leaves damp and too languid to do more than sigh when I stepped on them. Last night's storm had made mud of the path and it sucked at my feet, forcing me to go more slowly, to notice the rich earthy smells and the way that the sunlight came filtering down and the kiss of the mild morning breeze. I noticed the ground, too — the ruts in the mud and the rounded deep imprints of hooves.

So I should have been ready. I shouldn't have been as surprised as I was when I heard the horse coming behind me, not trotting but walking, quite leisurely, taking its time. And I should have expected the voice.

"God, it's you again." Gareth, on horseback, looked rather like one of those centaurs I'd seen as a child in my book of Greek myths — dark and not completely tamed, his jaw set high with arrogance, black jodhpurs and boots and thick-knitted black pullover blending right in to the midnight black mare till the two of them moved like one animal, towering over me.

They slowed to a halt, stomping a few times to flatten the deep mud, and Sovereign stretched her lovely neck toward me, nostrils flared to catch my scent. I fancied that her eyes held recognition. Gareth's, though, held something else. "Are you always this subtle when stalking a client?"

I looked at him, opened my mouth to respond and then closed it, deciding it wasn't worth the effort. Instead I simply turned my back and went on walking, as if he wasn't there. Sovereign followed along like a shadow.

"What, no comeback?" asked Gareth. "No protest? No speech about what a detestable bastard I am?"

"All right, then. You are a detestable bastard. Does that make you happy?"

"Ecstatic." He reined the horse closer, and slanted a searching look down at my face.

I stopped again, bending to make a great fuss over Chance, who had given up snuffing for rabbits and mice in the field and come running to greet me, his whole body wagging. Gareth gave a tight sigh and I glanced up. My eyes met his, warily, just for a moment, then darted away. But that was enough.

"Something's happened," he said.

"Don't be daft. Nothing's —"

"Tell me."

I don't know what possessed me, then. It might have been the sight of him on horseback, stirring memories of my riding days and friends I'd shared my life with at the stables. It might have been the silence of the wood, like a confessional, with Gareth putting me in mind of a medieval hermit priest, a warrior monk who'd turned his back upon the world. Or it might have been the aura of the man himself, the way his solid, sure demeanor made a contrast to the ever-shifting atmosphere of Castle Farm, demanding nothing, giving less.

Whatever the reason, I found myself telling him everything. I told him about the locked door, and the key, and *The Druid's Year,* and how yesterday had been the Light of Arthur, and the words tumbled out in a haphazard way like a litter of puppies pressed up to a gate that had suddenly opened. Gareth, no doubt, must have thought me quite mad.

When I'd finished, I said, ". . . and it's probably nothing, I know, but if someone *did* do that to Elen — trying to make her think there really *was* a dragon living in the tower that was wanting to take Stevie — then I think it was a horrid thing to do, and . . . well, that's all."

He didn't break the silence right away. He went on looking down at me as though I were an alien, while the mare danced a step in impatience and Chance went back to hunting mice. "I see," said Gareth, finally.

Embarrassed now, I cleared my throat. "I thought you had a right to know."

Something strange, imperceptible, flashed in his eyes, but I was already turning from it, wanting to escape. And since he was clearly headed west, I wheeled and faced the way I'd come — the route that seemed the safest. "Sorry I interrupted your ride," I said, trying to sound not the slightest bit sorry. For, after all, he was making me feel like an idiot, and he was meeting with Bridget, and . . .

"Thank you," he said. The phrase sounded rough in his throat, as though he hadn't used it in a long while. I stopped in my tracks to look back, but he'd already signaled the mare to walk on, and I couldn't do much more than stand there and watch them — black horse and black rider — melt into the shadows that dappled the path, with the little dog trotting behind.

CHAPTER 23

A hermit once was here,
Whose holy hand hath fashion'd on the
   rock
The war of Time against the soul of man.
                     — Alfred, Lord Tennyson,
                        "Gareth and Lynette"

If Bridget hadn't been a writer, I decided after lunch, she could have made her living on the stage. Sitting quiet and pale in her chair at the table, one hand to her forehead, she'd nearly convinced *me* the migraine was real.

"No, it's all right," she said, with the sigh of a martyr, "you go and have fun. I'll stay here."

Christopher frowned. "We don't all have to go."

Bridget glanced at him between her fingers, looking — if it were possible — even more pained. "But I want you to, really. I don't want to spoil your day."

"I suspect," James said, rising to carry his plate and cup to the sink, "you've a more selfish reason for wanting us out of the house." Then, before she had time to react, he explained, to his brother, "She can't bear the noise, any noise, when her head hurts like this. So the last thing she needs is to have us thumping round the place. Right?" he asked Bridget.

She relaxed with a nod and a grateful expression, enough to convince Christopher, who pushed back his chair. "All right, then," he said, "I suppose I could stand one more trip to St. Govan's."

I felt a bit relieved, as well. I hadn't fancied facing Bridget if things hadn't gone her way — especially since I'd almost ruined her plans by returning so late from my walk. Another five minutes, and James would have been in his writing room, lost to the world. Fortunately, it hadn't taken much effort to persuade him.

He had sat at the head of the scrubbed kitchen table, head tilted to one side, amused, as he'd finished his tea. "An agent who wants me *not* to write," he'd said. "How peculiar."

I'd smiled. "It rather defeats my own interests, I know, but it's such a lovely afternoon, and even writers need holidays, once in a while."

Christopher had drily said that writing, by its very nature, seemed one great long holiday, a comment that most certainly would have earned him a bruise on his arm had not Bridget been playing at having a headache. Eventually, I knew, she'd make him pay for that remark. Bridget had a long memory.

But happily, now, I appeared to be back in her good books, myself. And I knew I'd been forgiven when she offered me the last egg salad sandwich.

"You'll want to take your camera, Lyn," she said. "St. Govan's is your kind of place."

I remembered the name from my Pembrokeshire guidebook. "It's a chapel, or something, isn't it?"

"Mm. A little stone chapel set into the cliffs, with these bloody great rocks all around it. And limpets," she said, with a roll of her eyes. "You can't put a foot down without treading on limpets. You'll love it."

James rinsed off his dishes and turned from the sink. "Do you know, my love, I'll never understand how you can write the way you do about the fairies and the fields and things, and yet not like St. Govan's."

I knew how he felt. Bridget had such a

gift for imagery, for creating darkly tangled forests, flowered glens and magic places filled with beings of pure fancy, that it seemed unnatural, somehow, for her not to like ruins and castles and chapels built into a cliff.

She waved James's comment aside with an invalid's hand. "So I'm not keen on man-made constructions."

"Limpets weren't man-made, the last time I looked."

"Well, I don't have to love *all* of nature, surely," she said in defense, "and limpets are horrid."

"How can you not love a limpet?" James wanted to know, tongue-in-cheek. But he knew enough not to tease Bridget too long. She'd lost interest already, distracted by something she'd seen through the wide window over the sink.

"We've got company," she said, without enthusiasm.

From where I was sitting the window showed only a slice of the sheltered back garden, and the lone leaf dancing at the top of the viburnum. I couldn't see anyone there, but a knock at the door proved that Bridget had not been imagining things.

It was Owen's wife, Dilys, her face flushed from walking against the brisk wind. "You should all be outdoors," she said, after handing James the plate of warmly crumbling fresh mince pies that were, ostensibly, the reason for her visit. "It's a lovely afternoon, you know. You mustn't waste this sunshine."

James assured her we would not be wasting anything. "We were just making plans to go down to St. Govan's. Well, three of us, anyway. Bridget," he said, "has a bit of a headache. She thought she'd stay here."

"Nonsense," Dilys said roundly. "There's nothing like fresh air for curing a headache."

Bridget's smile was purposely wan. "Not *my* headaches. The only thing that makes them go away is a dark room and absolute quiet."

"It won't be very quiet here this afternoon," said Dilys. "Not with my Owen up cleaning the gutters. If the sound of him banging around doing that doesn't drive you mad, then his singing most certainly will. Thinks he's Anthony Newley, old fool."

Bridget's sighs, I decided, were growing more heartfelt. Having Owen hanging round the house all afternoon had not been in her plans. He'd be bound to see her sneaking off to Gareth's. "I don't suppose you could convince him to postpone the gutter cleaning till tomorrow?"

Dilys didn't think it likely. "He was saying there's a rather nasty blockage, and that storm last night just made things worse. He'll want to get it fixed before the weather turns again. But never mind," she said, to Bridget, "you can come and spend the afternoon with me. I've got a spare bed in the back room, for the grandchildren, and I'm only doing baking, so there won't be any noise."

Bridget's expression was priceless. I glanced at her sideways and choked on my tea, and had to be thumped on the back twice by Christopher.

"Sorry," I gasped, "it went down the wrong way." But I needn't have bothered. Nobody was listening.

"There you are, darling," James said, to Bridget, "your problem is solved."

"Oh, I wouldn't want to be a bother . . ."

"Nonsense," Dilys said, again. That one word seemed to capture her whole view of life. "It's no bother at all."

I could see Bridget's wheels working, trying to find an escape route, when James, with a well-meaning smile, closed the door of the trap. "We can drop you off on our way," he said, "and pick you up again when we come home. Then you won't have to walk in the cold."

"Wonderful." The flatness of her voice was lost on everyone but me.

By the time we set off on our afternoon's outing a half hour later, Bridget looked rather convincingly ill. So much so, I thought, that she probably *did* have a headache. When we stopped outside Owen and Dilys's house in the village to let her out, she went like a prisoner making the walk to the gallows, head down in dejection.

"Poor thing," James said, putting the Merc into gear. "It must be murder having migraines."

Not trusting my voice to reply, I turned my head and watched the passing street. The stone wall in front of Gareth's pink cottage was ablaze with cotoneaster, bright red berries thickly sprayed against the gray. Upstairs, one of the casement windows stood open, and a cheerful curl of coal smoke drifted upward from the chimney. He was in the house and waiting for her. Bridget, I felt sure, would find some way to keep the rendezvous, Dilys or no Dilys. Bridget, I'd learned, thrived on obstacles.

Christopher, shifting his legs in the back seat, remarked that an afternoon with Dilys was more likely to produce a headache than to cure one. "She simply will not stop talking. And if I hear one more word about her bloody son . . ."

"Ah yes." James grinned. "Cardiff's answer to Louis Pasteur."

"It's a bit much for someone who spends his days sorting through vials of semen."

"You're such a snob," said James.

Christopher, having bitten his tongue all through Dilys's short visit, had no trouble biting it now. He raised his arms and linked his hands behind his head, attempting to get comfortable.

I turned, feeling guilty. "Are you sure you don't want to trade seats?"

"No, I'm fine. I've got plenty of room." More than he'd had yesterday, at any rate. I'd shifted my own seat a few notches forward. "Besides," he said, "you ought to have the better view — I've seen this all a thousand times."

I wasn't sure a thousand times would be enough to tire me of the beauty of this landscape. We turned south this time, off the main Pembroke road, and kept to the coast, past a place where the red-tinged cliffs fell sharply away to a long sweeping crescent of pale sandy beach. The view was unexpected, and breathtaking.

James pulled the car over to let me have a proper look. "This is Freshwater West."

I looked with new eyes at the rough waves

that had picked up the tiny black speck of a surfer and hurled him at the shore. So this, I thought, would be the place where Elen's husband died. Christopher, behind me, read my thoughts.

"Tony was probably up on those rocks, when it happened," he said, leaning forward to point. "That's where he and Gareth always used to go."

There was no one there angling now, thankfully. That would have been too creepy. "Poor Elen." I bit my lip a moment. If either of the brothers was responsible for last night's crisis, they'd hardly admit it. But I couldn't help prodding. "Has anyone seen her this morning? I ought to have checked, to see how she was doing."

"She seemed fine," said Christopher. "No ill effects."

James glanced back over his shoulder as he started the car again. "When the devil were you over there?"

"Before breakfast. She's always up early. I thought I'd pop round and make sure she was all right."

Spotting an opening, I said, as casually as possible, "It's a pity there isn't a door, you know, linking the houses. Then maybe she wouldn't feel quite so alone."

"There is one," said James. "But it hasn't

been opened in years. I wouldn't think there'd even be a key for it, anymore. That reminds me," he said. "I did look for that key to the tower, you know, like I promised. Seeing you climb all those stairs at the castle reminded me how you had asked to go up. But no luck, I'm afraid."

"Never mind," I excused him.

We had dipped down now between the dunes, where the soft russet sand spilled out over the tarmac in heaps and the coarse marram grass bent to the wind, shivering in waves that showed an undercoat of green beneath the gold. "They've done a good job with this stretch of the coastline," said Christopher. "It's fairly unspoiled. There were caravans down here at one time, but they've been cleared out. And the dunes are protected — no holiday cottages."

Which was, I admitted, a rare thing indeed for any stretch of British coastline. The road brought us up for a last look at Freshwater West and the dangerous surf, with a red warning flag flapping high on our right. Then we turned briefly inland, through a small village and round an unusual round-about with a truncated stone turret set at its center. I might have asked what it was if we hadn't, at that moment, rolled down and over a bumpity cattle grid. It rattled my fill-ings, fragmenting my thoughts as I brought my eyes back to the road.

I couldn't see cattle, but sheep stood at odd tilted angles all over the banks at the sides of the road, blinking down at the car without any real interest. Twice we were forced to slow almost to stopping, to edge past a clog of the creatures. "I think I prefer the tanks to this," said Christopher.

I turned my head. "I'm sorry?"

"The tanks," he repeated, nodding out the window as we passed more red flags and a small unmanned guardhouse. "This is all Ministry of Defense land. We're on the Castlemartin firing range."

"I see. Should I duck?"

"Not to worry. They keep it closed off when they're blasting things."

"Unless, of course," said James, "it's the element of surprise they're after." He glanced over. "Speaking of surprises, I must say that what you did last night was not what I'd expected."

"Oh?"

"If I'd left Ivor in that house alone, he would have spent the night helping himself to my brandy and reading my manuscript. Whereas you, from what I can tell, didn't even go into the writing room."

Not for want of curiosity, I could have told

him. Ivor and I weren't so different on that level. But I did consider trust to be a vital part of my relationships with authors, and the thought of drinking James's brandy never crossed my mind. "And how do you know," I asked him, "that I'm not just good at sneaking into rooms?"

"Because I'm good at catching people sneaking into rooms."

Christopher confirmed this. "He used to set some damned clever traps, when we were kids. Hairs in the doorjamb, and that sort of thing. Like James Bond."

I leaned back with a smile. "Well, I'm glad I behaved myself, then."

"Perhaps," said James, "you're not so keen to read my manuscript . . ."

"I'm longing to read it, of course, but I don't need to read it to know that it's good."

"Is that a fact?"

"It is. Everything you write is brilliant," I told him honestly, and was rewarded with a pleased look that informed me I had scored another point. *Take that, Ivor Whitcomb,* I thought.

A second cattle grid jolted me out of my self-satisfaction. We were leaving the firing range, from the looks of things. A barracks compound loomed up on our right, its gates guarded by two enormous tanks, guns pointed outward. After that the hedged road ran without much incident to another roundabout, where a sign informed us that the road to St. Govan's was open.

I had to endure one final cattle grid before we came out onto a level stretch of vibrant green that ran along the cliff top, and a long, deserted car park with a dizzying view of the sea. There didn't appear to be anything here that would warrant a car park, except for the view, but I gamely followed Christopher and James as they got out and walked without fear to the edge of the cliff.

Here a winding set of steps wound downward through a fissure in the gray, imposing limestone, and between us and the sea below, a steep slate-tiled roof sat angled in among the boulders as though some giant hand at play had wedged it there, a square peg forced into an oddly shaped hole and forgotten.

"There's a legend," said Christopher, "that the steps to the chapel can't ever be properly counted."

"Why is that?" I asked.

"I haven't a clue. But I always get a different number going down than coming up."

Careful not to lose my footing on the sea-slicked stone, I counted the steps as I followed him down: Fifty-two. Lodging the number away in my memory, I ducked through the open stone doorway and into the chapel proper, blinking to adjust my eyes to the sudden dimness.

St. Govan, Christopher informed me, had been a sixth-century hermit, and his chapel reflected a hermit's austerity. It was small and high ceilinged, with one tiny window that looked on the sea and an even tinier square hole beside that, above the piscina. Stone benches had been built into the two side walls, and to my left, beside the rustic stone altar, a half flight of steps scrambled up to a cleft in the naked rock, lit from above by a pale shaft of daylight.

It was definitely, as Bridget had promised, my kind of place.

And in return, as thanks to Bridget, I did my level best to keep the men occupied, taking my time as I poked my way round every nook of the chapel. Not that James really needed occupying. He'd retreated into private thought, showing as little interest here as he had at Pembroke Castle, and leaving it up to his brother to lead me around. My favorite feature proved to be an odd little rock cleft with strange rib-like markings to show where the saint had supposedly pressed himself into the cliff in an effort to hide from marauders.

"And the rock opened up," Christopher said, telling the story, "and closed around St. Govan, sealing him inside, and he hid there until his pursuers had gone."

I touched the damp and time-worn stone. "So these are the marks of his ribs, then."

"Presumably. Just like a fossil. It's said to change shape to accommodate anyone, no matter how big or how small they are. See?" he said, fitting himself to the wall. "Now you try it."

Curving my back to the marble-like smoothness, I closed my eyes tightly and tried to imagine the feeling of being entombed in the cliff face, surrounded by stone. Something dripped in the darkness. A sigh, like the breath of a man, floated past me. I opened my eyes.

Christopher watched me, indulgent, hands thrust in his pockets. "There's not much more to see, after this."

He was clearly suggesting I might want to leave, but knowing that Bridget would want us to stay out till teatime at least, I tried to extend the tour. Venturing outside the chapel, I spent as much time as I could climbing over the boulders that tumbled down into the sea. It was slow going anyway. The boulders were huge, some as tall as me or taller, and I had to use my hands to

305

climb, and set my feet with care. And then there were the limpets, whole colonies of them, stuck to the rock where the tide had abandoned them, pointy hard shells that I tried to avoid for fear of crushing them underfoot.

"You needn't bother," said Christopher, stepping firmly to show me. "They're indestructible."

"Still, it can't be much fun to be trodden on," I said. I didn't go down to the water — I'd always had a healthy respect for the sea, and having just been reminded of how Elen's husband had died, I felt no great desire to go any nearer the waves. Christopher was braver. Picking his way through the limpets, he slipped through a shadowy cleft in the rock — more like a narrow tunnel than a proper cave — and disappeared.

"He's only gone around the corner," James assured me. "He'll be back."

He lit a cigarette while we waited. Bending, he plucked something from the edge of a tidal pool, near his feet, and straightened to show me. "Something for Bridget," he said, pocketing the empty limpet shell.

I smiled. "I don't know why she doesn't like them."

"They cling. Bridget isn't fond of anything that clings." He exhaled, rather thoughtfully, and watched the wind gather the smoke. "Her last two husbands, I believe, both tried to keep her on the lead. A mistake I intend to avoid." His tone was mild, confiding, as he turned his gaze to mine. "You should know that I'm planning to ask her to marry me."

"Oh?" I held my smile with an effort, recognizing the recipe for disaster. I could see it now — James proposing, Bridget amusedly turning him down, and me being stuck in the middle of everything. Smashing. "How . . . wonderful. When?"

"Christmas morning. Have you ever agented a husband and wife? No? Then we might be your first."

I wouldn't hold my breath, I thought. And if James's decision to sign with me depended on Bridget's accepting his ring, I was doomed. All my efforts were wasted. I looked away, watching the spray of the incoming waves on the boulders. "You're sure that Christopher's all right? He's been an age."

James raised his voice and called his brother. When nothing came back, he pitched his cigarette away and headed down toward the cave himself, to please me. "Won't be a minute," he promised. "He likely can't hear me, because of the waves."

Left alone, I watched the tidal pool awhile, seeing no real sign of life in the murky green water. The waves crashed again and the shadows shifted at the mouth of the cave, but the man who came out was neither James nor Christopher.

He was an older man, tall and thin with stooped shoulders and wispy white hair that blew wild in the wind. He was wearing some sort of a dark woolen wrap, like a cape, and its tattered edge trailed in the pools on the rocks as he made his way over the boulders toward me. But as odd as he looked, he seemed friendly enough. He stopped a short distance off and nodded a greeting.

"Hello," I said back. "It's a lovely afternoon, isn't it?"

But the weather didn't interest him. His eyes on mine were uncommonly wise, sharp as chips of gray granite, and his voice, when he spoke, held a melody hard to describe. "Take you care of the boy."

And with that quite remarkable speech he moved on again, smiling a secret, and vanished round the headland as the sea spat up a violent spray of mist.

CHAPTER 24

Here are snakes within the grass.
— Alfred, Lord Tennyson, "Merlin and Vivien"

"I saw him, too," said Christopher. "Quite the character. He recited that rhyme for me . . . you know the one, James. Mother used to say it. The one about the bell."

"Oh, right." We were passing through the dimness of the chapel, and I could only see the edge of James's smile. "How does that go, again?"

Christopher, having just heard it afresh, had no trouble remembering. "There is nothing to hope, and nothing to fear, when the wind sounds low on Bosherston Mere," he said, dramatically. "There is much to fear and little to hope, when unseen hands pull St. Govan's rope. And the magic stones, as the wise know well, promise sorrow and death, like St. Govan's bell." And then, to me, he added, "There, you see? I have a memory, too, for poetry."

"So you do," I congratulated him. "But what, exactly, does your poem mean? There's no bell at the chapel — the bellcote was empty. I looked."

"There used to be a silver bell, but it was supposedly stolen by pirates, and lost until a sea nymph brought it back to shore and sealed it for safety in one of the rocks by the water. Tradition says that if you tap the rock, it rings."

Resisting the impulse to climb down again and experiment, I started up the curve of stone steps after James, counting silently as I went. "Fifty-three," I announced, as I came to the top of the cliff. One more than I'd counted before.

Christopher, behind me, made it fifty-one. "It never fails."

So at least one of the legends appeared to be true, I thought — none of us had been able to number the steps of St. Govan's.

"Where did St. Govan come from?" I asked, as we started across the car park.

Christopher shrugged. "Nobody knows. He was probably one of the old Celtic monks who came over from Ireland around the same time as St. David, but I always preferred the Arthurian angle."

"And what might that be?"

"That St. Govan was really Sir Gawaine."

"Of the Round Table?" James glanced back. "I thought Sir Lancelot finished him off."

Christopher shrugged in defense of his argument. "Perhaps it was only a flesh wound."

"Like something out of Monty Python," I suggested.

"More like something out of Mother's daft imagination," said James. "She goes all potty over Arthur, always did. She'd have named me Galahad, if Father hadn't put his foot down."

Christopher admitted that his father's intervention had saved them both the trauma of countless playground fights. "Although I must say that Galahad Swift would have looked smashing on a book jacket."

"Well, I'm happy being James, thanks all the same. Bad enough that she read us those same bloody stories, over and over."

I looked at him. "So how did you escape hearing about the prophecies of Merlin?"

"What?"

"Escape?" Christopher laughed. "You must be joking. I can practically recite the prophecies. We both can, can't we, James?"

"My memory, as you're so fond of reminding me, is not as keen as yours."

We'd reached the car. The conversation died. But I couldn't help feeling uneasy, as I always felt when I suspected someone wasn't being truthful — a sort of sixth sense that I'd learned to rely on after all my years of contract negotiations and dealings with difficult people. Of course, I reasoned, James might not be lying — he might really have forgotten the tales that he'd heard as a child. It happened. But if that were the case, why then hadn't he suggested I ask Christopher about the prophecies, instead of sending me to Gareth?

James felt my sideways glance, and turned. "Are you bored, yet?"

"Not a bit."

"Good, because I thought we might make a short stopover . . ."

His brother knowingly pointed out that it was only half past three. "The pubs are closed."

"Well, naturally," said James, whipping the Merc round the bends in the village of Bosherston. "But we haven't stopped in yet to say Happy Christmas to dear old Aunt Effie, at Stackpole. She always keeps a little something tucked away, for visitors."

I hadn't stopped to think that James had gone since lunch without a drink. He must be near exploding. I thought I detected a certain urgency in his driving, now, and he did seem unusually focused on the road ahead.

Again, it was left to Christopher to tell me what sights we were passing.

". . . and if you can bear yet another local legend," he said, leaning forward so his head drew level with my shoulder, "King Arthur's sword, Excalibur, supposedly lies just a stone's throw over there. You'll be able to see better in a moment."

I turned to look past James, the way Christopher was pointing, as we turned again along a road with forest to the right of us and a steep field rising to the left. Through the thick screen of trees I could see the flash of sunlight on still water.

"Bosherston Pools," announced Christopher.

I looked at the lily ponds, frowning. "I thought Excalibur got given back to the Lady of the Lake, when Arthur died."

"That's right. Arthur told Sir Bedivere to take it to the nearest lake and chuck it in the water, and then the hand came up and caught the sword and waved it round three times, and took it under."

"And that happened over there?"

He nodded. "That's what they tell me."

As he spoke, something moved at the edge of my vision, and Christopher noticed it, too. He squinted to see better. "That's not our friend from St. Govan's, surely?"

I'd wondered that, too, when I'd glimpsed the dark clothing and wild white hair, but already the tangle of branches had swallowed the shape of the man, and I couldn't be certain.

"Not unless he grew wings," James pointed out the obvious.

He was quite right, of course. No one could possibly have walked this far in such a short time. Still, I thought, the man that I'd just seen had looked familiar, just as the man from St. Govan's had looked familiar, though I couldn't for the life of me think where I would have met him. *Take you care of the boy,* he had said. I assumed he'd meant Christopher, since they'd just been talking to each other and it would have been quite natural for him to think I was Christopher's girlfriend. A word of friendly romantic advice, from an old man.

"Whoever it was," James remarked, "he's gone now."

The wind hit my window and, over its laughter, I fancied I heard in the distance the faint silvery warning of St. Govan's bell.

■ ■ ■ ■

It always amazed me how quickly the sun dropped in winter. Five o'clock brought the dark and a bone-chilling cold that breathed round my window and huddled me into my seat as James opened his car door. The fumes of the idling engine mingled sharply in the night air with the thicker scents of coal smoke and, from somewhere, roasting chicken.

"I'll just run in and fetch her," James said. "Keep the car warm."

Christopher woke as the door slammed. He'd slept all the way back from Stackpole, having dropped off the instant we'd left their Aunt Effie's house. She had turned out to be a delightful old woman who, not being much of a drinker herself, thought that Scotch should be poured to the top of the tumbler. "And where are we now?" he asked, groggily.

I twisted round. "Owen and Dilys's."

"Terrific." He watched the front door open in a flood of light as Dilys came to answer James's knock. "We'll be stuck here the rest of the night, now. Just watch."

"Oh, I don't think so." I watched Dilys's

gestures. "I believe Bridget's already gone home."

"I don't blame her. This place would be hell with a headache. That woman would drive me to drink." Returning Dilys's wave with a forced smile, he went on, "She used to be a nurse, you know."

"Oh, really?"

"God, yes. Sister bloody Casualty. You want to get her started on *those* stories, sometime," he said darkly. "I tell you, it's a treat."

It didn't surprise me that she'd been a nurse. In fact, it explained a good deal — her bustling, take-charge manner and her open impatience with what she perceived to be Elen's incompetence. And her tidiness, too. That would come from the nursing.

"Well," I said, "Owen seems quite happy with her, so she must have some good qualities."

"I can't think of any."

"Not even one?"

"Her cooking," he conceded, "is a cut above average."

"There, you see?"

"And she's quite good with children, believe it or not. It's a shame that her own is such a flaming idiot."

"She only has the one son?"

"One's enough, believe me. We're of an age. I used to have to play with him when we came down for summer holidays, and even then I couldn't stand him. And he's not the perfect angel Dilys makes him out to be. You know he got a young girl pregnant in the village, here? Quite the scandal, that was. Everything worked out all right, the baby was adopted, but Dilys damn near died of shame."

I could well imagine. She looked the sort of woman to whom shame was a palpable thing, a great burden to carry.

She was still in the doorway and talking to James, hands on hips, her face firm with righteousness. Christopher yawned and sat back again, closing his eyes. "We'll run out of petrol before she stops talking."

But a minute later James returned to join us in the car. "It seems we've missed a bit of excitement."

"Where's Bridget?" asked Christopher.

"She went home. Drank one of Dilys's healing teas and felt immediately better, so I'm told."

"Clever girl," said his brother.

"I doubt she found much peace and quiet back at Castle Farm," said James, stretching his words out for maximum effect. "Elen had some company this afternoon."

Christopher frowned. "Oh? What sort of company?"

"A couple of social workers from the local authority."

"Christ."

I felt something flip in my own breast. "They didn't take Stevie?"

"Not yet. Elen must have impressed them."

"Well of course she did." Christopher's words came out hard, like a slap. "Damn it all, she's a good mother."

"Anyway," James said, "I'm quite sure we'll get all the details from Bridget."

But Bridget, when we arrived back at the house, proved to be of little help.

"I was sleeping," she defended herself, stretching like a kitten in her chair beside the Christmas tree. Her eyes caught mine and glanced away, and I knew that she was lying. Besides, I had a good idea how she'd really spent her afternoon. "You'll want to ask Owen, he knows the whole story. Or Gareth — he's over there now."

Something in the offhand way she spoke his name made me seek her gaze a second time. She shook her head faintly in warning as James crossed to pour himself a before-dinner brandy. "Oh, I'm sure I can wait," he said smoothly. "I've had most of the story already from Dilys."

"Well, I haven't." Christopher, not so patient, left us abruptly to check for himself.

James shook his head. "I can't get used to seeing Christopher this way, it's not his style. I mean, it wasn't so long ago he was trying every trick he knew to get in Elen's knickers, and now he's gone all noble . . ."

"James," Bridget interrupted, "would you be a darling and fetch me a couple of aspirins?"

"Still have the headache?"

"Yes."

"Dilys's miracle cure didn't work?"

Bridget pulled a face. "Dilys's miracle cure tasted rather like pond scum. I had to tell her I felt better, or she would have made me drink the whole pot."

"Poor baby." He smiled. "Yes, I'll get you your aspirins. Where are they, upstairs? Right."

She waited until he had gone to recover. Shifting forward in her chair, she rolled her eyes expressively. "God, what a day!"

I took the chair opposite, stretching my legs. "I thought you liked a challenge."

"Challenge, hell. It took me an hour to break free of that woman, and then she only let me go because her bloody son rang. Although," she admitted, "she did send me off with a plate of mince pies to deliver to Gareth. That worked rather well with my plan. Now, if Owen says he saw me coming out of Gareth's cottage, I have an excuse."

I agreed that she'd been fortunate. "And was it all you'd hoped for?"

"What?"

"Your interlude with Gareth."

"No." Again the rolling eyes. "Why didn't you tell me the man was so *dull*?"

I lifted my eyebrows, surprised. "Well, I —"

"Honestly, Lyn, it took all of my effort to keep my eyes open. He just went on and on . . ."

"About what?"

"Bloody everything. He knew your husband, did you know that?"

"Gareth knew Martin?"

She nodded. "They went to the same parties, apparently."

Which was possible enough, I thought, in retrospect. Martin had had several friends within the theater circles. But still, I found it strange to be reminded just how small the world could be.

"Gareth didn't think much of him," Bridget said. "I believe the term he used was 'sodding little —' "

"How did you get on to Martin?"

320

"Do you know, I can't remember. We must have been talking about you, mustn't we? But I really can't recall the conversation. Like I said, it was hard enough staying awake. Such a pity. He *looks* like a brooder — those dark eyes, and everything — but behind it all there's not a shred of passion. Hopeless," she pronounced him, with a sigh.

I couldn't help but wonder if she'd met the same man I had. I could think of many qualities that Gareth lacked, but passion, I suspected, wasn't one of them. "So that's that, then?"

"Mm. Mind you, there is still Christopher."

"And James."

She stiffened her jaw, holding back a yawn. "So did he take you to St. Govan's, or did you all get stuck in a pub somewhere?"

James, coming through the doorway, answered smoothly, "No, the pubs were closed, my dear. We stopped by Aunt Effie's instead. I couldn't find your aspirins, but I found these in the bathroom. Will they do?"

She took the bottle from him and shook two tablets onto her palm without reading the label. "At this point, I'll try anything." Ever the convincing actress, she drooped wearily onto the cushions, as though the

321

simple act of swallowing had left her de-
pleted. "What shall we do about supper
tonight?"

James refilled his brandy glass and came
to sit with us beside the tree. "Well, you
can't be too ill, if you've still got your appetite."

"I always have my appetite."

I'd had one myself, half an hour ago, when
we'd stopped in the street outside Dilys's. It
was the chicken that had done it — the
smell of roasting chicken always gave me
that deliriously hollow Sunday morning
feeling, making me want nothing more than
to sit down and eat for the rest of the day.
But that had been half an hour ago. I wasn't
hungry now.

Some nagging emotion had intruded,
blunting my senses. For one awful minute,
I'd thought it might be jealousy of Bridget,
only that was absurd. There was nothing of
Bridget's I wanted. And then something
twisted inside, like a knot, and I named the
emotion with certainty: guilt. I felt guilty
for not being here when the social workers
had come to question Elen.

Not that I'd ever *promised* her I'd be her
son's protector, but part of me was beginning to think he might actually need one.

Because dragons, I knew, came in all shapes and sizes.

CHAPTER 25

Now days are dragon-ridden, the nightmare
Rides upon sleep . . .

— W. B. Yeats,
"Nineteen Hundred and Nineteen"

I was wet through and shivering, chilled to the bone, but the child asleep on my shoulder felt warm, his face pressed to my neck and his breath coming evenly, trusting. The mist swirled and parted and showed me a flickering fire through the reeds at the water's black edge. I took a deep breath, pulling strength from the night, and pushed on, hearing only my rustling steps and the blood in my ears.

Through the long night of running I'd wished and I'd prayed for the screaming to stop, and now it had stopped and I found the dead silence more frightening. I no longer knew where the creature was — out in the mist somewhere, following, hunting

us. Or maybe in front of us, stealthily waiting. Maybe it had set the fire itself, to draw
us in.

The thought slowed my pace for a moment. I looked and saw nothing.

And then the flames leaped higher as a
shadow passed before them and a woman's
voice began to speak. A voice I knew.

"You have done well," she said, "but there
is further yet to go."

She held out her hand and the firelight
chased down the billowing skirt of her blue
velvet gown.

I shook my head. "Please, I can't. I need
to rest. Surely you could take the boy from
here?"

Pale as porcelain, very proud, she faced
me. "He has chosen you to help him. And
the night is not yet over."

I took another dragging step toward her,
struggling to lift my leaden arm, to reach
her outstretched hand, but the wind rose
wailing through the reeds and suddenly the
fire, the woman, everything was gone, and
in its place was only darkness and the cold
and clinging mist. And as I pushed the wet
hair from my eyes the ground began to
tremble and a shriek of rage, inhuman,
drowned the wind.

The child woke, crying. I gathered him

closer and started to run.

I hoisted one foot on the stile and stood for a moment, quite still. Then I heard it again, the faint snap of a twig in the bracken behind me that told me I wasn't alone on the path.

It hadn't been too brilliant, I suppose, to choose to walk along the coast path in the first place, but I'd wanted the sea and the solitude, and this section of path that I hadn't yet walked had looked clearer and safer, at first, than the part that I'd been on before. Now though, I wished I had listened to Gareth's advice. He'd been right — this was probably not the best place for a woman alone. My heart gave a nervous leap into my throat and I swallowed it down, deliberately. Swinging my leg up and over the stile I hopped to the leaf-littered path and walked on, a little faster now, holding my chin at a brave angle. I tried humming, too, to show I wasn't worried, but it came out tense and unconvincing so I stopped. Besides which, I needed the breath.

The air here was heavy and thick with the smell of decay, like a greenhouse fallen into neglect, and I longed to be clear of the trees and the brambles, the ferns with their slapping wet leaves and the gorse prickles spearing the legs of my jeans. Another branch behind me snapped, and then another, and I broke into a half run, bursting from the thicket with a backward look as though I expected the horrible snout of the beast of my dreams to appear in pursuit, breathing fire.

So it was something of an anticlimax when, after a pause and a rustle, the undergrowth parted and out came a little white dog, with his stump of a tail wagging happily.

"Chance!" I couldn't control the relief in my voice as I bent to scratch his tufted ears. "What are you doing up here, hmm? What are you doing?"

He snorted an answer and groveled a moment, bellying into the mud. I looked up and waited for Gareth, but no one came out of the trees. "On your own, are you?" Standing, I smiled and turned, inviting the dog to follow. "Well, you might as well stick with me, then, for protection."

I had rather more need of his protection than he had of mine. Although he was only a small dog, I knew he'd do damage to anyone trying to hurt me, and it helped my confidence tremendously to see him bouncing ahead of me, his stout legs a blur as he dug at the hillocks and trotted from side to side of the wandering path. We were close to the edge of the reddish-black cliff — uncomfortably close, in some places — with a view of the Haven that would have been stunning in sunshine. This morning a fog hovered over the flatly gray water and clung to the opposite shore, though I still could see partway across to a jagged rock island topped by a stern-looking building. A prison, perhaps, or a fortress.

"What is that, Chance?" I asked aloud. "What is it, do you know?"

"Thorn Island."

The voice spoke from under my feet, and I jumped. "God, don't *do* that! I might have gone over."

Perilously near the edge, I balanced myself and peered over as Gareth, fearlessly perched on a ledge just below me, his back to the cliff, answered without looking up. "I told you that walking the coast path alone wasn't safe."

"I'm not alone. I have Chance."

"He'd be no help at all. He's a right little coward."

"And I suppose what you're doing is safe, is it?"

"Perfectly." He did look up at that, a hint of challenge in his eyes. "I thought you weren't bothered by heights."

"I'm not."

"Well, then." He shifted over, holding up a vacuum flask. "There's plenty of room. And I even have coffee."

My pride, as always, triumphed over prudence. Not wanting to appear a coward, I lowered myself rather gingerly over the edge and sat beside him on the folded groundsheet he'd set on the coarse grass to keep out the damp.

"It's a communal cup," he said, filling the lid of the flask with hot coffee and passing it over, "but I can promise you I'm not contagious."

That, too, was a challenge. I took the makeshift mug and drank. "So," I said, fitting my back to the cold of the cliff face, "what exactly is Thorn Island?"

"Used to be a defensive fort, in the last century. Since then it's been a hotel, and a private home."

"That?" I looked again at the imposing building, all angles and solid gray stone. "Someone actually lived in it?"

"One of the most famous bits of our local history happened out there," he informed me. "The wreck of the *Loch Shiel,* a Scottish ship bound for Australia. 1894, I think it was, in January — nasty night. The ship broke apart on the Thorn Island rocks, and the Angle lifeboatmen managed to get all her crew and passengers ashore. Hell of a rescue, from all accounts." He drew up one knee and propped a booted foot against the rock. "I've been with the Angle lifeboat myself for three years, and I've seen some hard rescues, but nothing like that. Still, they had compensation. The *Loch Shiel* was carrying cases of whisky. They washed into shore the next morning, and everyone scrambled to get them before the customs men arrived."

"Just like *Whisky Galore*."

"Exactly. The bottles that didn't get drunk right away wound up buried, or bricked into walls. They still turn up from time to time, when people dig their gardens out or do a spot of renovating." He shrugged. "I haven't found any myself, though, for all the walls I've torn out of the cottage."

I wondered what he'd do with one, if he did find it. A recovering alcoholic must be tempted enough without having whisky bottles dropping from the rafters. But then, I didn't know. Perhaps the need for drinking passed, in time.

I looked away, before he caught me watching him. "So," I asked him, lightly, "do you come here often?"

He shook his head. "First time."

"Ah. And you're sure this ledge is sturdy?"

"Don't worry," he said. "If we get into trouble, the lifeboat's just round the corner."

Watching the waves swirling white round the rocks at the base of the cliff, I doubted that the lifeboat could do anything to help us, if we fell. Chance seemed to share my misgivings. Putting his head over the edge, he gave us a reproachful look before settling with a sigh and a thump on the path, so that only his nose showed.

"So," I asked Gareth, "is this recreation or research?"

"Might be research," he told me. "Henry VII was landed just over the way there, at Dale, when he came back from exile in France. And his followers might well have sat in this very spot, waiting for the sight of Breton sails on the horizon. Only you can't see the horizon this morning, or Dale. Too damned foggy. And that's not why I came up here." He turned. "If you must know the truth, I was waiting for you."

"For me? Why?"

"You stole my dog."

"I never did!"

"Well, he saw you come out earlier and take off up the coast path, and traitor that he is, he took off after you."

I glanced up at the terrier's black eyes and

331

panting grin. "He did?"

"Like a rocket. So I thought, the hell with chasing after *him,* I'll just come here and intercept you both."

"There really was no need, you know." I stretched one hand to scratch the satin underside of Chance's jaw. "I'm sure he would have found his own way home."

"He might have done. But anything can happen on the coast path." And his tone plainly told me that it hadn't been the dog at all that worried him. He had waited here to see that I came through the path all right.

Such acts of chivalry were usually wasted on me — implying, as they did, a certain lack of ability and reason on my part, as though I were incapable of taking care of myself. Ordinarily, I would have felt resentful. But I didn't. Instead, I felt an oddly small and spreading warmth, a pleasant sort of feeling.

Encouraged by my silence, he went on, "In fact, there's no place where a woman can walk safe alone, these days. You only have to read the papers."

I challenged him, on that one. "That's a rather chauvinistic thing to say."

"No, it's not. I'll admit that in a perfect world you women should be able to go anywhere you like, but this is not a perfect world," he said. "There are too many nut-cases roaming around."

"Even in Angle?"

"Everywhere," he said, with firmness. "And you'll find them in all shapes and sizes."

"Like dragons," I mused. Glancing up in the silence that followed, I found myself facing his curious stare. "Sorry, I know that sounds foolish. It's only that I dreamed of dragons, last night." And that made me think of Elen, so I asked him how she was.

He shrugged, and slid his gaze away again. "She's been rather more level about this whole thing than I thought she'd be, really. She thought the social workers were very kind to want to visit Stevie. Kind." He spat the word out, in contempt. Taking the empty flask lid from my hand he pitched the dregs over the edge and refilled it for himself. "Bloody interfering bastards. Can't leave well enough alone."

"They probably had good intentions . . ."

"Oh, they're always well intentioned, social workers. But it wasn't them I meant. I meant whoever called and set them on to Elen."

I hadn't thought of that, myself. But of course someone must have reported Elen to the social services — they didn't go round

333

making random home visits, as far as I knew. I frowned. "Who would do such a thing?"

"I don't know." He brought his head round again, met my eyes darkly. "But I'll lay odds it's one of your lot."

My frown deepened and I looked down, poking fiercely at a clump of roughened grass.

"You're not surprised," he said.

"Not really, no."

He watched me a long moment, thinking, then finished his coffee and rose to his feet. "Time to see to the horse," he said, screwing the lid tightly down on the flask. "If you don't mind the smell of the stables you're welcome to come."

Damned infuriating man, I thought. Always shutting his feelings down, changing the subject. But I took his hand anyway, letting him pull me back up to the path.

It was the first time we had touched. I felt the strength and power of the man, immovable as stone, and something else . . . a tiny jolt of pure sensation that coursed through me like a shock and made me draw my hand away, confused. And then I met his eyes and found my voice.

"I don't mind the smell of a stable," I said.

CHAPTER 26

Yet now, I charge thee, quickly go again
As thou art lief and dear, and do the thing
I bade thee, watch, and lightly bring me
   word.
— Alfred, Lord Tennyson, "Morte d'Arthur"

The shed at the top of the paddock looked larger, close up, than it had from the road. Inside there was room for a box stall at one end, with metal-barred window and sturdy Dutch doors. Behind their wire cages in the ceiling strong electric bulbs gave light to banish the gloom of the gray winter morning. I sat in the opposite corner on one of the straw bales stacked up to the wall and inhaled the warm scents of sweet hay and leather and steaming damp horse. Sovereign turned in her stall, dark eyes fixing on Gareth.

"Keep your shirt on, you bloody big cow," he told her, but he said it with affection. He was quite a different person, with the mare. Even his appearance changed. His eyes had grown kinder, and his face had lost its bitterness. And the lines beside his mouth that looked forbidding when he spoke to me, now seemed to have been carved by constant smiling. I watched as he bent his head, mixing the feed. His black hair flopped forward and into his eyes, and he shook it back firmly. He looked like a boy when he did that, I thought.

"What?" he asked, without looking up.

"Sorry?"

"You look like you're wanting to say something."

"Oh. I was thinking, that's all."

He seemed to accept that. Straightening, he set the mare's feed bucket in place and swung the bottom section of the Dutch door shut, pulling the latch across. "So, which one of them did it?"

My train of thought had gone off track. "What?"

"Which one of your friends rang the social services?"

"I don't know. It couldn't be Bridget."

He raised an eyebrow. "Oh? Why not? She doesn't think too much of Elen."

I could have told him Bridget didn't think too much of anyone, besides herself. But loyalty to my client bound my tongue. Instead I said, "It's not her style. You'll have to take my word on that. Besides, there's not just the phone call to worry about — I still think that someone *did* go in the nursery that night. Not to hurt Stevie, or anything, but maybe to play a joke on Elen, to make her think there really was a dragon. There are people whose senses of humor are that warped," I said. "They might think it's funny to see Elen panicking, maybe that's why they reported her to the social services. And if it *is* one person doing this, then Bridget's in the clear, because she was with me when Elen heard the noise in Stevie's nursery."

Gareth thought that through a minute, following my logic. "All right," he said. "Assuming that I take your word, we're left with Christopher and James."

"And Owen."

"What?"

"Well, he has as much freedom as anyone, inside the house. And I thought I saw him in the garden that night. He could have —"

"It's not Owen." He shook his head, definite. "You'll have to take *my* word, for that one. Owen's far too fond of Elen."

"All right, then," I conceded. "Christopher or James." I linked my fingers round

337

my knees and settled back against the straw bales, thinking hard. "I suppose either one of them could be the culprit, really. I mean, when Elen heard the noise in Stevie's nursery James was supposedly in his writing room, but I expect he could have gone upstairs and through that door and no one would have seen him. Christopher was sleeping," I explained. "Or it could have been Christopher using the door while James was downstairs working. Either way . . ."

"Christopher was sleeping? At five o'clock in the evening?"

"Half past five, actually. Bridget had worn him out, shopping."

Gareth sympathized. "She'd wear anyone out. I've known toddlers with longer attention spans."

His tone of voice surprised me. "Well, then why did you . . . ?" I stopped myself, realizing how the question would sound, and not wanting to admit, even to myself, that I might be a little bit jealous.

"Why did I what?"

"Oh, nothing. Just forget it."

"Why'd I ask her in to tea?" He finished the question, not missing a beat. "I thought you might hear about that."

"It's none of my business."

"You're right. Found me boring then, did she?"

He clearly expected an answer, so I gave him a truthful one. "Yes, she did rather."

"Thank God for that." Leaning an elbow on top of the stall door he sent me a very superior look. "I reckoned that might be the way to get her off my back."

"What, you did it on purpose?"

"Of course. I have to bloody concentrate to bore a woman."

I couldn't help but smile at his conceit. "I don't know that anyone's *tried* to bore Bridget, before."

"She was after me, wasn't she? Being a nuisance. But that sort of woman just thrills to the chase. You stop running away, let her catch you, the thrill disappears."

He'd pegged her exactly. "That's very astute."

"There were plenty of Bridgets in London," he said with a shrug, reaching over to stroke the mare's neck. At his touch she turned lazily, nibbled his sleeve, and he warned her with a word. "She's a mouthy one, Sovereign is. People keep feeding her treats. Makes her nippy."

I opted not to tell him about Bridget and her carrots. "You didn't like London."

"That's very astute."

Not put off by the sarcasm, I asked him why.

"Because it's a ravenous beast that'll eat you alive if you let it. It drugs you first, with lights and praise and all the little luxuries, so you won't know what's happening. But in the end, you feel the teeth. You know." The bitter lines were back, but only briefly. As he went on stroking Sovereign's neck, they faded until only his eyes showed the depth of his disillusionment.

I watched him for a moment. Then I said, "The West End isn't all there is to London."

"It's enough." His tone was definite. "I won't be going back."

"Ever? That's rather limiting for a play-wright, don't you think?"

"Why? They don't need me to be there when they're putting on a play. That's bloody rubbish. It's the play that brings the people in, the play and the actors. No one gives a damn who wrote the thing."

"Oh, I don't know," I said. "It seemed to me a lot of people cared who wrote *Red Dragon Rising.*"

"No, they didn't." His sideways glance knew better. "It's all just a matter of fashion — who's seen with whom at the right cocktail parties. And it's been my experience that the ones who give the loudest praise and pat you on the back and say you're absolutely brilliant haven't seen the play at all, and never will. It's only fashion."

I couldn't really argue that. It was the same with publishing. Martin had thrived on the glittering social scene, moving from party to party with the ease of someone born to live a life of leisure, working over and over the same bits of rarefied prose to ensure that he didn't lose his privileged status. I had to admit I'd enjoyed the glamour in small doses — still did, when the job demanded it — but the artificial luvviness could wear a little thin, sometimes, and reveal the emptiness beneath, like a cheap tin brooch with its gilt rubbing off. I'd never been deceived enough to think that world was real.

But there were *people* in that world, I knew, who were sincere, who meant the words they said, who made it possible for me to keep my faith. I tried to explain this to Gareth. "It isn't all fashion," I told him. "Not everyone's like that. I could introduce you to a dozen people who not only went to see your play but who truly were touched by it, thought that it mattered."

"Could you, now?"

"Of course. You'd have to come to London, though."

"No chance of that. I've told you, I'm not going back." With a shrug that dismissed the whole city and everyone in it, he said, "I'm much happier here."

"Happy" wasn't exactly a word I would have chosen to attach to Gareth, but watching him with Sovereign I admitted that he did look quite content. I was working up the courage to ask him why he'd chosen Angle, out of all the places he could have gone to, when he said, "But that's enough of that. We've gone a mile off topic."

"Yes, well, that wasn't my fault," I said. "You started on Bridget, and —"

"So what we want to do, it seems to me, is keep an eye on Christopher and James, to see they stop their pranks before they do real damage, right?"

"All right. I'll do my best."

"And if you learn which one of them it is, you come and tell me, and I'll have a little chat with him."

I felt better, somehow, having Gareth involved. The problem already seemed smaller.

Chance, who'd been off chasing things in the field, bounded in through the doorway and came to me, grinning a terrier's grin. I reached down to pet him, the small movement bringing my watch into view. "Lord, is that the time? I should get back before Bridget starts calling out search parties." I very nearly made it to the doorway.

"Miss Ravenshaw."

I turned, expecting more instructions. "Yes?"

"Yesterday, when you said I had a right to know . . . what did you mean by that?"

"Oh, well, you know," I said, casting round for words, not wanting him to learn that I'd been listening to gossip. "You were friends with Elen's husband, and you seem to take an interest, so . . ." My voice trailed off, unable to compete with the intensity of Gareth's watching eyes.

The silence stretched, while he considered something.

"Stevie's not my son," he told me finally, "if that matters."

It shouldn't have mattered at all to me, really. But it did. And I discovered, as I walked across the wet grass of the paddock, that it mattered very much.

Owen saw me coming up the lane and waved a greeting. He was halfway up a ladder outside Bridget's bedroom window with a hammer in his hand. "Morning," he called down.

I stopped at the base of the ladder. "Do-

343

ing a spot of burglary? Or is it still the gutters?"

"Gutters. Your friends are all up," he informed me, "I made sure of that." He held up the hammer and winked. "You've been off with Mr. Morgan, have you?"

I realized Owen's perch atop the ladder would have given him a clear view of the paddock and the road beyond. "I met him on my walk," I said, "and stopped to see his horse."

Owen nodded, and whistled a snatch of a tune. "He's a popular man, these days."

From which I gathered he hadn't missed Bridget's visit to the cottage, either, yesterday afternoon. I tilted my head back and showed him an innocent smile. "Must be his warm and winning personality."

Owen laughed.

"Are you ready for tea?" I asked.

"Well now, there's a thought. I tell you what, if you'll go put the kettle on, I'll finish up this bit and take a break."

Bridget had beaten me to it. I found her in the kitchen, standing guard over the kettle as it wheezed toward the boil. She'd apparently just woken up — she hadn't combed her hair yet and her eyes weren't fully open and her dressing gown was trailing on the floor.

I did my Dr. Frankenstein. "It lives!"

"But only barely," she said, yawning, then midyawn her eyes came open and she stopped to sniff the air. "What *is* that smell?"

"What smell?"

"Ugh, it's you," she accused, with a wrinkling nose. "You're all horsey."

"Oh, well, I've been playing with Sovereign."

"Who?"

"Gareth's mare."

"I can't eat with you smelling like that," she complained. "It'll spoil the taste of my food."

I wasn't worried. I'd never yet seen anything put Bridget off her feed. "What's for breakfast?" I asked as I kicked off my boots, shrugging out of my jacket.

"That depends. Are you changing your clothes?"

"Maybe."

"Waffles."

"All right, then, I'll change." I caved in to the bribe. Bridget's waffles were worth it. She'd had the recipe from one of her previous men, an American actor who, to me, had been unremarkable in everything except his cooking, and that had been stupendous. He'd made waffles to die for, pale golden and crisp, heaped with cinnamoned apples, transparently tender, and dollops of whipped double cream. If he'd only been slightly more clever, he would never have let Bridget copy the recipe. She might have married him, then.

On my way upstairs to wash and change, I met James on the landing. Like Bridget, he'd only just got out of bed and although he was dressed he looked anything but awake, his jaw still darkened by the night's growth of beard. "There's a queue for the bathroom, I'm afraid," he said. "My brother sneaked in first." He yawned, and looked me up and down, taking in the state of my clothing. "Another walk? You're putting us to shame."

I wasn't sure how to react to him this morning, knowing he might be the one who'd played those tricks on Elen. The hero-worshipping agent part of me, in love with his books and his talent, didn't want to believe he could do such a thing, but the rest of me, more analytical, wondered and doubted. His moods could shift so easily, I thought, charming one minute and distant the next, and for all I admired the work of the writer, I couldn't claim to truly know the man.

"Where did you go this morning?" he asked.

"Just round the coast path to that big beach, you know . . ."

"West Angle Bay."

"Right. Then home through the village."

"Meet anyone interesting?"

It might have been a harmless question . . . then again, I fancied that I read some deeper interest in his eyes. "Not really, no."

"Well, I'd expect that everyone's indoors. The weather isn't —" Breaking off, he sniffed experimentally and frowned. "Do you smell something?"

"Oh. That's me, I think."

But James's face was clearing. "Waffles!" he exclaimed with pleasure. "Bridget's making waffles." And he absently excused himself and hurried down the stairs.

Which left me first in line for the bathroom. Since there seemed no point in changing clothes until I'd had a wash, I leaned my back against the wall and waited, trying to gauge Christopher's progress from the splashing sounds within. There, I thought, he was out of the bath now. A yank of the plug and the bathwater gurgled away down the drain, while footsteps slopped across the floor. More water, and humming

347

that grew strangely hollow as he brushed his teeth, then the tap of the toothbrush against the sink's rim, and . . .

"Could you do me a favor?" The bathroom door opened and Christopher leaned round, bare-chested and damp from the bath. "Oh, sorry," he said, when he saw me. "I thought you were James."

"What's the favor?" I asked him.

"Well, I'm rather short on towels, here." He hugged the door for modesty. "And I think my dressing gown's still hanging on the back of my bedroom door, so I wondered if maybe . . . ?"

"Of course. Just a second."

He thanked me and closed the bathroom door to keep the warmth in while I headed for the linen cupboard. Grabbing an armful of stiff folded towels, I pushed his door open to look for the dressing gown. I hadn't been in Christopher's room before. It was smaller than my room, square-walled and decidedly masculine, colored in mustard and brown and rich walnut, with one window looking out over the slope of the dining room roof to the dovecote and fields.

It took me a minute to find the dressing gown, not where he'd told me it would be, but on a chair beneath the window. Folding it loosely I draped it on top of the towels and was turning back toward the open door when I noticed the book.

He'd been reading it in bed, apparently, and had left it facedown, half hidden by the tangle of the blankets. A large hardback book with a glossy white jacket and vivid green letters that spelled out its title: *The Druid's Year.*

CHAPTER 27

Moreover, that weird legend of his birth,
With Merlin's mystic babble about his end
Amazed me . . .

— Alfred, Lord Tennyson,
"The Last Tournament"

"Christopher did it." Owen pointed the finger of accusation as Bridget reached to take the empty plate. "He ate the last one."

Christopher grinned. "Why, you lying old sod. I never did. And besides, there were two waffles left on that plate, last I looked."

"Well, I can't stop here arguing." Owen stood, clapping one work-worn hand to his belly. "I've got gutters to fix."

Watching him leave, I admired his energy. The rest of us sat round the table like sloths — the waffles had weighted us all to our chairs. Across from me James sat, eyes closed, still in ecstasy, smoking a cigarette. "So," he said, as the door to the garden banged shut behind Owen, "does anyone have any plans for the day?"

Christopher glanced at the clock on the wall and reminded his brother the day was half over. "We never do seem to get off our behinds till it's too late to do much of anything."

"That," Bridget said, "is the whole point of being on holiday. But if you're so keen to do something . . ." She set the trap neatly, and smiled, and he wandered right into it.

"Yes?"

"You could give me a lift into town to buy coal."

I couldn't think, at first, why she'd asked Christopher. Owen would seem the more logical person — he had, after all, been the one she had turned to for help with the Christmas tree. Christopher wasn't the coal-hauling type. And he couldn't be of much use information-wise to Bridget, now that she'd abandoned her pursuit of Gareth. Even so, I thought, watching her face, she *was* flirting, and flirting with purpose.

And then I saw her steal a look at James, and I knew what she was doing. He'd been rather attentive to me over breakfast, refilling my teacup and telling me jokes, and Bridget meant to show him she could play that game as well. She watched with satisfaction as his eyes came open.

"Why?" he asked.

"Well, darling, I can't lift a sack of coal alone, you know. And my car's hardly big enough, and since you don't like getting dirty I thought Christopher —"

"No, I meant why would you want to get coal? There's a shed up there full of the stuff."

"No, there isn't," she told him. "Whatever we've got in the house, that's the last of it. Owen didn't know that we were using it, you see, so he didn't think to order any more, and now the coal man doesn't come again till next week, so . . ."

James exhaled a thin impatient stream of smoke. "But we don't *need* coal. We've got central heating."

"Darling," crooned Bridget, "it's Christmas. And you can't have a proper Christmas without —"

"All right." He waved his hand, surrendering. "You do what you like. You will anyway."

"Actually," Christopher said, with another quick look at the clock, "I'm not sure I'll have time. I should probably check in on Elen, you know, and make sure she's recovered from yesterday."

"I can do that." The words came out before I'd really thought them through, surprising me as much as anyone.

Christopher looked at me strangely. "It's kind of you to offer, but . . ."

"I really don't mind. And anyway, if I'm meant to be Stevie's guardian, or whatever, I ought to at least pay a visit."

"There you are then," said Bridget, "that's settled." Her gratified smile made it clear she believed that I'd said what I'd said for her sake. Bridget, being Bridget, wouldn't think that I could have another motive. Her wants, her needs, were such a focus of her life, it seemed quite natural to her that they should drive my actions, too.

James wasn't totally convinced. "You know, you needn't feel compelled to play along with Elen's fantasies. She and Stevie got on fine before you came, and I've no doubt they'll both survive when you've gone home, and in the meantime you've come down to have a peaceful Christmas holiday. You shouldn't let them ruin it."

"I am having a peaceful holiday," I lied.

"Yes, well, I can't imagine that it's been too Christmassy, thus far." He stubbed out his cigarette, struck by a thought. "What we need is a party."

Bridget stared at him as though he'd grown an extra head. "A what?"

"A party. Oh, nothing big, nothing grand.

Just invite a few people for nibbles and drinks, say tomorrow night."

Bridget reminded him that tomorrow was Christmas Eve.

"Yes, I know. That's why I suggested it. I thought we could have the party first, and then all go from here to the service."

"The service . . ." echoed Bridget, faintly dazed.

"Well, darling, it's Christmas," he pointed out, benignly. "And you can't have a proper Christmas without going to the midnight service, can you?"

And with that he rose and left us to get started on his writing for the afternoon, leaving Bridget staring after him, astonished.

"It won't happen, you know," said Christopher wisely. "He'd have to spend money on canapés, drinks . . . and I've never seen James in a church Christmas Eve. No, he's just temporarily mad." Turning to Bridget, he folded his arms and leaned back, eyebrows raised. "What on earth did you put in those waffles?"

Elen came to the door in her working clothes, with sawdust clinging to her hair and flakes of old paint — pink and burgundy — splotched up one pale freckled arm like a rash. Beneath her denim smock she wore a T-shirt that had once been white, and her jeans were a canvas of color, ripped out at the knees. Standing barefoot on the freezing tiles, she looked about fifteen.

"Oh," she said, pleased to see me, "hello. Did you come to see Stevie? I've just put him down for his nap." She drew backward, inviting me into the porch. "He normally goes down right after lunch, only Owen was pounding things outside the nursery for the longest time, and of course Stevie couldn't sleep with all that noise, so I couldn't get him settled until now. But he won't sleep long, he never does."

The stained glass windows made the porch feel warmer, streams of red and gold and amber shifting softly over Elen as she opened the door to the hall. "I was just stripping paint off some shutters for Gareth, that's why I'm such a mess."

I couldn't smell solvent. "Do you work in the house?"

"No, it wouldn't be healthy for Stevie to breathe all those fumes. I do most of my work in the back porch, or outside. Depends on the weather." She brushed off one sleeve. "Can I get you some tea?"

She looked so pleased at the prospect of having company that I relented, though I wasn't sure where I would fit the tea. Since

I'd eaten the waffles, an hour ago, they'd expanded to fill every inch of my stomach.

"I'm afraid I'm out of biscuits," Elen told me as she led me down the passage to the kitchen, "but I have mince pies and Welsh cakes. Owen brought them by this morning. He always brings me treats, you know — just leaves them on the table."

"Don't you lock your doors?" I asked her, lightly.

"Yes, of course. But Owen has a key. He keeps the spare keys to the houses and the barns and things, when Pam and Ralph aren't here."

"And you keep the cats," I said, stepping over a sleeping bundle of fur beside the doorway to the kitchen.

"That's right. They're lovely, aren't they?" Scooping up the sleeping cat, a placid-looking ginger tom, she set him on a nearby chair and crossed to the sink, where she scrubbed like a surgeon. For someone so tiny, I thought, and with such a huge house, she kept everything spotless. The kitchen gleamed copper and pale oak and warm yellow tile, with braided rag rugs on the floor and potted herbs arrayed along the window sills, by size.

I didn't wonder that the social workers yesterday had failed to find fault with her.

356

They'd seen a healthy, happy baby and a clean, well-ordered house. Hardly the mark of an unfit mother. Or a madwoman.

I had the feeling Owen might be right, that Elen simply used her fantasies to help her cope with what she'd lost. That underneath all her talk about Margaret and Merlin and dragons, she knew exactly what was going on around her, what was real.

She went on talking, brightly. "Chance — that's Gareth's little dog," she said. "He doesn't like the cats at all. He chases them and worries them and barks and makes the biggest fuss. So Gareth doesn't bring him anymore. Have you met Chance?"

"I have. He's quite the character."

"Like Gareth. Chance and Tony used to have a thing — they used to fight each other. Well, pretend to fight. Like boxing. Chance would bring his paws right up, you know, and Tony would make fists, and they'd pretend to have a fight." She smiled, and dried her hands, and turned away to put the kettle on. I couldn't see her eyes, but her voice had a catch in it. "Tony liked dogs. We were going to get one, before he . . . well, one of the places where Gareth was working had puppies, Jack Russells, and Tony thought maybe he'd get one. I sometimes wish he had, you know? But maybe not. My hands are full enough, with Stevie."

I'd got stuck a few sentences back. "I thought Gareth worked from his home."

"Well, he writes there, if that's what you mean, but he can't pay his bills just from writing, he says, so he does things with horses for people."

"And what does he do with them?"

She shrugged. "That depends on what people want done. Sometimes it's just plaiting and clipping, you know, for the hunt. But mostly he breaks them and trains them and takes them to the shows at Tenby."

"Ah."

"He's very good," she said. "Everybody wants him, and he's always telling people no, he hasn't got the time."

I had no doubt that he'd be good at breaking horses — he was stubborn enough, and one look at that jaw would make any horse throw in the towel. But I hadn't come round here to talk about Gareth. "Elen," I said. "You remember the night when you heard that noise in the nursery?"

"Yes?"

"What sort of noise was it?"

She wrinkled her nose as she tried to remember. "Well, the window rattled — I was just coming out of the bathroom, then, and I thought that was strange so I went to look into the nursery, you know, and just before I got there I heard a sort of scrabble sound, like something clawing at the wall. And that's when I got scared, because I'd heard that sound before," she said. "The night before you came."

"I see." I pulled out a chair and sat down at the table, and the cat rose and arched and came onto my lap as I tried to decide how to phrase my next question. "And why do you . . . what makes you sure it's a dragon?"

"There's always been a dragon in that tower. My mother told me all about it, growing up. I just didn't know it was a *white* dragon until Merlin told me."

I nodded the same way my mother had nodded when I had gone on about Truffles, my imaginary pig friend who lived in our garden. I took pains, as she had, not to appear patronizing. "Does Merlin talk to you often?"

"Not really," she said, stretching up on tiptoe to get teacups from the cupboard. They were china cups, expensive, and stacked on their saucers they rattled precariously in her hand. "He goes away for months, sometimes, without a word."

I'd rather suspected as much. I waited till the teacups had been lowered safely to the counter. Then I asked, "He doesn't sound like Christopher, by any chance?"

She thought the question curious. "Of course not. Merlin has an old man's voice, you know. And he doesn't have an accent."

"Oh, right." I nodded again. "So, these conversations that you have —"

"They're more like lectures, actually. He tells me what to do for Stevie, what I ought to teach him, things like that. He tells me Stevie's future."

"Really?" Absorbing this, I stroked the cat, who sighed and stretched and rolled onto one side to test his claws against my knee. "What does he say?"

"That Stevie's going to be a leader, an important one, and people are going to come from everywhere to hear him and to follow him." The kettle boiled. She made the tea, an ordinary act, and yet when Elen did it somehow it took on the air of ritual. "I didn't understand, at first. I was angry with Merlin, because he had tricked me, but then I remembered how Arthur was born and I thought, it's no different, really. It happened the same way to Igraine."

"I'm afraid you've lost me."

"Igraine," she said, "Arthur's mother. *She* thought that the man in her bed was her husband, you see, but it wasn't. Her husband was already dead."

And then it sank in, and I knew what she was telling me — what the gossips had already told me.

"I thought it was Tony," she told me, quite innocent. "But it couldn't have been, could it? Because the coroner's report said Tony died at eight o'clock — this woman was walking her dog on the beach and she saw him on the rocks, and when she came back he was gone, that's how they fixed the time. And it was later, near eleven, when . . ." She stopped, and slowly poured the tea.

I thought of what Owen had said that first day, about guilt, how it twisted a person's mind, and I wondered whether guilt had twisted Elen's, whether she'd been having an affair and Tony's death had left her feeling so remorseful that she'd had to wrap the whole thing up in legends, myth, and fantasy, to cope.

"It couldn't have been Tony," she repeated, setting out our teacups on a tray. "But sometimes, I like to let myself believe it was. Does that sound very mad?"

I looked at her, the small face and the large eyes turned so hopefully toward me, and I gently shook my head. "No."

"It's only that I miss him," she said, simply. "Does it ever stop, this missing someone?"

I was thinking, not of Martin, but of Justin — of the empty cot, the grave beneath the churchyard yew, the smile I'd never see. *No, I could have told her,* but instead I answered truthfully, "It changes."

"Good." She added the plate of mince pies to the tray and lifted it carefully, stepping away from the counter. "Let's go have our tea in the sitting room, shall we?" she said, switching subjects. "I do want to show you my Christmas tree."

CHAPTER 28

The gale and the storm keep equal pace;
It is the work of the wise to keep a secret.
— *The Red Book of Hergest*
(trans. W. F. Skene)

"Well, I can't see how it could be better than *our* tree," said Bridget. Behind the upraised magazine, her posture was defensive.

Even the tree seemed to bristle, indignant, its fairy lights twinkling more sharply than usual. Kneeling beneath it, I centered a book in the bright square of gift wrap and sighed. "I didn't say that hers was better. I just said that it looked rather nice, the way she had it done, with all the ornaments from nature, and the ribbons, and no lights. It's very rustic."

Bridget sniffed, to show me what she thought of all things rustic. "Anyone who makes a crib from bits of twig and nuts . . ."

"She's creative."

"She's something, all right." Shifting round in her chair, Bridget swung her legs over the arm and lay back, shaking out the pages of her magazine. "Such a shame she won't be coming to the party."

"I thought she told James maybe."

"She won't come. She'd never leave her precious boy with someone else."

I couldn't resist. "Perhaps she'll bring him."

"Oh, that," Bridget said, "would be brilliant. A baby at a cocktail party. That would . . . what are you laughing at?"

"Nothing." I straightened my face, looking down.

"I can always switch agents, you know."

"I wasn't laughing."

"I hear Ivor Whitcomb is taking new clients."

James chose that moment to enter the dining room. "What's that about Ivor?" he asked.

"Nothing," Bridget said, mimicking me. Looking over her shoulder, she watched James start opening drawers in the sideboard, with purpose. "What is it you're wanting?"

"A pen that works."

"Well, darling, I should think this is hardly

the right room to —"

"Ah." He pulled the fourth drawer out and smiled. "The mother lode." Rifling through the contents of the drawer, he selected a handful of pens and wandered over to inspect my work. "Is that for me?"

"Don't tell him," Bridget said. "The man is horrible with gifts. He pokes and rattles."

"I do not."

"You nearly broke your birthday present last September."

"A fine French brandy," he informed me. "Smashing stuff."

"Yes, well, you nearly *did* smash it," said Bridget.

"But this one won't break." He looked down at my gift. "It's a book."

I smiled at his persistence. "It's not for you. It's Christopher's."

"Ah yes, my baby brother." Eyebrows raised, he turned to Bridget. "What the devil have you done with him, by the way? I haven't seen him anywhere since you came back."

She shrugged, not looking up. "He helped me put the coal into the shed and then took off again. I don't know where."

"How odd."

"No odder," said Bridget, "than you making plans for a Christmas Eve party."

His mouth curved. "That bothers you, doesn't it?"

"It's just so out of character."

"Yes," he mused. "I suppose it is." And then, with pens in hand, he grinned and left us.

Bridget lowered her magazine, meeting my eyes. "Men," she said. "They love to be mysterious."

"And you love mysterious men," I reminded her.

"Lucky for James." Watching me do battle with a length of curling ribbon, she asked, "Is that really for Christopher?"

"Mm. I'm giving him the naval murder mystery."

"Oh. Because I meant to tell you earlier, you could have given him the Welsh one that Lewis sneaked into the heap."

"Does Christopher know Welsh?"

"Yes. He said his mother taught him. James never took any interest in learning it, Christopher said, but then James hasn't got an ear for languages. I've heard him butcher French," she told me. "Christopher, though, is a wonderful mimic. You ought to have heard him today, going on like the man at the coal yard. He got the Welsh accent down perfectly."

The flat blade of the scissors slipped and

left the ribbon, nicking the side of my thumb. I sucked the tiny wound a moment, wondering if Christopher could imitate an old man's voice, as well.

Bridget didn't notice my accident, nor my frown. "So I thought," she went on, "if you wanted that book off your hands, you could give it to Christopher."

"Well, I've got this one wrapped now," I said, attempting the ribbon again with more care. And besides, I had somebody different in mind for the Welsh book.

Gareth looked larger, somehow, in the dark. With the light spilling out from the passage behind him, his face was in shadow, unreadable. "A what?" he asked, as though he hadn't heard me right the first time.

"A Christmas present." I thrust the small parcel toward him. "Here, take it. It's not going to bite."

"What the hell'd you do that for?"

The wind struck my back and I shivered on the doorstep, losing patience. "Look, either take it or don't take it, I don't much care. But I can't stand here freezing all night."

He took the book warily, studied my face, and stepped back from the door. "Come in."

The Aga, nestled in its nook within the kitchen wall, had chosen to behave this evening, burning cheerfully and radiating warmth. With the fire cover off, the play of thin blue flames across the glowing mass of coals gave the illusion of an open hearth and made the room feel cozy. Chance was dozing on the flagstone floor close by the Aga's feet, too comfortable to do much more than wag his tail in greeting. Gareth clearly had been thinking about putting supper on. A can of Irish stew, unopened, sat beside the cutting board, with a generous hunk of cheddar and a whole-grain cob. He shoved them to one side and set his gift on the work top, reaching to plug in the kettle. "Tea?"

"Lord, no." I put a protesting hand to my stomach. "I've had tea with breakfast, tea with Elen, and tea at four o'clock. I really don't think I could face another pot."

He considered the problem. "I have instant chocolate," he said. "Any better?"

"Heaps. Thank you."

Retrieving the tin and two mugs from the cupboard, he glanced at me over his shoulder. "So you've been to see Elen today."

"Yes."

"And?"

"We had a long talk, about Tony. And Stevie."

He knew what was coming. "She said Tony wasn't the father."

"She did, yes."

"Bloody rubbish. If there's one thing I know about Elen, it's that she would never have cheated on Tony."

"She seemed very sure."

"She's confused in her mind about what really happened the day Tony died, that's all." He challenged me, "Can you remember everything about your husband's death?"

That caught me off guard. Till now I had nearly forgotten what Bridget had said about Gareth knowing Martin from the time he'd spent in London all those years ago. And of course, if Gareth and Bridget had talked about me, he would know I was widowed. "I wasn't with him when he died," I answered, very calm. "But yes, I have a fairly vivid memory of the day, and what I did, and who was with me."

The kettle boiled. He frowned and looked away. "Well, Elen doesn't." And then, in a completely different tone of voice, he asked, "How did you end up with a sod like Martin Blake? You hardly seem the type."

"What type is that?"

He met my eyes again. "You know the sort

369

of man he was." He handed me the mug of frothing chocolate and I took it with a shrug.

"Like you, I met him at a party. He was sober then. He dazzled me. I wasn't very bright."

"Would you have stayed with him?"

No one had ever asked me that before. Would I have stayed with Martin if he hadn't died? I wasn't sure. I'd always thought — still did — that marriage was a promise, a commitment, not a thing you walked away from. But with Martin . . .

"Sorry," Gareth said. "That's not a fair question, is it?"

I replied without thinking, "I wouldn't have thought that you cared about fairness." Then, hearing how tactless that sounded, I hastened to soften the statement. "What I meant was —"

"I know what you meant." His dark eyes assessed me, expressionless. "You do have a high opinion of me, don't you?"

"Well, you haven't made it easy."

Frowning, he unplugged the kettle and lifted his mug from the work top. "Come on through to the study. It's colder in there, but the chairs are more comfortable."

Chance came with us into the adjoining room, and settled himself with a sigh and a thump on the hearth, his shaggy back pressed close against the fire screen.

"You'll singe yourself, you idiot. Get out of that." Gareth nudged Chance aside with his foot before lifting the screen away, letting the fire's full heat spill out into the room. He was right — it did feel a bit chillier here, but the armchair he offered me cradled my back with more kindness than the hard wooden one in the kitchen.

"So." He sat at his desk by the half-shuttered window and swiveled the chair round to face me. "You think I'm an ill-mannered bastard, is that it?"

I didn't back down, this time. Lacing my fingers, I met his gaze levelly. "I think you like to give people that impression, yes."

"And why would I want to do that?"

"I don't know. To keep them away, I expect, or to keep up your image — the angry young playwright at war with the world."

To my astonishment, he smiled. "Not so young, anymore. And there are some who might dispute the 'playwright' part. My muse doesn't speak as freely as she used to."

Now, I thought, we'd moved to more familiar ground — an agent and a writer talking shop. But still, I couldn't help but hesitate, uncertain of his smile, not wanting

371

to put a foot wrong. "Have you been working on this play for long?"

"I started it years ago, right after *Red Dragon Rising*. But after I came out of London I chucked the whole thing, put the play in a drawer and just left it there rotting."

I assured him that a lot of writers did that. "I think when your first work has been such a stunning success, there's so much pressure to repeat the trick that . . ."

But Gareth was shaking his head. "The last thing I wanted," he said, "was another success. I was sick of the whole bloody business."

There was no use, I thought, in pointing out the pleasure that his work had given people, and the eagerness with which we'd all awaited his next play. I knew he wouldn't thank me for the praise. He'd only think it hollow flattery, and bracket me with all the hollow people that he'd so despised in London. I held my tongue, accepting his decision. "So what changed your mind?"

"Stevie's birth." He said that without hesitation. "Elen going around spinning tales about dragons and talking to Merlin . . ."

"You know about that, then?"

"Oh, yes, it's all part of the same thing, it

372

makes Stevie special — a fatherless baby, a child of prophecy. Once she got on to all that, all her prophecy business, I couldn't help thinking of Henry VII. And once I start thinking," he told me, "I write."

"Well I, for one, am glad of that. I do like your writing — you have such a poetic way with words." So much, I thought, for my determination not to praise him.

He didn't seem to mind. He shrugged. "It's not the words that worry me. The value of a play is in its silences."

"How so?"

"The silences," he said, "are when the actors get to act. That's where the magic happens. Without the actors, all you have are pretty words on paper."

Tearing my eyes from the uneven stack of pages at his elbow, I tried to shift the conversation out of the abstract and into the concrete. "And does it have a title, this new play of yours?"

He measured me a moment. "I call it *The Long Yellow Summer,* from an old song the bards passed around in the summer of 1485, while everyone waited for Henry's return from his exile in Brittany. 'When the bull comes from the far land to battle with his great spear,' that's what they sang. 'When the long yellow summer comes and victory comes to us . . .' Henry, of course, was the bull — that was one of his symbols. Like Owain Glyn Dŵr, he knew how to play on the prophecies."

"I imagine, like Owain, he'd make quite an interesting hero."

He shrugged. "Henry's not in the play. It's a couple of months in the lives of those waiting for him to return and do battle — much more scope, there, for intrigue. I wanted to steer clear of Henry."

"Because you don't connect with him?"

"Because we have too much in common."

"Ah." I shifted my gaze to the fire, reluctant to ask him the obvious question. Knowing nothing of his private life, I didn't want to pry. The flames dancing round one large coal to the rear of the grate disappeared with an audible puff in a trail of thin smoke, then sprang to life again, like magic.

I felt Gareth's eyes on my face, but I left it to him to break the silence. When he finally did, his voice was calm and even, making conversation. "He was taken from his mother as a young boy; so was I. Raised by strangers; so was I. He never knew his father." As I turned my head to look at him, he said, "Writing Henry would be little more than putting my own words in Henry's mouth. I bloody hate that kind of self-indulgence on the stage."

I didn't know what to say. "I'm sorry."

"Why be sorry? I survived."

Watching his jaw settle into the now familiar stubborn pose, I tried to picture what he would have looked like as a little boy, a child of five or thereabouts. I had no right, I knew, to ask him anything, but as someone who'd carried a baby myself I couldn't help wanting to know. "Your mother . . ."

"Drank herself to death, I'm told. A minor family illness she was kind enough to pass to me." The bitterness, I thought, was not for her. Not for his mother. It was meant for those who'd stepped between them, taken him away. "She couldn't stop the drinking, so they said she wasn't fit to raise a child. But she tried. She wanted help, not a bloody care order."

I understood now why, when he'd talked about social workers this morning on the cliff, he'd been so harsh. And I understood something else, too.

"So you see," he said, taking the thought from my mind, "why I do what I can to help Elen and Stevie, the way someone should have helped us. And why I'd like to kill whoever made that call to the social services."

I nodded, saying nothing. I had meant to share my suspicions of Christopher, but looking at Gareth's face I decided that wouldn't be wise. Not, at least, till I'd come up with actual proof.

"Nothing new on that front?" he asked.

"No, not really. I'm keeping an eye on what everyone does, like you said, but so far —" I broke off as a great hurling spatter of rain hit the window, surprising us both. It came down the chimney as well, landing on the coals with a scattering of tiny hisses.

Gareth leaned over and twitched back the curtain to look. "It's really coming down," he said. "You'll have a wet walk home."

"Oh, that's all right, I've got my raincoat. And I'm only going to the pub, just up the road. I'm supposed to meet the others there at eight."

He let the curtain fall. "I'll run you up there in the car."

"No, really, I'll be fine. You needn't —"

"I take it they don't know you're here, with me?"

Actually, I'd told Bridget some story about needing to phone through to Canada and discuss some nonexistent crisis with my brother, but I didn't want Gareth to know I'd gone to such elaborate lengths just to bring him a Christmas present. I was trying to decide what I should tell him when he shrugged and said, "No problem. If they notice me dropping you off you can tell them we met in the lane and I gave you a lift."

"Thanks." And then, remembering how deeply he valued his privacy, I added, "I won't tell anyone, you know, about . . . well, what you said."

He'd finished his chocolate. Shifting the papers aside with his elbow, he swiveled to set the mug down on his desk. "If I'd thought there was any real danger of that, I'd have kept my mouth shut in the first place, now wouldn't I?"

Which was probably, I reasoned, as close as he would ever come to paying me a compliment.

CHAPTER 29

And thro' the tree
Rushed ever a rainy wind, and thro' the
    wind
Pierced ever a child's cry . . .
        — Alfred, Lord Tennyson,
           "The Last Tournament"

No one seemed to notice that I wasn't soaking wet. Except, perhaps, for Christopher, who flicked me a curious glance but said nothing, mainly because he was too busy fending off questions about where he himself had been. "Nowhere, really."

"You had to be somewhere," said James.

"I just went for a drive. Oh, and rented some videos."

That got Bridget's attention. "Videos?"

"Mm. *Miracle on 34th Street* and *A Christmas Carol* — the old black-and-white one, with Alastair Sim. Uncle Ralph's got a video recorder, we might as well use it."

Bridget, predictably, thought it a brilliant idea. For once, she didn't linger over after-dinner coffee, but herded us into the car and straight home to make popcorn. Not that I minded — it made a nice change from our usual gather-around-by-the-Christmas-tree evenings. It was heaven to lounge in the dark on the sitting room sofa, with everyone silent and no need to make conversation.

I even did rather well, staying awake, but it was nearly midnight when we slipped the second tape into the video, and though I tried my best to follow Scrooge's nasty undertakings, by the time Marley's ghost finally clanked through the bedchamber, sleep was attacking in waves. Yawning, I leaned my head back on the cushions and let my eyes close. It was Marley's voice, really, that finished me off — that drab, mournful monotone, lecturing Scrooge.

As I drifted, I heard the ghost rise in a shrieking of chains, but the shrieking became something else, full of menace and terrible . . .

Something behind me.

It roared again, gaining, and clutching the child I dragged myself free of the water and reeds and climbed onto the hard, frozen turf of an unknown field. I was too tired to run now, my legs moving leadenly. Soon it would be at our backs, it would catch us, and then . . .

"Almost there," a voice whispered, ahead in the darkness. "Seek the light and then follow it. There you'll find safety."

I looked for the speaker. "Where are you?"

"Follow the light," came the answer, more faintly.

And a small, steady gleam like the flame of a lantern chased over the cold ground ahead of me, beckoning. It paused when I stumbled but never stopped moving, leading me swiftly across the strange field while the mist swirled around us and hid us from view. And then, when my strength had all gone and I felt I would faint if I went one step further, the light led me out of the mist altogether. I might have stepped over a threshold — a nebulous wall shifted shape at my back, as though held in place by some invisible force, while before me the moonlight struck pale through the perfect clear night to shine upon an ancient grove of oaks.

Their tangled branches, silvered by the moon, dripped thick with mistletoe, and somewhere in their twisted depths an owl hooted out a warning. The light had halted, quite abruptly, in the center of the grove. And slowly the shadow beside it turned round and resolved itself into the shape of a man.

The old man I'd seen at St. Govan's.

His eyes met mine kindly, his hair blowing white as he took a step forward and held out his hands. "It is time," he said. "Give me the child."

I tightened my hold. "No, I can't."

"It is time," he repeated. "Your journey is done. The boy's path lies with me now. Let him go."

"No." My hand closed protectively over the tousled fair curls, pressing his head to the curve of my shoulder. "He chose me. I have to protect him."

"If you would save him, you must give him into my care now or all will be lost. This is the boy's destiny."

My eyes filled. "Please, you can't take him from me."

The old man stood firm, hands out-stretched. "So have I prophesied; so must it be."

"No." I turned, and in that one unguarded instant came a flash of flame that brought the night alive.

The shadows writhed in fury and an evil yellow eye, too close to mine, rolled over white as one thick grasping claw slashed through the wall of mist to steal the child from me. And the creature screamed its triumph, wheeled and vanished in a sudden flap of wings while I stood stunned and empty-handed on the scorched and barren earth.

I heard the child cry in terror; heard him cry, but couldn't follow. I could only stand and listen as the crying grew more distant, till it sounded somehow smaller, like the wailing of a newborn.

Then a sudden swell of music rose to underscore the drama, and I forced my eyes to open.

On the screen, Scrooge was leaving the room where his sister had died. *Almost* died, I corrected myself . . . she revived for a moment and murmured in fever, too late for her brother to hear her. "Promise me you'll take care of my boy," she implored him. "Promise me you'll take care . . ."

Bridget stirred in her chair and glanced over with glistening eyes. "I know. It always gets me, too, this part," she said, and handed me a tissue.

CHAPTER 30

Then this is the Deciding Day . . .
— John Dryden,
Merlin, or The British Enchanter

There was only one shop in the village, but it seemed to sell everything, tidily organized into a space that was barely the size of my parents' front room.

". . . and the sprouts . . . yes, that's it." Bridget finished checking through the box of fruit and veg assembled to her order on the counter. "That's brilliant, Sheila. What do I owe you?"

The small dark-haired shopkeeper tallied the bill while I struggled to get a good hold on the turkey. It was fresh and enormous and kept slipping out of my hands.

"Having company, are you?" the shopkeeper asked.

Bridget smiled. "No, I just adore food."

"Well now, Elen from over your way came

this morning to pick up her turkey, and I thought she said you were having a party."

"Oh right, yes, tonight. Just a few people over for drinks and things, really, before we go out to the Christmas Eve service."

The shopkeeper nodded approval. "Very nice of your man to ask Elen, I thought. She doesn't get out much, poor thing."

I couldn't resist throwing Bridget a smug look as we edged out the narrow shop door with our purchases, but sticking to her guns she shook her head.

"She won't come. She never wants to socialize when Gareth isn't there."

"Gareth's not coming?" I said that too quickly, but Bridget, absorbed in herself, didn't notice.

"Apparently not. He said thanks very much, but he likes to stay in Christmas Eve, on his own."

"Oh."

Misinterpreting my tone, she nodded. "Yes, I thought you'd be happy to hear that. I know you don't like him."

I hefted the turkey and followed her across the street to the green-painted gate leading into the playground, my gaze drifting sideways to the low gray stone wall with its bright sprays of cotoneaster, and the quiet pink cottage behind, nestled up to the trees.

The gate clanged behind us, disturbing the crows in the branches above so they rose in a black flapping whirl, hurling insults.

"Doesn't look like he's home," Bridget said, with a glance at the cottage. "I don't see his car."

I turned my head deliberately, taking the positive view. "Well, at least I won't have to worry tonight, then, about how to keep James distracted."

"Has it been such a worry? I'm sorry. I never do think, do I? Here you are, meant to be having a holiday . . ."

"At least you're feeding me," I said, and hugged the turkey with a smile. "I can't complain."

"I do owe you a break, though. Tonight," she vowed bravely, "I shan't flirt with anyone. Not even James."

I laughed, I couldn't help it. "Now, *there's* an empty promise if I've ever heard one."

"You don't think I can do it?"

"Well, maybe if you were unconscious . . ."

"All right then," she told me. "I'll bet you ten pounds."

"That you go a whole night without flirting? You're on."

Indignant, she wedged herself, box and all, into the kissing gate. "I could go a whole week if I wanted to."

She very nearly lost her bet when Christopher came out to meet us at the bottom of the drive, his hands outstretched. "Here, let me take that. It looks far too heavy."

As she handed him the vegetables her mouth began to form the wide and slightly breathless smile she only showed to men, but in time she remembered and caught herself. "Thanks," she said simply.

"You're welcome to take this one, too, if you like," I told Christopher, offering my turkey. It was meant as a test of his chivalry, really — I didn't think he'd take it. But he rose to the challenge.

"Right." He extended the box. "Chuck it in."

"Only if it doesn't crush the veg," instructed Bridget.

"You can't crush sprouts," he said. "They're hard as bullets."

She took his word and led us up the drive, past the grassy spot where the Merc should have been. "Where's James?"

"He's gone into town."

"What, again? He'll be wearing great grooves in the road," Bridget said. "What on earth was he after this time?"

"More champagne and smoked salmon."

"Oh, God." Her eyes rolled. "You'd think the Queen was coming."

I flexed my strained arms, massaging the quivering muscles. "Who *is* coming?"

"Owen and Dilys, of course, and a bunch of local people you don't know." She named them anyway, and she was right — the names meant nothing.

"And Elen," I added, straight-faced.

But Christopher shook his head. "No, she's not coming."

Trying my best to ignore Bridget's gloating expression, I asked him why not.

"She said she wasn't feeling well — a touch of this flu that's been going around, maybe. It wouldn't surprise me, she doesn't take care of herself." I thought I detected a note of complaint in his voice, and that struck me as odd, but it had vanished by the time we reached the back door. "Mind you," he added, "I don't think she'll miss much. I can think of half a dozen ways I'd rather spend my Christmas Eve."

"Oh, I don't know," said Bridget. "I rather like a good party."

"So do I." His tone was dry. "But it's my brother throwing this one, don't forget. That spells disaster."

Inside the back passage, the whine of the hoover drowned everything, prim and industrious. It seemed strange to see Dilys here, doing the cleaning — I'd have thought that cleaning house for someone else would be beneath her. But James had assured me that wasn't the case. "No, no," he'd told me, earlier, "she always does this, honestly. It's a matter of pride with her, having the place looking spotless. She doesn't bother when it's only Christopher and me, but if we dare to entertain . . ." He'd rolled his eyes expressively. "She won't have anybody saying Owen doesn't take good care of Castle Farm, while Uncle Ralph's away. She was in here scrubbing floors, you know, the day before you came."

She didn't look like any cleaner I'd ever met. In fact, I decided, the way she looked now must be quite like the way she had looked in her Sister Casualty days. Bustling round in her floral-print pinafore, carefully lipsticked and smelling of hand cream, she made me feel wet and incompetent.

"Now mind you wipe your feet," she said, switching off the hoover as we tramped in. "I've done this bit already; I'm not keen to do it over."

Bridget defiantly shrugged off her jacket and shook out the damp before tossing it anyhow into the corner. "I'm off to have a bath," she announced.

Christopher stepped through to set his box down in the kitchen. "Just shout if you

388

need me to come scrub your back."

I saw what it cost her to let that line pass without making some equally flirty reply, but she'd taken our wager to heart and she didn't like losing. Her gaze flicked toward me, to make sure that I'd noticed, before she tossed her head and walked away.

Dilys bent to pick up Bridget's jacket, lips compressed in disapproval. "She'll make a proper pair with James — they'll have to have somebody living in to clean up after them. I've never seen such a mess as that room that he writes in."

Christopher, who'd gone through to the kitchen, poked his head back round the door. "You didn't clean it, did you?"

"Well, of course I did. You never know where guests are going to look," she said. And looping the hoover's cord over the handle, she rolled off to see the dining room.

Christopher watched her go, shaking his head, and then slid his gaze sideways to me. "Just a word to the wise: when my brother gets home, keep your head down — he's bound to explode."

But James, quite surprisingly, took the invasion of his writing room in stride. "Oh, well," was his only comment, after seeing his papers and books stacked with knife-edge precision on the gleaming rosewood table. And then he turned and closed the door and went upstairs to wash.

He came down whistling, riding the crest of a good mood that lasted through supper and left Bridget mystified.

"Maybe you've caught Elen's flu," she said, feeling his forehead.

"I do wish you'd stop that. I've told you I'm fine." Smiling, he leaned back in his chair and lit a cigarette. "Shall I help with the dishes?"

"You see? There you go again," Bridget accused him. "It's like one of those films, where an alien takes over somebody's body . . ."

He laughed. "I'm no alien."

"That," said his brother, "is open to argument. What time is this party supposed to begin?"

James shrugged. "I said nine thirtyish."

"Well, I'd better get dressed, then."

"I'll check to see everything's organized," James said, and pushed back his own chair to rise.

Bridget frowned. "It won't help you, you know."

"What won't?"

"Running away. I won't rest till I know what you're up to."

"Who says I'm up to anything?" He smiled

and bent to kiss her. "It's Christmas, darling."

As he left us, Bridget looked across at me, one eyebrow arched. "God bless us, every one."

The dining room looked different with the table pushed against the longer wall, beneath the windows, and the high-backed chairs turned round to face the room for extra seating. At one end the Christmas tree, gracefully sparkling, soared to the ceiling, while at the other end the sideboard had been heaped with heat-and-serve treats.

The party appeared to be constantly swelling, a mingled confusion of laughter and talk and new faces, all friendly, and in their midst James moving round with the skill of a chef, stirring people together. Bridget, in her element, played hostess — though I noticed she never strayed far from the sideboard. She was into my smoked salmon roll-ups again when I came to refill my champagne glass.

I searched through the platters. "What happened to all of those cheese things?"

"Mwuf," Bridget said, with an innocent shrug.

"You're impossible."

Smiling, she poured my champagne. "So,

do the tights fit all right?"

"Mm. That just goes to show you, I'm not nearly as organized as my mother. She would never have forgotten to pack an extra pair of tights."

"At least you remembered the little black dress," she pointed out. "And very fetching it looks, too."

"Thanks."

"Having fun?"

"Yes, I am, rather." I picked up a bowl that was empty except for a few scattered crumbs. "Did you eat the crisps, too?"

"There are more in the kitchen."

"I'll get them. Here, hold this." I gave her my glass. "And for heaven's sake don't finish anything else while I'm gone."

In the kitchen I found Christopher, standing by the corner cupboard looking at something he held in his hands. He glanced up quickly as I came in, and my eyebrows came down in suspicion. I'd been trying to keep him in my sights all evening. Having decided that he was most likely the person who'd been bothering Elen, I had wanted to be sure he didn't get a chance to spoil her Christmas Eve.

He must have sensed the change in me. His smile tried too hard. "Enjoying the party?"

"Very much. We need more crisps," I said, holding out the empty bowl as evidence.

"Oh right. I think they're by the toaster, there."

"I see them." Shaking out the bag, I stole a sideways look to see what he was doing. "Are you after food, as well?"

"What? No," he said, smiling, and hung something up on a hook in the cupboard. He swung the door shut. "No, just poking about."

"Well, if you're going back in, could you carry these, please? I should heat up some more of those cheese things."

"Sure." Taking the bowl of crisps from me he scooped up a rattling handful and sauntered off into the passage. I waited till his footsteps had been swallowed by the general party din before I crossed the kitchen floor to check the cupboard.

He'd been looking at a ring of keys — a large, old-fashioned ring with keys of every shape and size slung round it, crowded right together.

Lifting my head, I looked toward the door, the way that Christopher had gone, and frowned again. I couldn't be sure that he'd taken a key from the ring, but I rather suspected he had. And I thought I knew, too, just which key it would be. Well, if he meant to play another trick on Elen, I thought stoutly, he would have to come through me.

Damping down my anger, I went back to join the party.

Bridget was still by the sideboard. "I thought you were bringing more cheese things," she said, as she handed me back my champagne.

"I couldn't find them." Which was an outright lie — I hadn't looked. But my mind was occupied with other things. My gaze wandered over the clusters of heads, touching briefly on James's dark blond one before settling in on its true target, Christopher, standing at the far end of the room beside the Christmas tree.

Owen stepped in front of me and blocked my line of vision, cheerful in his bright red reindeer pullover. "You can't be a wall-flower, lovely — especially not in that frock. Go and mingle."

I assured him I'd been mingling. "I just thought I'd better get some food, before it disappeared."

He glanced at Bridget, grinning. "I was thinking the same thing myself," he said, taking two plates from the stack at the end of the sideboard. "Weren't there cheesy things here just a minute ago?"

Bridget smoothly deflected the question. "*Two* plates, Owen?"

"Well, I thought I'd make one up for Elen. A shame that she couldn't be here."

"Mm," said Bridget, keeping a critical eye on his choices. "I don't think she's keen on smoked salmon."

"Who, Elen? She loves the stuff." Owen forked a third slice onto the plate, added lemon, and turned. "Now, I'll just run this over . . ."

"I'll take it," I offered, my gaze still fixed on Christopher.

"That's nice of you, lovely. I'm sure she'd rather see your face than mine."

"Don't be daft. I just want to see she's all right, that's all." Setting my empty glass down on the sideboard, I took the plate. "I won't be long."

Seen from outside, through the long narrow windows, the party looked strangely surreal, bright and glittering, laughing white faces that floated about in their own private world behind glass. With the wind blowing bitterly cold up my skirts and my elbows hugged close to my sides, I chattered past in my high heels, wishing that I'd thought to wear my jacket.

Elen didn't answer when I knocked — she likely couldn't hear me for the wind, I reasoned — and after a minute of waiting I let myself into the porch and then, when she still didn't answer, I opened the inner door, poking my head round. The hall was in darkness, but just round the corner I saw light spill out from the sitting room. "Elen?"

I waited. It didn't feel right, going in uninvited, but then I remembered she hadn't been well and concern overrode any qualms about manners.

"Elen?" I called again, coming right in this time, swinging the door shut behind me. Stepping out of my shoes, so as not to leave marks on the polished wood floors, I went to look in through the sitting room door. She was curled on the sofa, half sitting, one hand tucked beneath her pale cheek like a child's. The remnants of her supper tray still littered the low table in front of her — a soup bowl, two browned apple slices, biscuit crumbs, a teapot. As I came into the room, her lashes fluttered, lifted, fell again.

"Didn't you hear me?" I asked.

"Too sleepy."

"I've brought you some food from the party."

She murmured and tried to sit up.

"No, don't bother. I'll just put it down on the table."

She mumbled again, and I leaned closer.

"What?"

"Knew you'd come. Margaret said . . . Margaret told me . . ." Her voice trailed away as her head sank again to the cushions. Her breathing came deeply — too even and deep for a woman who'd just been awake. Either she was very ill, I thought, or she had taken some sort of medication. Leaning over, I joggled her shoulder.

She didn't respond.

As I looked round, trying to decide what I should do, my gaze fell on the homemade crib set out across the mantelpiece — the stubby little walnut sheep, the Magi made from pine cones wrapped in moss, the painted pebble Christ Child in his manger. The child . . .

A knot of apprehension twisted slowly in my breast. A cold draft gusted down the empty chimney and it seemed to breathe the warning of the old man at St. Govan's: *Take you care of the boy . . .*

"Stevie." I took the stairs two at a time, but I needn't have panicked. The nursery was filled with his smell and the sound of him sleeping, curled snug in his cot. Relieved, I stood and watched him for a moment, then I lightly, very lightly, stroked my hand across his curls and tucked the blankets in around him, as I'd never had the chance to do with Justin.

My hand was still holding the blankets when I heard the first scrape of the key in the lock.

The sound brought my head up and sharply around to stare, transfixed, at the cupboard built into the corner, and as I stared the doorknob started turning.

What I did next went well beyond reason, beyond conscious thought. Reacting from instinct much older than memory, I picked up the baby and ran.

CHAPTER 31

And through back waies, that none might
    them espy,
Covered with secret cloud of silent night,
Themselves they forth convaid . . .
    — Edmund Spenser, *The Faerie Queene*

I really don't know why I chose the back
door. Maybe because I'd come in that way,
and like an animal whose path had brought
it face-to-face with danger I'd blindly
doubled back upon my tracks and made a
bolt for safety.

I'd have gone right round the back of the
houses again if I hadn't seen the shadow
slanting suddenly in front of me, and then
the flash of dark blond hair above it. I didn't
stop to reason that the devil couldn't be
behind me and before me all at once — I
turned and darted up the ankle-breaking
flight of steps behind the shed, my stock-
inged feet making no noise on the stone,

399

gathering Stevie against me and ducking my head as the gnarled branches of the fig tree scrabbled and clawed at us. One caught my hair but I tugged myself free and pushed on, up the hill to the shed.

The padlock hung loose from its hook — Elen never did shut it properly, Owen had said. Grateful for her carelessness, I jiggled the lock free and pulled the door open, then jumped as the wind grabbed it, flinging it hard to the side so it banged on its hinges. I stopped. Held my breath. Looked at Stevie.

He slept like a stone. He hadn't moved once since I'd lifted him into my arms, but the sound of his breathing came rapid and soft and the warmth of it brushed on my fingertips as I folded the trailing corner of his blanket over him to shield him from the cold, to keep him quiet.

Below me, the man's shadow stopped in a hard square of window light, head turned to listen. And then I saw the angle of it change and knew that he was starting to look up, that any second now he'd see us, and I couldn't let that happen.

I slipped sideways through the open door that blew again and sharply banged behind me with a force so great it shook the shed's four walls. And then the wind, as though it tired of the game, released the door and let it swing back slowly, creaking, sealing me in darkness. There were no windows here, and the air had the thick, musty smell of a cellar. Forced to grope my way into the tangle of furniture, I curved my body round Stevie's to give what protection I could, holding him with one arm while the other strained forward, my hand feeling into the blackness.

I might have been moving through some sort of nightmarish forest, with creatures and trees grabbing at me from all sides. Hard corners stabbed me and upturned legs pummeled me, bruising my ribs as my fingers raked surfaces greasy with dust. At one point I touched the face of a carved beast — a lion, I think — and I snatched back my hand without thinking, only to have something slash at my shoulder, a searing swift pain like the pass of a knife. I cried out and caught myself, biting my lips into silence.

He was coming.

I heard the hard ringing footsteps on stone climbing steadily closer, unhurried. And then he was there, at the door, and with a silent prayer I crouched and huddled in among the table legs, cradling Stevie warm against my heart.

The door creaked open.

In the moonlight he was featureless, the outline of a man and nothing more, but I could tell it wasn't Christopher. I felt myself relaxing and I might have called his name if someone hadn't done it for me.

"James?"

He turned. "Up here."

More footsteps, this time running, and another shadow joined him in the doorway. "What are you doing?" *That* was Christopher. Panicking, I tried to scuttle deeper into my hiding place as James spoke again.

"The shed door was open. I thought that I'd better . . . hold on, did you hear that?"

I froze in my awkward position, not daring to draw back the leg that had just kicked the corner of something.

Christopher listened. "It might be a cat."

"Where's your torch?"

The beam clicked on smartly. It found a wardrobe up against the farther wall and steadily, methodically, began its sweep toward me. My mouth dried as I looked from the light to the shadows that held it, knowing if I could see them, they'd see me when the torch swung my way. I couldn't think of anything to do. Dear God, I couldn't think of anything . . .

Already the beam was beginning to broaden and dazzle, the edge of it misting against the cold darkness. I saw the wooden lion's head gleam briefly on a newel post, and then for an instant the shape of a dragon flashed sharply in silhouette, wings furled behind it and talons outstretched. I flinched before I saw the thing for what it really was — a sheet metal ornament perched on the top of a weather vane. Feeling the wetness of blood soaking into my sleeve from my now-throbbing shoulder, I realized that this must have been what I'd bumped against, slicing myself on its razor-like edge.

The light left the dragon's contemptuous sneer and came on, growing brighter. I was turning my head from it, closing my eyes, when it suddenly stopped.

"There," said Christopher. "That's your intruder."

The little gray jumping cat, pinned in the torchlight, arched up with a plaintive meow. "Bloody nuisance," James pronounced it. "Come on, then, we're wasting time."

He switched off the torch and the darkness rushed in once again to fold round me as my forehead slowly sank to rest on Stevie's. I heard them shuffling round the door, and heard the door swing shut.

And then something rattled. I lifted my head as the padlock shot home with a small, final click, as though someone had just cocked a gun. It rattled again as he checked its strength, locking us in.

"And remember," said James, fainter now, "I don't care about Elen. It's Lyn that we're after."

Their footsteps moved off, down the stairs to the East House.

Blind, I felt the flutter of hysteria rise steeply in my chest, and pushed it back. No time for that. I had to think. From the dark came a scrabble and thunk as the cat, unperturbed, leaped down onto the floor, padding past me on soft, certain feet. A square of moonlight flashed low in the door and I watched the small pale form slip through before the flap slapped down again.

On cramped legs, I cautiously felt my way forward, gritting my teeth as I shifted the baby's weight onto my uninjured arm. The cut in my shoulder was deep and still bleeding. I could smell the blood now, feel it sticking warm against my skin, feel it running down my arm to trickle wet between my fingers. I bumped the door and leaned against it, letting it support me as I slid down to the ground again, my knees against the cat flap.

In my right mind, I would never have attempted it. Even with the enlargement that

Owen had made, it still looked a very tight squeeze. But I wasn't in my right mind, I was running still on instinct, and I knew we couldn't stay here trapped and freezing in the shed.

I pushed the flap out a few inches and listened.

A dim sliver of light angled through the square hole, touched a small chest of drawers not two feet from me. Struck by a sudden idea, I shifted the baby again and reached with my good hand to yank one drawer free, skidding it over the ground till its edge nudged the door to one side of the cat flap. Wrapping the blanket more tightly round Stevie, I lowered him carefully into the small makeshift cot. Safer for me to go first, if I could, and bring Stevie out afterward.

I dropped to my belly and, pressing my cheek to the flap, looked out toward Elen's house. Nothing was moving. It had to be now, I thought. Reaching both arms out, I forced myself into the hole. The rough wood scraped painfully under my arms as I thrust myself through, and my shoulder caught fire. Gasping, I managed to slide six more inches . . . and stuck.

Below me, a light went on in Elen's kitchen window. They were searching the house, I thought. Looking for me.

With one last desperate surge I exhaled all the air in my lungs and kicked out with my legs. Something scraped at my hip and I felt my legs sting as I laddered my tights and tore the softer velvet of my dress, but I'd come through the hole. I was out.

Scrambling round on my knees, I reached back for Stevie. My hands shook as they closed round him, easing him out. I nearly had him through when at my back the night exploded with a sudden boom, like cannon fire, and a flash of red set fire to the sky above the Haven. It startled me so badly that I lost my grip and fumbled to regain it. Stevie slipped sideways and bounced against the hole's edge, but he didn't wake. He didn't make a sound.

Pulling him onto my lap, I looked down at his face in the light of the flare. Surely it couldn't be natural for a baby to sleep so soundly. Whatever drug they'd given Elen, they must have given some to Stevie, too, so that he wouldn't wake and start to cry. His breathing sounded normal still, but that no longer reassured me. I knew how quickly things could take a turning for the worse, without a warning.

I had to get him somewhere safe, and soon. *Gareth,* I thought, on a rush of relief.

I could trust him, he'd know what to do. I'd take Stevie to Gareth.

Lifting the baby and holding him tightly, I turned and picked my way across the drive. Without shoes, I would never be able to run fast enough on the gravel. I'd have to get into the field. The fence by the dovecote was easy to climb. As my feet came down soft on the grass of the pasture, the sound of a second boom rolled down the hill and a second flare traced a bright arc through the sky, but I paid no attention.

What worried me more were the sounds I could hear from the back of the house now, the human sounds — voices and footsteps, confusion.

I ran.

I might have been back in the dream, racing over the field with the child in my arms, only this time I knew I had no hope of waking. The danger behind us was real. Behind Gareth's cottage the warm amber light of the Globe Hotel shone like a beacon to show me the way, spinning a shimmering thread down the length of the long wire fence at the foot of the pasture and guiding me over the obstacle. Then, stumbling over the pebble-rough lane and through shivering grass, I ducked round the stone wall into Gareth's back garden.

Panting, I flung myself hard at the door, pounding on it like a madwoman. *Hurry,* I silently urged him. *Please hurry.*

But nobody came.

Biting my lip, I half turned on the doorstep and noticed the window a few feet away, with the light seeping out at its edges behind the thick curtains. Surely that was the room we had sat in, the one where he did all his writing. He must be in there, and unable to hear me because of the wind.

I banged on the glass. Called his name. No one answered.

But I did hear a sound, rather faint, from behind me. The roar of a car motor revving to life. Glancing over my shoulder, toward Castle Farm, I saw headlights flash at the top the drive. They dipped towards the tower and I held my breath. Perhaps they'd go the other way, across the bridge . . .

The headlights reached the gate, and turned.

"Oh, God." They'd see me if I tried to run. I left the window, shifting Stevie higher on my shoulder as I darted through the shadows of the garden to the shelter of the wall. Crouching there among the bins, I wrapped my body round him, closed my eyes, and turned my face against the frozen stone to listen as the Merc came crawling down the lane toward us.

Chapter 32

One refuge only remained
— Thomas Heywood, *The Life of Merlin*

It seemed an age before I heard the rolling crunch of tires approaching. Twice the sound slowed almost to a stop and then came on, as though the car itself was hunting me, a predatory creature pausing now and then to test the wind for any scent of fear.

I didn't dare to breathe. I hugged the stones of Gareth's garden wall and screwed my eyes shut tighter as the rolling tires drew level with us . . . slowed again . . . moved on.

At the end of the lane they turned into the village street, and I could hear the motor thrumming past the front of Gareth's cottage, heading back toward the bay. I was so busy listening, marking their progress — they'd just passed the church, now — that I didn't notice any of the noises in the garden, and I nearly jumped a mile when the wet nose nudged my hand, inquisitive.

"Jesus," I whispered. "You scared me to death."

Chance sat back on his haunches, a ghost in the moonlight, and tilted his head. He looked first at Stevie and me, then the cottage, and back again.

· "Where on earth is he?" I asked the dog. "Where's Gareth?"

At the sound of his master's name, Chance sneezed with a force that brought him up on all fours, tail wagging helpfully. Turning, he trotted off a short distance and stopped to look round. We'd played this game before; I knew he meant for me to follow. But I hesitated, huddled in among the bins.

I could no longer hear the Mercedes. They might have turned off somewhere — down through the houses and over the bridge, round the rim of the bay, or the other way, up the hedged road toward Pembroke. But they wouldn't go far. I was running on foot, in the dark, with a baby. They would know that I'd still be close by.

Whatever choice I made involved some risk. I could stay here hidden, waiting for Gareth to come home, but he might be hours yet and in the meantime I would freeze and Stevie's health might take a turn. Or I could follow Chance, and pray that he would lead me to his master, and that nobody would see us.

The little dog wagged again, whining, deciding the matter.

I'd been afraid that he would lead me out along the village street, beneath the lamp and in full view of anyone who might be watching. But he didn't. His legs moving briskly, he guided me out of the garden and into the fields again, taking the longer route up and behind the next house. There were more fences here. Chance squeezed under and waited while I struggled over them, every movement of my injured arm an agony, but then I saw the warm light gleaming in the darkness and I knew where he was leading me. The light came from the paddock, from the window of the little shed where Gareth stabled Sovereign. He was there, I thought, and seeing to the horse.

The wind stole my sob of relief as I summoned the strength to climb over the last fence and into the paddock. No longer caring if anyone saw me, I gathered up Stevie and ran for the light. A woman's voice called from the gate by the road, but I didn't slow down. All that mattered was getting to Gareth.

I must have looked a perfect sight, bursting through the shed door with my torn frock and laddered tights and bleeding shoulder, like the lone survivor of a horror film — but there was no one there to see me. Only Sovereign. The black mare glanced warily over the boards of her stall, hooves rustling the straw as she stepped sideways, tossing her head in alarm. Whether it was recognition of my scent or seeing Chance run fearless rings around my ankles that reassured her in the end, I don't know, but her ears came slowly forward, and she calmed.

I barely noticed. I was looking round bewildered in the bright lights and the sudden warmth, refusing to believe the shed was empty. "Gareth?"

There were footsteps behind me, too light to be his.

Dilys wasn't a woman accustomed to running. Her breath came in gasps. "I shouted," she said, "from the gate. You didn't hear." And then she seemed finally to focus on me, see my true condition. "Oh, my dear. What's happened?" Her gaze fell to the quiet breathing bundle in my arms. "The baby? Is the baby all right?"

The warmth had made me groggy, slow of thought. "I must find Gareth."

"My dear, you're bleeding. Let me see." She took charge, Sister Casualty again, turning me into the light with a nurse's firm touch.

"Gareth . . ."

"He'll be out with the lifeboat, I expect. The signal just went up, didn't you hear it?"

The cannon booms, I thought. The flares. So that's what they had been in aid of — calling all the lifeboat men to duty.

"This is deep," Dilys said, of the wound in my shoulder. "You'll need to have it stitched. Have you had an injection for tetanus?"

I couldn't remember. Even the simplest thoughts were becoming a struggle.

"And you're sure that the baby's all right? Is that blood on his blanket?"

I tightened my arms round him. "Mine."

"Your blood? Oh yes, I can see. It's all over your hand, poor dear. Still, he should be home in bed, shouldn't he?" She was still Sister Casualty, brisk-voiced and practical, reaching to take Stevie out of my grasp. And then, for an instant, I saw something flash at the back of her eyes.

"No." I backed away sharply, and startled the mare. Her quick sidestep rattled the door of her stall and Chance perked up his ears.

"Don't be silly," said Dilys. "I'm not going to hurt him. Now give him to me."

She looked perfectly normal now, so normal I might have imagined the thing I had seen, like the slip of a mask, but I kept shrinking backward, my arms hugging Stevie. I was feeling peculiar. A line of black mist had begun to rise over my vision, and my heart sounded loud in my ears. Vaguely aware that someone else had joined us in the shed, I tried to turn my head toward the door.

"That's enough." Owen's voice. He came forward, a half-shadowed shape behind Dilys's shoulder. Above the black mist I could see his hands, outstretched and waiting. "It's all right now, lovely. I'll take him."

I was sinking in a sea of mist, sinking . . . and suddenly where Owen's face had been I saw the wise and weathered features of the old man from St. Govan's. His knowing eyes met mine. He smiled. "It is time," he said. "Give me the child."

The black mare pawed behind me like the creature from my nightmares and in panic I thrust Stevie toward the old man, into his hands, and then the sea of mist surged higher and my head began to ring and I was falling . . . falling . . .

Strong arms caught me, held me, drew me clear of the abyss. Gareth, I thought. He had come. I was safe. I leaned against his body while the world swirled round and steadied.

But when my eyes came slowly open, he was gone.

I'd never fainted in my life; I had no frame of reference, no idea how much time had passed. I blinked into Owen's face, hovering close to my own. "There, lovely, there now, you're all right now, aren't you? Just sit here a moment, that's right, keep your head down." Still squatting beside me, he turned on his wife. "What the hell were you thinking?"

Sitting on a bale of straw, she seemed to have grown smaller, though her voice still held defiance. "I was thinking," she informed him, "of the boy."

"You're mad."

"She isn't fit to raise a child."

"And you are, I suppose." His tone was acid. In my dazed confusion, it took me a moment to realize they weren't talking about me. Folding my arms round my knees, I leaned my head to one side, watching Owen as he straightened and stood facing Dilys, holding Stevie close against his chest. "You surely can't have thought I'd go along with this," he said.

"I'm not a fool."

He looked at her, frowning. "No," he said, after a moment, "you're not. You didn't mean for me to know at all, did you?"

She stayed silent, but her eyes supplied the answer.

"But if you didn't plan to take the baby home, then where . . . ?"

His voice trailed off, his eyebrows lowering. "I should have bloody known. Where is he?"

"Where is who?"

"Our son. That priceless piece of work *you* raised. He'll be in this mess up to his neck, if I know him."

I saw Dilys bristle, defending her son. "He only wanted to help."

"I don't doubt it," said Owen. "What price are they paying for babies, these days?"

"It isn't like that. He knows a couple who've been coming to the clinic, a nice couple — professional people, good people — who can't have a child of their own."

"So you thought you'd let them have Elen's."

She refused to be shamed. "I've told you, I was thinking of the boy. What's best for him."

My head felt hollow but I lifted it and cleared my throat to find my voice. "He needs a doctor," I told Owen, thickly. "He's been drugged."

The older man looked from the still-sleeping baby held warm in his arms to his wife's face. "You didn't."

"He might have cried," she said. "It's only Marzine."

"My God." Owen lowered his head, and in the moment of silence that followed I watched his anger fold inward. "I should have stopped it sooner. When I found that key in the old upstairs door, I should have stopped it then. But I thought no, you're only looking at him, seeing he's all right. I thought, my Dilys wouldn't ever harm a child."

"You're right, I wouldn't."

"No, you'd only fill him full of drugs and sell him off to perfect strangers. And did you spare a thought for how the boy would feel tomorrow, waking up without his mother there, how terrified he'd be?"

"He's just a baby. He'd forget her."

"Would he, now? And what of Elen? You're so quick to call her mad when she says someone's after Stevie, but an empty cot's an empty cot. You couldn't call her liar then." And then he stopped, eyes narrowing. "Or did you mean to call her something else?"

"Of course not. Don't be —"

"You thought everyone would think she'd killed the boy," he said, and from his face it looked as though the words had left a foul taste on his tongue. "Another mad mother who kills her own child, such a pity that nobody noticed the danger. God, I can hear you now, telling the press all about it." He shook his head slowly. "What did she ever do to you, for you to hate the girl so much? She's such a loving person . . ."

"Yes," said Dilys, rising very calmly to her feet. "Yes, she's like her mother that way, isn't she?" And gathering her dignity around her like a blanket, she gave Owen one last icy look and walked straight past him, out the stable door.

He stood with his back to me, rigid and still, for so long I thought he must have forgotten I was there, but then the black mare banged against her stall and Owen roused himself, his shoulders lifting in a sigh. "I'm sorry."

I wasn't sure who the apology was meant for, or for what, but he looked so alone that I felt I should answer. "It isn't your fault."

He turned then, and his reaction to my own appearance made me glad I didn't have a mirror. "Christ," he said, and setting Stevie very gently on the bale of straw beside me, Owen knelt to take a close look at my shoulder. I was sitting forward now. The dizziness had faded to a hollow-headed throbbing at my temples, and with the protective effects of adrenaline starting to wear off I felt every move of those fingers against my bruised flesh. I couldn't help the indrawn breath.

"Sorry, lovely. Here, you hold that on there," he said, handing me a handkerchief. "Hold it good and tight now, lots of pressure. That should stop the bleeding." He eased one arm round my back, helping me onto my feet. I nearly trod on Chance, but he stepped smartly to one side as Sovereign arched her head above the stall a second time, soft nostrils flaring questingly toward the sleeping baby.

Following her gaze I looked at Stevie on his bed of straw, surrounded by the warmth and the smells of the stable and animals watching. And then Owen cocked his head and said, "Listen," and I heard it, too, rising over the wind: the sound of the church bells, the Christmas bells, ringing out pure and clear through the turbulent night.

Owen's smile was slow to come, but it transformed his weary face. He tightened his arm round me, glancing at Stevie, his eyes very gentle. "Perhaps we ought to wait here for a minute," he suggested, "just in case the Magi come."

CHAPTER 33

For this my son was dead, and is alive
    again;
he was lost, and is found.

      — Luke 15:24

Bridget, in a rare show of concern, came up to see that I was safely tucked in bed. "I've brought you something warm to drink." She handed me the mug and sat beside me while I hitched myself a little higher on the pillows.

"What is it? Cocoa?"

"Not exactly."

My eyes swam from the alcohol fumes as I took the first sip. "God, Bridget, that's strong."

"Yes, I know, but it's wonderful stuff. It's an old family remedy. Helps you to sleep."

"I've no doubt. But the question is, will I wake up?"

"Of course you will." Curling her legs

underneath her, she settled back against the bedpost. She looked, I thought, astonishingly alert, considering it was just gone four in the morning and she'd been drinking all night. "So how are the stitches?"

I told the truth. "Hurting like hell."

"You know, James feels just awful for leaving you locked in that shed."

"I know."

He had apologized a hundred times while driving me to hospital to have my shoulder seen to. "But you see," he'd said, "I didn't think that anyone was in there. I only went to shut the door, because the wind was banging it. And then Christopher came along and we saw that blasted cat . . ."

"I thought you were looking for me," I'd confessed.

"I was, as a matter of fact. Only not in the shed. Owen said you'd nipped over to Elen's," he'd said. "You couldn't have had worse timing, really. I was just getting ready to make my announcement. I needed you back at the party."

I'd frowned. "What announcement?"

"Well, question and announcement, actually." He'd qualified the statement, and in a terribly casual tone he'd explained, "I had meant to ask Bridget to marry me, you see, but I'm afraid that with all the distractions . . ."

"Oh, James. I am sorry."

He'd glanced at me, reading more into those words than I'd intended. "You don't think she would have said 'yes'? It's all right," he'd gone on, as I'd floundered, "I know all about her aversion to marriage, she's told me herself enough times. But I really do love her, you know. And I've learned the trick of handling her."

"You have?" I'd smiled. "I don't suppose you'd tell me what it is?"

"Freedom," he'd said. "Give her absolute freedom to do as she likes. It's rather like letting a child run loose in the house, you just keep all the dangerous things out of reach." His gaze had slid sideways, to mine. "I'm afraid I've made use of you there, this past week."

"Really? How?"

"Well, shunting you off onto Gareth, like that. When you asked about the prophecies of Merlin," he'd elaborated, to my blank expression. "I knew them myself — I'd have had to be bloody deaf not to, the way that my mother went on — but I thought, if I sent you to Gareth and you kept him occupied, Bridget might not have a chance then, to get him alone."

He had used me in other ways, too, I

424

thought. All the attention he'd shown me, the smiles and the charm, that had all been for Bridget. Nothing held her interest like the threat of competition. But I hadn't called him to account. Instead, because I'd thought he ought to know, I'd told him he needn't worry about Gareth. "Bridget thinks that he's boring."

"Does she? Saves me throwing down the gauntlet, then. A pity," he'd remarked. "Pistols at twenty paces would have been very dramatic, and you know how Bridget likes drama."

I recalled his words now, as I lifted the rum-scented drink for another lung-searing sip, thinking that his observation might explain why Bridget looked so pleased tonight. From what I'd been told she'd had drama in spades.

There had been some sort of scene, I knew, with Christopher. "He thought you'd snapped," had been Bridget's succinct way of putting it. And who could have blamed him? Finding Elen as I'd found her, drugged and unresponsive . . . finding Stevie gone, and me nowhere in sight, and knowing — thanks to Bridget — that I'd lost a child . . .

No, I thought, I couldn't blame Christopher. In his place I'd have reached the same conclusion. And I had to admit his suspicion of me made a good deal more sense than my distrust of him.

At any rate, he'd had it out with Bridget, who'd defended me — from all accounts — spectacularly. James had confessed his decision to get in the car and come look for me had had less to do with his wanting to find me than with wanting to get clear of Bridget's wrath.

She looked harmless enough at the moment, twirling a fiery strand of hair round her fingers and thinking. "I wonder what will happen now, to Dilys."

"I'd imagine that depends on whether Elen wants to lay a charge."

"Rather creepy, really, having someone coming into your house without you knowing. I gather that Dilys had done it a few times — sneaking into Stevie's room while Christopher and James were at the pub. Apparently she thought it was unhealthy, Elen keeping Stevie's window closed."

I'd missed all this, earlier. Bridget must have had it from Owen, while I was in Pembroke Dock having my arm stitched. "I wonder why she bothered reporting Elen to the social services, then, if she'd planned all along to take Stevie?"

"Well," said Bridget, linking her hands round her knees as she plunged ever deeper in hearsay, "James thinks that she probably *didn't* plan it."

I disagreed. "She drugged Elen and Stevie beforehand. I don't know how she did it, but —"

"Chicken soup."

"Sorry?"

"On her way to our party she took Elen chicken soup — you know, for her flu. And she very kindly heated Stevie's bottle."

"Well then, how could James believe it wasn't planned?"

"What he means is, she probably started out just wanting to see Stevie taken into care, and with Elen going on about dragons in the nursery, Dilys saw her chance to get the social workers to make a care order. But when they came and didn't do anything, *that's* when she decided that she'd do the deed herself. Well, not entirely herself," she said. "She had her son to help her."

Owen thought so, anyway. He'd found tire tracks down by the little stone bridge, deeply impressed in the soft mud to show where somebody had pulled a car over and waited, without getting out. Presumably Dilys had planned to take Stevie down there, a short walk from the house, hand him off to her son and return to the party before we had noticed her missing. She'd likely have got clean away with it, too. I, for one, hadn't seen her go upstairs, and even Owen had thought she was still in the room somewhere, talking to someone.

She'd been at his side minutes later, when Christopher had burst in on the party with the news that I'd stolen the baby. But in the confusion she'd slipped out the back door, determined to run me to ground before James did. She hadn't expected that Owen would follow.

"Poor Owen," said Bridget. "Why is it that nice men can sometimes have such horrid wives?"

"I don't know." The mention of wives made me glance at her left hand, but seeing no ring there I kept my mouth closed. James still hadn't asked her . . . or else he *had* asked her and she'd told him "no." Either way, I should mind my own business. Even though, in a way, it was my business too what she answered, because if she said "yes" then I'd have a new client . . .

She looked at me. "What?"

"Sorry?"

"Well, you're wearing that look, so —"

I cut her off, raising my eyebrows. "What look?"

"The one that means you're weighing something."

I shook my head. "It's nothing."

"Ah."

"You shouldn't be so sensitive to how I look," I told her, and then cringed because that sounded so exactly like my mother.

"If you say so. God, is that the time?" She checked her wristwatch, yawning. "I ought to be getting to bed myself, or Father Christmas won't come." She stood and stretched and shuffled to the door, and turning, said, "You're sure you'll be all right?"

"I'm sure."

"I'll see you in the morning, then. And Lyn?"

"Yes?"

"Happy Christmas."

I returned the words and smiled with an effort through the alcoholic fog that had begun to wrap around me. I was half asleep already when I reached to put the light out. Through my window I could see the stars revolving in the still-dark sky. The morning star, I knew, was out there too, somewhere toward the east. I tried to find it in amongst the others but my eyelids felt too heavy to hold open and I couldn't focus properly. I murmured "Happy Christmas" once again, though, for good measure. And I thought I saw one eastern star gleam brighter than the rest before my lashes drifted closed.

The dream came, as it always did, just before dawn.

I was standing alone at the edge of a river that wound through a valley so lush and so green that the air seemed alive. The warble of songbirds rang over the treetops from branches bent low with the weight of ripe fruit, and everywhere the flowers grew, more vivid and more fragrant than any flowers I had ever seen before. Their fragrance filled me with an incredible thirst, and kneeling on the riverbank I cupped my hands into the chill running water and lifted them dripping, preparing to drink.

A shadow swept over me, blocking the sun.

Beside me the grass gave a rustle and parted, and out came a serpent, quite withered and small. The shadow behind me moved swiftly. I saw the bright flash of a blade and the serpent's severed body writhed a moment on the riverbank and then lay still, and lifeless.

The shadow moved again, and looking up I saw a young man of perhaps twenty-five, with a lean handsome face and blue eyes. He might have stepped out of a Renaissance painting, in his black velvet gown belted low on his hips and cut above the knee, with a cap of black velvet to cover his red-tinged fair hair.

"Be not afraid," he said. "It is but me."

I shook my head. "I do not know you."

"Yes, you do." He lowered his sword to the ground and a woman stepped out of the wood. A pale woman in blue — not so young, now. She smiled. "You have given me my son. Now I give you yours."

And from out of the trees came the sound of a small baby crying. Bewildered, half hoping, I rose to my feet.

"Go now," she said, and I went where she pointed, uncertain at first, and then starting to run, plunging deep in the wood with its green dappled light spilling soft all around me. The undergrowth dragged at my feet as I ran and the branches and leaves tangled into my hair, but the crying grew stronger and beckoned me on till I came all at once to a clearing.

At its center grew an ancient, gnarled oak, and in the shadow of the oak there stood a man with wild eyes and whitened hair, and in the man's arms lay a baby.

The man stepped forward, and his eyes were very knowing, very wise. He held the baby out toward me. "It is time."

With trembling hands I took him then and felt my baby living, felt him warm against my breast, and as I passed my hand over his hair he stopped crying. And in that whole wood nothing stirred.

All was silent.

CHAPTER 34

'Tis time that I were gone.
— Alfred, Lord Tennyson, "Morte d'Arthur"

"He's quiet this morning," said Elen.

I slid a little forward on the sofa, shifting Stevie higher on my lap so that his curls just brushed my chin and I could smell the warm, freshly bathed baby scent of him. All the excitement last night didn't seem to have bothered him any. Head bent, he was deeply absorbed in the red curling ribbon and bow that his mother had given him.

"It isn't much," I told her as she carried on unwrapping the gift I had brought. "It's only a book, and far too old for him right now, of course. But I thought that when he starts to read, you know, it might be nice." I wished that Lewis had thought to include a picture book in the package he'd made for me.

Elen slid the gift wrap off and looked.

"Oh," she said. "It's one of Bridget's."

"Yes, that's the first book she ever had published. And I had her inscribe it, right there in the front, so it might be worth money someday."

"Thank you." She said that with sincerity. "I wish that I had something I could give you, in return."

"I really don't need —"

"I know," she interrupted, brightening a little. "I could let you have a look around the shed, and see if there's anything you like in there."

"You don't have to give me a gift."

"Please. I want to. I want to do something to thank you, for all that you've done."

"It was nothing."

But Elen refused to be convinced. She looked at her son, sitting happily there on my lap with his tangle of ribbon clenched tight in one fist. He fluttered it up and down, clearly impressed by the rustling noise, before cramming it into his mouth. "Da!" he told us, triumphant.

"He's safe, now," Elen told me. "Owen said I needn't worry about Dilys, anymore."

Remembering the words that had passed between Owen and Dilys last night in the stable, I couldn't help casting a curious eye over Elen's frail features, seeking some trace of the older man there. Finding none, I said simply, "He seems very fond of you."

"Owen? Oh, yes. He takes care of me," was how she put it, in a tone that didn't question his affection. "It's because of my mother, you see. They were friends. He took care of her, too."

Stevie, apparently liking the taste of the ribbon, held it with both hands now, chewing more lustily, leaning his heavy head back on my shoulder and watching his mother with wide-open eyes.

Elen reached across to touch a finger to his cheek. "He's Owen's namesake, Stevie is. His proper name is Owen Stephen Anthony — I named him before he was born — but he looked like a Stevie, so that's what I called him. The Anthony's after his father," she said, as an afterthought.

I caught the fleeting upward glance she sent me; saw her bite her lip and look away, as though there was something she wanted to tell me but couldn't. I tried to make it easier. "I thought you told me Tony wasn't Stevie's father. Don't you remember? You said Merlin tricked you."

"Yes," she said, as her head came round gratefully. "Yes, I was tricked. I would never have done it, otherwise. I loved my Tony."

"I know."

435

"But I'd been drinking, you see. There was wine, and I'm never too clear when I'm drinking. And he kept refilling my glass . . ."

I waited a moment, debating the wisdom of saying the name, but I had my own idea as to who here would have wanted to seduce her, and in the end my intellectual curiosity won out. "You mean Christopher, don't you?"

Biting her lip even harder, she nodded. "I wouldn't have done it, you know, only . . ." Sighing, she folded her hands in her lap, and looked down. "I just made a mistake."

I understood completely, and told her so.

"Afterwards, well, you can imagine how I felt. And it wasn't just me — he felt awful as well," she said. "Really he did. He still does. I mean, not that he's said it in so many words, but I know that he wants to make everything better for Stevie and me. He asked me to marry him once, even."

I couldn't help raising my eyebrows at that. "*Christopher* asked you to marry him?" I could see him supplying her needs, out of guilt — writing checks, maybe putting her up in a nice little cottage. But *marriage . . .*

She nodded, thinking back. "He'd bought a ring and everything. I told him no," she said. "Because . . . well, he's just not the sort of man one marries, is he? And besides,

436

I really don't know he's the father, do I? I mean, there's still a chance . . ." With hopeful eyes she looked at Stevie, nestled quiet in my arms. "He might be Tony's, mightn't he?"

"It's an interesting thought," said Gareth, several hours later. We were sitting in his kitchen, with our chairs hitched round to face the glowing fire in the Aga. He stretched out his legs, careful not to disturb Chance, who had fallen asleep on his back on the brick hearth with all four feet up in the air, looking for all the world like something that had just been struck by a lorry.

"Interesting," Gareth said again, still sorting through the Elen-Tony-Christopher connections, "because if what James said was right, about his family coming down the wrong side of the blanket from Henry Tudor, and if Christopher — the bastard that he is — is Stevie's father, then . . ." He left the sentence hanging, and I finally had to prompt him.

"Yes?"

"Well, Henry Tudor claimed descent from the ancient Welsh kings. From Cadwaladr."

Again that haunting speech from Gareth's first play chased through my mind in the voice of the rebel Glyn Dŵr, five hundred years dead: *The blood in my veins is the blood of Cadwaladr, last of those kings who were named of the dragon.*

Although perhaps, as Gareth said, Owain Glyn Dŵr had never really died. He'd been given no grave. Just like Arthur, he slept in the hills somewhere waiting to wake, or perhaps to be born once again . . .

Gareth smiled, as though following my thoughts. "And the name of the divine child, as he's usually foretold, is Owen. So," he said, "young Owen Stephen Anthony may yet surprise us all." He tipped his chair back on two legs and balanced it there, with his shoulders to the wall. "Mind you, it won't stop me ripping out Christopher's liver."

"Gareth."

"I'd try for the heart, but I don't think he's got one, the selfish bloody —"

"Gareth," I reminded him, "you promised."

"I promised not to kill him, and I won't. But Tony was a good kid, like the brother that I never had. More than that, he was a good friend, and you don't find those too often. You, of all people," he told me, "should know what it means to lose someone who matters."

That confused me at first. I thought he

was speaking of my losing Martin, and knowing Gareth's opinion of Martin I wouldn't have thought he'd have classed him as "someone who matters." But then I saw his face and realized he hadn't meant Martin at all. I looked away and watched the dance of blue flame in the Aga.

"Who told you? Bridget?"

"Elen," he replied. "I'd imagine the chain of events was that Bridget told Christopher, who told Elen, but I don't know for certain. It's hard to keep secrets, you know, in a village." And then he said, "I'm sorry." Only that. Nothing trite about time healing wounds, or the usual things people said to the grieving.

I liked him the better for that. "Thank you."

We sat there in silence and stared at the fire and the shared moment passed. Gareth shifted his shoulders, adjusting his chair in its tilted position. "So you're leaving tomorrow."

"Yes." I'd be driving Bridget's car back to London for her. She and James had left this afternoon, to see his mother, and tomorrow they'd be going on to Bridget's family in the Cotswolds.

"A shame you can't stay on a few more days," he said. "I've got three new horses that need to be exercised, down at Cresselly. I'd hoped you could give me a hand with that."

"Me?"

"Well, I reckoned a woman who'd ridden Prix St. Georges dressage could manage to gallop a horse round a field."

I turned to look at him, surprised. "How did you . . . ?"

"I know a lot of things," he said. He leaned his head back, closed his eyes. The lifeboat had been out all night, attending to a tanker that had floundered in the Irish Sea, and Gareth was showing the wear of his efforts. "There's one thing that I don't know, though."

"And what is that?"

"Why you thought to bring Stevie to me, last night."

I floundered a little myself, on that question. "I don't know . . . it just seemed like the thing I should do." And then, because he went on sitting there, eyes closed, not saying anything, I felt a pressing need to fill the silence. "I wasn't really thinking very clearly, at the time. It's a good thing that Chance came along when he did, or I might have sat crouched in your garden all night, waiting for you to come home."

"You'd have had a long wait," he agreed,

as the dog on the hearth twitched one ear at the sound of his name.

I hadn't meant to tell him what I'd imagined last night in the stable, but to my surprise I heard the words slip out in my own voice: "I thought you *had* come, actually, when I was up with Sovereign. Someone caught me when I fainted, as I fell. I could have sworn that it was you."

"It must have been Merlin again, shifting shapes."

I watched his face, trying to judge if he meant it. And as I watched, his eyes came open.

The room seemed too warm, suddenly. Blaming the Aga, I started to gather my things. "I should really be thinking of getting back."

"Don't go," he said. "Stay to supper."

"I can't. I'll have an early start tomorrow, and I'm still beastly tired . . ."

"You only have to lift a knife and fork."

"I can't." To emphasize the statement I pushed back my chair and stood, fumbling with my coat. Where *was* the blasted left sleeve? There. I straightened the collar and faced him, composed. "Good-bye, then." I held out my hand. "It's been . . . well, it's been . . ."

"Quite." I caught the wry twist in his

voice, though his face didn't change. The handshake seemed ridiculously formal, after all that had happened this past week, but I didn't know what else to do. One didn't hug a man like Gareth Morgan, or give him that glancing false kiss on the cheek that was the favored way to greet and part, in my profession. Gareth, I suspected, wasn't the type that went in for all that. I doubted he would show affection lightly, if at all.

Chance, though, was entirely different. His tail nearly wagged itself off in his efforts to show me how much he thought of me, and when I gave his ears a final scratch and turned to leave, he let out a sharp whine of protest.

"He'll miss your walks," said Gareth.

"And I'll miss him. He's good company."

"Better company than me, you mean."

"I never —"

"As you said, I haven't made it easy."

I couldn't argue that, I thought. Instead I frowned, considering the problem. "Bridget," I said, "seems to think it's because of our names, you know. Gareth and Lynette."

"A sort of name-based incompatibility, you mean?"

"That's right. Because they didn't get on in the story."

"She's never read Tennyson, then."

I was tempted to ask what he meant by that, but he'd already moved past me to open the door, so I simply let it pass. "Good-bye," I said, again.

"Good night."

It was already dark, and bitter cold. I thought he'd waste no time in going back inside, to where the Aga burned its steady heat upon the hearth. But when I reached the halfway point along the lane between his cottage and the farm, and turned my head for one last look, I saw him standing in the doorway still, a solid shadow fixed within the light. And something told me he'd stay standing there until I'd reached the house and shut the door behind me, and he knew that I was safe.

CHAPTER 35

And he that told the tale in older times
Says that Sir Gareth wedded Lyonors,
But he that told it later says Lynette.
       — Alfred, Lord Tennyson,
          "Gareth and Lynette"

I closed the book of poetry and pushed it to one side. Taking a deep breath, I reached for the telephone, my fingers not quite steady on the keypad. It had taken my assistant, Lewis, the better part of an hour this morning to track down the ex-directory number, and it had taken me an hour more to find the courage to use it, but it was all for nothing. Gareth didn't answer.

I replaced the receiver as Graham, passing in the corridor, put his head round the door of my office.

"You're an idiot," he told me.

"Oh? And why is that?"

It was our first day back after the holidays,

and no one was up to speed yet, except Graham. He never slowed down. "I've just come from a meeting upstairs with the powers that be," he informed me, "and somebody said you'd turned down a directorship."

"I did, yes. There were strings attached."

"But we're talking about a *directorship,* Lyn. Your name on the letterhead, all of that."

I told him I could live without my name on the company's letterhead. "Besides, when I'm made a director, I'd rather it be because I'm brilliant at my job, and not because I nabbed some poor sod for our client list."

"My dear girl, you're an agent. Nabbing clients for the list *is* being brilliant at the job." He settled himself in the doorway. "Which reminds me, I hear you've signed Swift."

"Yes."

"Well done," he said, pleased. "How'd you manage it?"

"Actually, I didn't do much at all. It was Bridget who clinched things."

"Bridget? How so?"

I didn't often know a tidbit Graham didn't know, and I played it now for full effect. "Let's just say you'd best keep all your

Saturdays in June free, and dust off your morning dress."

He stared. "She isn't."

"I'm afraid so. Third time's a charm, so they say."

Graham thought it terribly inconsiderate of Bridget to get married. "This will ruin my finances, you know. When I think of the winnings I'll have to pay out . . ."

"Cheer up. You can always take bets on how long it will last."

"True." His idle gaze, scanning the room, came to rest in the corner. He lifted his eyebrows. "Good God. What the blazes is that?"

"A Christmas present," I informed him, "from a friend."

"Indeed." He looked at the weather vane leaning against my office wall, with the gleaming metal dragon perched on top of it, long claws extended, threatening. "You want to be careful where you put that thing. It looks like it might bite."

"It does." I flexed my healing arm in memory.

"On the subject of dragons," he said, "did I hear them correctly upstairs when they said it was Gareth Gwyn Morgan they'd asked you to get?"

"That's right. He lived round the corner

from where I was staying."

"He's an arrogant bastard, from what I recall. I don't wonder you couldn't convince him to sign."

I didn't bother telling him I hadn't even tried. Instead, I rose to Gareth's defense. "I shouldn't think it arrogance so much as a desire for privacy."

"Privacy," said Graham, "is the price of fame."

I reminded him that writers all had different motivations. "They aren't all of them in it for fame."

Unconvinced, Graham shifted aside as my young assistant, Lewis, pushed into the doorway. "Lyn? Ivor Whitcomb's on line one."

"Oh, hell. I'm at lunch," I said, scrambling to gather my things.

"Right." Lewis turned and left Graham alone in the doorway to watch me, amused. "You don't really have to go to lunch, surely? I mean, it's only twenty past eleven."

"You don't know Ivor. He'll never take Lewis's word that I'm out — he'll most probably come round to see for himself."

"Ah." He twisted his head to read the title of the paperback on my desk. "*The Idylls of the King?* I didn't know that Tennyson was one of your clients."

"I'm just checking a reference." I scooped up the book with my handbag, preparing to dash. "Care to join me?"

"For lunch? No, I can't. I'm already promised to an American film producer, I'm afraid. Reservations, twelve o'clock," he told me, gloating, "at the Savoy."

My own budget didn't quite extend to the Savoy, but I'd seen a new place on the Strand that looked promising.

Outside the air was sharp with petrol fumes and the various smells of warm bodies pressed close on the pavement. Stripped of its Christmas cheeriness, London looked bored with itself, dull and flat beneath skies that felt heavy with gathering rain. I found myself missing the clean Angle air and the winds off the coast and the deep, quiet calm of the morning.

I'd been restless since my return. The only moment's peace I'd had had come two days ago while I was standing by the yew tree in a little Kentish churchyard, looking down on Justin's grave. I'd only been there twice since the day of the burial — once when they'd laid the headstone, and once on the first anniversary of his death, but I'd found it too hard and I hadn't gone back. This time had been different.

It was as though my holding him at last,

alive, if only in a dream, had sealed us both together in a way that went beyond the grave and touched on the eternal. As I'd stood there in the churchyard, where the tiny ivy tendrils had stretched over from my grandmother's grave to twine around the glossy leaves of holly at the base of Justin's stone, I'd felt a sense of continuity — of life returning and repeating endlessly, and falling into slumber.

Someone jostled my arm. Coming back to the present, I took a step sideways to give them more room, but they nudged me again so I stopped altogether and sighed, turning to the nearest shop window in an effort to control my rising temper.

The window glass cast back a dark reflection . . . mine, and someone else's. Someone who stood watching me from several feet behind.

I whirled.

Gareth looked distinctly out of place here. Moodily brooding in black jeans and jacket, he looked like Lucifer himself, cast down from heaven.

"You," I said, a little stupidly.

He came closer but kept to his edge of the pavement, so the crowds of bustling people flowed between us, but I scarcely noticed. In one movement they vanished like spokes of a fast-spinning wheel, and I saw only Gareth.

"What on earth are you doing in London?" I asked.

"Following you." He thrust his hands into his pockets and widened his stance. "I was just getting ready to pay you a call when I saw you come barreling out of the building. So I followed."

"Oh." I couldn't keep the pleasure out of that small word. And then I said, not thinking, "But you told me you'd never come back here again."

"Did I, now?"

"Most emphatically."

He neither denied nor confirmed it. He simply went on standing there and watching me with thoughtful eyes. I'd thought he would be ill at ease in London, perhaps a bit awkward, but instead he looked like . . . well, like *Gareth,* solid and immovable as ever, planted firmly on the pavement making everyone flow round him as a stream flows round a rock. "In Celtic myths," he said, "there is another well-known character, apart from the divine child. Shall I tell you who he is?"

I nodded, waiting.

"His name changes, of course, but in essence he's always the same. A young hero, of dubious parentage, searching for something — that changes, as well. But the form of his quest," Gareth said, "doesn't change." He was storytelling, speaking levelly across the ever-shifting crowd as though there were no one between us. "This hero, he comes to a wasteland, a place ruled by a dying god, a barren place, and empty."

I knew from his expression he was speaking of himself, and London. "And then what happens?"

"Then there's a woman." His gaze met mine, held it. "A woman of pure heart, who travels to the underworld and heals the dying god, and brings the wasteland back to life."

It would, I knew, be an enormous challenge, trying to restore his faith in people, to convince him that the world in which I lived and moved — the world he'd turned his back on seven years ago — was not the evil place that he'd imagined it to be. I asked, "And does the hero find the thing he's after, in the end?"

He crossed the pavement then, and stood beside me, looking down. "I think he does, yes." Someone brushed past and joggled us both and my book fell. He bent to retrieve it. Reading the title, he handed it back with unreadable eyes.

As our fingers touched, a glancing touch, I felt again that spreading warmth, the sense of promise. "Would you like to come to lunch?" I asked. "I know this little place nearby that's very trendy, full of actors."

He frowned in hesitation, and I tossed his own words back at him.

"You've only got to lift a knife and fork."

I didn't realize how much I'd missed Gareth Morgan's smile until I saw it. He suppressed it deliberately, studied my face. "Will Simon Holland pay for this?"

"Well, naturally."

"Right, then. I'll come to lunch. But I will not be held responsible," he told me, "for what happens."

And with one hand at my back he steered me back into the ebb and flow of life along the pavement.

AUTHOR'S NOTE

If you should chance to go to Wales, and if the road should lead you down to Angle, where the Haven meets the sea, then you'll find Castle Farm standing as I've described it, the green hills behind, and the cows peering curious over the fence from the field where the ancient stone dovecote still sits, and the cats coming round from the little back garden to give you a proper Welsh welcome. Above the western door the blind-eyed Gerald Stone will fix its gaze beyond you to the tower by the gate, where round the high and roofless walls the wind tells its tales in a whispering voice and the crows keep restless watch. I know these things because I passed a winter in the old West House of Castle Farm, with Pam and Ralph Rees as my landlords and friends, and the people of Angle as warm and helpful as family.

It began with my good friends Margoe

and David Hammon, whom I met some years ago in Chinon, France, while doing research for *The Splendour Falls*, and who were most insistent that I should journey down to visit them, in Pembroke. "We have a castle, too," they said, "and you could write about it."

So they do. And so I have.

ABOUT THE AUTHOR

New York Times and *USA Today* bestselling author and RITA Award winner **Susanna Kearsley** is known for her meticulous research and exotic settings from Russia to Italy to Cornwall, which not only entertain her readers, but also give her a great reason to travel. Her lush writing has been compared to that of Mary Stewart, Daphne du Maurier, and Diana Gabaldon. She won the coveted Romance Writers of America RITA Award for *The Firebird* and hit the bestseller lists in the United States with *The Winter Sea* and *The Rose Garden,* both RITA finalists and winners of RT Reviewers' Choice Awards. In the UK, she won the prestigious Catherine Cookson Fiction Prize for *Mariana* and has been a finalist for the Romantic Novel of the Year Award and the National Readers' Choice Awards. Her popular and critically acclaimed books are available in translation in more than twenty countries and as audiobooks. She lives in Canada, near the shores of Lake Ontario.